Rebecca & the RENEGADE

MICHAEL J. SCHNEIDER

Rebecca & the Renegade
Copyright © 2024 by Michael J. Schneider

All rights reserved. No part of this publication may be reproduced, distributed, or transmitted in any form or by any means, including photocopying, recording, or other electronic or mechanical methods, without the prior written permission of the author, except in the case of brief quotations embodied in critical reviews and certain other non-commercial uses permitted by copyright law.

ISBN
978-1-963254-47-1 (Paperback)
978-1-963254-48-8 (eBook)

This book is dedicated to Denise Poling
who has faithfully edited more than one of
my books.

TABLE OF CONTENTS

CHAPTER 1

CAPTURE AND ESCAPE

The birds stopped singing. Rebecca just noticed. The Western Pennsylvania woods, normally alive with the music of the *Scarlet Tangier, Oriole and Bluebird*, now were strangely silent. A shiver propagated through Rebecca's nineteen-year-old body. She gathered her shawl about her shoulders. Although the spring of 1781 had barely arrived in Westmoreland County, until now, Rebecca had felt warm enough in her wool petticoat and shortgown. It was the thought of redskins that made her shiver. Visiting neighbors had brought stories of Indian attacks in other townships. Although she had previously thought the bloody stories to be exaggerated, violent visions flashed through her mind.

It was now quiet, too quiet! How long had it been that way? Had the birds just stopped singing, or had it been that way for some time and she was just realizing it? Could they be watching her right now? Maybe it wasn't Indians. Could it be an animal? What kind of animal would frighten birds? A panther perhaps? No it had to be human. She'd best make for the cabin. The berry picking could wait until she was sure all was right at home. With only a single layer of berries in the bottom of the basket, she brushed back her red-brown hair and headed for the cabin her father, Henry Walker, had built when she was but five years old.

Rebecca had taken but a few steps when the report of a rifle rang out. Her mother's terrified scream followed the rifle, then the blood curdling whoops of savages. Rebecca dropped the basket she carried and ran toward the cabin. She paused by a beech tree at the clearing. Before her, just outside the door to the one and one half story log cabin, her mother knelt, bent over the prostrate body of her father. Two of the Indians held fast her 14 year-old brother, Philip, who struggled with all his might to free himself from his muscular captors. Two more Indians rushed upon her mother and snatched her away from her husband, whereupon another scalped her father.

Rebecca's mother, upon seeing this last act, broke loose from her captors, her internal rage providing the needed strength. Before the Indians could lay a hand on her, she swung the ax, bringing the blade down into the closest Indian's skull.

Rebecca watched in horror as her mother tried to draw back the ax to strike at the second one. Her mother wasn't fast enough as the second Indian fell upon her and tomahawked her, rising with her mother's bloody scalp in his hand.

Overcome with grief, Rebecca let out an involuntary shriek, which drew the attention of all the living at the cabin to her direction. Philip spotted her first and cried out.

"Run, Becky, run!"

Rebecca darted back into the woods. Which way should she go? West, toward Fort Pitt, but that was so far away. Nevertheless, she was helpless against the redskins, having no weapon. Surely the militia commander at Fort Pitt would send troops to free her brother. Her brother, what would the Indians do with him? If she went for help at Fort Pitt, it would be days getting there and days to return. The Allegheny woods would swallow up Philip and his captors and she may never see him again. She had a more pressing problem, however, for now she could hear the rustle of brush and twigs snap behind her, meaning the Indians were closing fast on her. She spotted a dark silhouette, not a person, but a dense growth of plants to her right. It appeared to be a mass of thorns and briars. It flashed into her mind that her brother liked to hunt rabbits in this sort of brush because as he had put it.

"This vegetation is so inhospitable to the view, that the rabbits feel safe within."

Without considering the matter further, Rebecca made for the cover, diving to the ground and crawling into it. She stayed low, hugging the ground. She squirmed and twisted like a snake, the thorns tearing at her face, hands, and clothes. She stopped and hugged the ground, wishing somehow she could bury herself within the earth. Then came the crunch of brush as her pursuers arrived. She saw only one pair of moccasins, but heard two voices.

"Yu undachqui!" one said.

"Lachpi," the other answered.

The sounds from the two Indians began to recede, indicating they were leaving. Cautiously, Rebecca began to raise herself up from the prone position she'd been in. She wiped spider web from her face and knelt back on her heels for a moment. Not hearing anything more, she slowly untangled herself from the briar. Standing up, she spotted a deer trail a little to the right of the briar patch. *So that's where they went,* she thought. It made sense that they assumed a white woman would have followed a trail, any trail. *What to do now?* She first thought of returning to the cabin to bury her parents, but then there was her brother. He might still be alive. The Indians must have wanted him for a prisoner or they would have killed him before she'd arrived on the scene like they did her father. Maybe she could find him, but how? Then she thought of the two redskins she'd just closely encountered. *Yes, sooner or later they would rejoin the ones who held her brother.* She started down the trail to follow them.

After about twenty or thirty paces, she spotted the silhouettes of two moving figures in the trees before her. She halted. They were coming toward her! She quickly ducked behind a white oak tree. Quietly she slid to the ground to take advantage of the additional cover of the forest understory. The two Indians passed by her without taking notice. She waited a few moments; then rose to her feet and inched forward. Keeping in the cover of the understory, she observed the Indians. They had stopped by the mass of briars and thorns, which had formerly been her refuge. One of the two cut a sapling with his tomahawk and used it to probe the dense vegetation. A few moments later, apparently satisfied that their quarry wasn't there, one shrugged at the other and they headed back toward the cabin. Rebecca followed, keeping behind them far enough that she could barely see the dark silhouettes of their bodies in the forest foliage before her.

The Indians did not return to the homestead. Instead they were met on the way by the rest of the party who had attacked Rebecca's home. Rebecca was close enough to determine two were escorting Philip, two were carrying the body of the Indian her mother had slain on a hastily constructed bier, and the other carried her father's flintlock, power horn, and bullet bag, as well as a sack which she surmised contained anything else the redskins had deemed valuable enough to pilfer from the house. Her brother's arms had been wrapped around a pole and fastened to a strap in front, making it easier for his captors to control him. The two Indians who had chased Rebecca exchanged a few words with the others then fell into a more or less single file line, one taking the lead and the other at the rear. Again Rebecca followed, determined to find a chance to free her brother.

Rebecca managed to follow this part, uphill and down, through forests, streams and thickets until they decided to make camp at dusk. She was hungry, having not eaten since breakfast that morning, and tired. She longed to sleep on her feather mattress and pillow; she'd made with her own hands. The image of her mother being slain burned in her mind and kept her awake. She silently cried at the thought that her mother would no longer be there to comfort her. Just yesterday, in fact, her mother told her that rumors of Rebecca's beauty were being spread throughout the valley. Rebecca's father had commented something to the effect that he had enough to do and he didn't need the added trouble of dealing with every eligible bachelor in the country coming around and making a nuisance of himself. Now, two of the people she loved most dearly were dead. The third was a prisoner in the hands of these murderers. No, there was no sleeping tonight!

Rebecca found a spot at the edge of the Indian encampment where she could observe without being observed. Leaning against an oak tree, she saw two of the Indians disappear into the brush on the far side of her. She assumed these went off to hunt meat for their supper. In the meanwhile, the two who had carried their dead companion set him to the side of the trail. Rebecca noted that a blanket, undoubtedly stolen from her cabin, covered the dead body. These two headed toward the brush with tomahawks in their hands. Rebecca froze for a moment, thinking they had spotted her; but they entered the woods a little to her left and set about cutting some saplings. The redskins were dressed in deerskin shirts, with leggings and moccasins to match. Their faces bore strange painted images. One appeared to have the head of a woodpecker while the other that of a hawk.

From her vantage point, Rebecca soon learned the purpose of the tree cutting. They cut a pole about the thickness of a man's thigh and hollowed notches into it. Then they untied Philip's hands from behind his back and retied them in front. They made him lay on the ground on his back and put the log with the notches over his ankles. To hold this log in place they lay poles, with the diameter of a fat sausage, on either end of this log. These poles they held in place by stakes made from branches where the notch created by the branch held the pole in place. Then they wrapped a strap around Philip's neck and fastened it to a tree. Rebecca watched as Philip tried to squirm loose, but he was effectively confined to his back. By this time, one of the other Indians had built a fire, and all the others set about gathering dead sticks to feed the fire. As darkness began to settle in, the two Indians returned, carrying the lifeless body of a doe on a pole between them. All the Indians joined in the work of dressing and butchering the deer. Before long, the smell of roast venison permeated the air, causing Rebecca's stomach to knot with pangs of hunger.

A little later, as the redskins gathered around the fire to eat, Rebecca noted that Philip was unattended; but the fire illuminated the night camp enough that she would surely be spotted if she tried to get near him. She would have to wait. Her best chance would be after dark. She huddled herself next to the tree, trying to cover as much of her body as possible with the tree and her shawl, for a chill descended with the nightfall. As she watched the Indians enjoy the warmth of the fire, rage rose within her. This aided in the fight against the cold.

As the noise of the night took over, the crickets, and a distant howling of a wolf, Rebecca's eyelids grew heavy. In her effort to stay awake she plotted the rescue of Philip. She decided together they would go west to Fort Pitt. She and Philip would lead soldiers back to handle these murdering savages; but what then? She was afraid to return to homestead. Sure, she and Philip could rebuild. Philip was strong from cutting wood, threshing grain and other farm chores. It wouldn't be long before he would be able to handle the chores as well as any full grown man. Rebecca was afraid to stay at the homestead though. These savages could show up at any time and destroy the two of them as they did her parents. As she pondered her brother laying at their mercy in the darkness, Rebecca suddenly felt remorse for every wrong, real or supposed she'd ever inflicted on her brother. For instance there was the time he stuck a frog down her dress. He's managed to sneak up on her and drop it down her dress at the back collar without her knowing what it was. When she felt the wet slimy flesh, she screamed and nearly stripped herself naked to be rid of it. Her father, upon hearing her screams, came running to what was wrong. When her father observed the scene and Rebecca told him what happened. Her dad "wailed the tar" out of Philip. Philip hurt so bad that it pained him to sit down for a week. Surely Philip must be enduring the same sort of pain right now, only it was worse. For presently the worst was likely to come and fears of all manner of tortures must be coursing through his mind.

Rebecca envisioned that sandy-haired face of a boy grown, but not yet a man. Just this morning she'd made a comment about the wisp of a mustache growing under his nose. She said.

"I should put some milk on it and let the cat lick it off."

In response Philip muttered some insult about her having a face like a horse and that her father probably should take her to a fair and trade her for a better looking one (horse). Rebecca had been searching her mind for some equally nasty reply when her mother called her away to help with breakfast. It was amazing how her world could be turned upside down between dawn and dusk!

Rebecca looked back toward the fire. All the Indians save one appeared to be asleep. The fire burned low. Apparently the deerskin clothes the redskins wore provided adequate protection against the night chill. Rebecca scrutinized the lone Indian sitting up. He was rocking back and forth in a rhythm not unlike a slow pendulum. *Could it be he was dozing off and might not notice if she moved to her brother?*

She decided to chance it. Rebecca moved silently. Creeping on all fours, she lifted each hand and knee in turn and carefully set them back down again. Her progress was agonizingly slow. On the edge of the brush, she lay flat and crawled like a snake. She crawled up alongside her brother's ear and whispered.

"Phil, it's Becky. Stay quiet. I'm going to try to free you. Stay still until I tell you it's all right to move."

Philip nodded that he understood. Rebecca worked on the strap that held him by the neck first. She suddenly remembered something. She dug into her "pockets" and found a scissors she had there. Actually it was her mother's scissors; but she had been doing some sewing yesterday and forgotten to return it to her mother's sewing box. With she went to work on the rawhide strap. After a few strokes, it separated, freeing Philip's neck. She slid down opposite his body and went to work on the strap that bound his hands. The Indian by the fire stood up. Rebecca froze. The Indian started to come toward them. Rebecca wasn't sure whether to make a dash to escape now, or stay motionless and hope he wouldn't come any closer. She held still.

That was the right decision. The Indian stopped to pick up a couple of sticks to add to the fire and turned with his back to them as he fed the sticks into the fire. Rebecca saw this as a great boon. She decided to abandon the bond on her brother's hands in favor of releasing his legs first. She moved to where the first stake held fast the pole holding the log across his legs. She wiggled it back and forth until she was able to start working it upwards out of the ground. With effort it was soon removed enough that she could slide the pole out. She crawled over to the other side and started working on it. A few moments later, her efforts were rewarded and she removed the second pole. She lifted off the log and Philip's legs were free. He started to sit up, but she squirmed up alongside him and pushed him back down.

"Let me cut the bonds on your hands first. Then crawl out; follow me and don't make a sound." She instructed.

"Okay," Philip whispered.

Rebecca went back to work on the strap that bound her brother's hands. Her eyes darted toward the fire from time to time to check on the solitary guard. He was squatted with his back toward them– Good! She had to take more care not to stab her brother with the scissors as she worked to cut the strap, but finally the scissors cut through and Philip unraveled the strap from his wrists, rubbing them afterwards.

"Let's go," Rebecca whispered and rolled over on her stomach, crawling toward the brush again. She now was facing away from the Indian at the fire and wasn't aware that he'd moved to the far side to avoid some smoke as the fire began to regenerate. The Indian now faced them again, and the new fuel burned brightly again, illuminating much more of the area than before. About the time Rebecca became aware of the additional light she heard.

"Pennau!" the Indian shouted and darted toward them.

"Get up and run," Rebecca shouted, then she added, "Split up."

Rebecca looked back over her left shoulder to see the rest of the Indians scrambling to their feet. Philip followed her command and ran for the woods far to her left. Rebecca pressed straight ahead, fighting her way into the brush. She frantically pushed the branches aside before her as though swimming through a field of vegetation. In the darkness, she struggled to bury herself in the dense foliage of the forest. In a few moments, the snap of branches and rush of leaves told her she was being pursued. She dare not look back now; to look back would waste precious seconds and she was afraid of what she would see. No, she must press on. Perhaps she was drawing the Indians away from her brother. At least it would be some compensation for Philip to escape. *Well they hadn't caught her yet either. Maybe she had a chance.*

Then it happened. She tripped on a root or stone protruding from the ground and went down, face first, sprawling on the earth below. As Rebecca started to push herself to her feet again, two mighty hands grabbed her arms just below her shoulders. She was lifted into the air and set back on the ground; but the hands didn't relax their grip. She was turned to face an Indian with white stripes painted on his face across the cheeks. The Indian withdrew a knife from a sheath on his belt and reached for Rebecca's hair.

"Atta ta," the Indian restraining Rebecca shouted at the one with the knife.

Rebecca watched as the Indian, who was about to scalp her, returned his knife to its sheath in disgust. The Indian holding her then addressed Rebecca.

"White woman, you not fight, I keep you for my squaw. Not let brother scalp you."

Realizing the futility of trying to fight when one Indian held her arms fast and the other was ready to kill her, Rebecca answered.

"I won't fight."

With this commitment, the Indian who held her, turned loose of her arms and shoved her in the middle of the back.

"Go," he commanded.

The Indian in front of Rebecca turned around and started back through the brush toward the campfire. She followed him, not wanting to look back at her captor. She cringed with disgust at the thought of what she might be expected to do as his "squaw". There had to be some way to escape, and she was determined to find it. For now, she would try to be cooperative in the hope that they might relax their guard. When they reached the clearing that was the campsite, no one else was there. Rebecca's heart leapt for joy. Apparently, Philip was leading the others on a merry chase. She knew her brother could run. He might just outrun them all together!

"Lie down here," the Indian who captured her ordered.

Rebecca looked down and noticed she was now at the same spot where her brother had been trussed-up for the night. She did as ordered, and the two Indians began to secure her legs as they had her brother. When the Indian who captured her came to bind her hands, she noticed he did not look as fearsome up close as she imagined he would in the woods. He was younger, perhaps only a year or two older than her. His face was painted also, but only a couple of streaks on either side of his forehead and several concentric circles on his chin. The skin stretched taunt over the bone like a deer's hide over a deer's hind legs. This almost "human" appearance prompted her to ask.

"Do you have a name? Something they call you?"

"What does it matter to a white woman? To you we are all the same—animals to be chased off the land so your grain can grow and cattle can graze."

"If I am to be your squaw, I should know your name, should I not?"

Her captor moved to fasten the strap around her neck.

"Enough talk, woman. You are not of this land like the Lenape. You clear large areas of land of the trees the Great Spirit has given us. This drives the deer and turkey far from village. Then you bring your disease, the one known as "Small Pox" to our village. Many die, my father, mother, two brothers born of my mother, all die. Whites must die if Lenape are to live!"

"But you killed my father and mother and now are after my brother," Rebecca responded, reduced to tears as the vision of her mother being scalped flashed across her mind again.

"No more talk." Her captor said and left to join the other Indian at the fire.

Rebecca lay in the dark, just staring at the star filled sky for a long time. Fatigue was taking its toll now and she was beginning to drift off to sleep when the noise of other Indians returning to the camp awakened her. She rolled her head to the right. In the darkness she could only see silhouettes. Two Indians returned to camp. She could tell by the crown silhouette formed by the feathers on their head. She started to sigh with relief; but the sign aborted when she saw two more Indians enter, pushing Philip before them. Before long they had Philip staked out on the ground alongside Rebecca. When the Indians had finished securing their new prisoner and left, Philip spoke to Rebecca.

"What happened to you?"

"I tripped on a tree stump or something, fell flat on my face. They had me before I could get up again." Rebecca explained.

"What do you think they will do with us, Becky? I've heard rumors they torture prisoners." Philip asked anxiously.

"There is nothing you can do now but be brave, brother. And look for a chance to escape. Oh, and if you see a chance, take it. Don't worry about trying to take me with you and don't try to come back for me without militiamen, promise?"

"But Becky," Philip protested.

"Promise."

"I promise."

"Let's try to sleep then. We'll need all the strength we can muster to deal with these barbarians." Rebecca admonished.

To Rebecca's surprise, sleep did come. She didn't dream, but was awakened by the Indians releasing her from her neck and leg restraints. She opened her eyes and found she was staring into a blue sky.

"Get up," a voice barked.

Becky rolled over to her knees and stood up. She looked around her. The Indians were all standing in line, more or less, ready to travel. Two of them had Philip between them up front. They were followed by the two carrying the litter with the body of their dead companion. Rebecca's captor held a ling strip of roasted deer meat before her.

"You take. Eat. Day's journey long. Don't want white woman to faint before we reach village." He said.

Rebecca took the meat.

"The name is Rebecca," she said indignantly.

"Whatever, you white women all look alike to me. Now go."

Her captor then took hold of Rebecca's shoulder. He first pulled her toward him; then pushed her ahead of him. Rebecca started walking behind the Indian who had wanted to scalp her last night. Rebecca felt offended because the remark her captor had just made seemed to hurt as much as the loss of her parents. Although it was awkward, she began to nibble on the strip of dear meat. She was so hungry that she thought it was the best thing she'd ever tasted in her life. She tried to savor it, not knowing when, or if, she would ever eat again.

The hike was rigorous. Rebecca wondered how fast they would have gone if they didn't have the dead Indian. She noticed that each member of their party, including her captor, took turns carrying the litter. By the time the sun was at its highest position in the sky, Rebecca was now parched with thirst. They began to travel a path where the ground squished under her feet. The Indian party stopped. Rebecca watched as her captor, like the others, stopped, took out his knife and dug a small hole in the ground. Water oozed into the hole, murky, brown water.

"You drink," he said and motioned toward the hole.

Rebecca, repulsed at the muddy liquid, hesitated. But, as she paused, the murky water began to clear up. She dropped to her knees, bent forward, putting lips to the water surface and sipped the liquid. It tasted as cool and sweet as any water she'd ever tasted. She drank and drank until she felt her sides would burst.

"You drink like horse, not like woman," her captor commented.

"When she rose, he took a drink from the same hole. Rebecca noted he took several modest swallows and stood up.

"We go again," her captor prodded, pointing to the other members of the party who were on the move again.

A little before sundown they reached the village. Rebecca's first impression was that she had arrived in a land of giant turtles. This was what the Indian houses looked like. As they entered the village amongst cheers from its inhabitants, she could see that the houses were made from poles, buried in the ground at one end and bent over and tied together. Upon this frame were sheets of bark or thatched reeds. A hide hung over a single doorway. Women and children piled out of many of these to see what the excitement was all about.

The Indians in her party then gave a bone-chilling yell. It sent shivers racing through Rebecca's body. After this, the men, women and children of the village lined up in two lines alongside each side of the path of the party. Rebecca suddenly noticed some had sticks and some had tomahawks in their hands.

The two Indians escorting Philip took him to the head of this path between the two lines of Indians. They removed all his bonds.

"You see that painted post in front of the large lodge before you?" One of the Indians asked.

"Yes," Philip answered.

Rebecca looked to see what they were talking about. Just in front of the largest of the shelters in the camp, she saw a thick round pole, painted mostly in white, but other colors besides.

"If you want to escape torture, you must touch that post." The Indian continued.

Philip started to take a step forward. An old squaw raised a stick to strike at him.

"But those on either side of you have lost loved ones to the whites. They will do their best to see you don't make it." The Indian continued.

With these words both sides of the parallel lines of people let up yells and whoops, nearly as chilling as the war party had done when they entered the camp. Her muscles tense, Rebecca watched her brother. He nervously looked at one side of the two columns of Indians, then the other, then at the painted pole. He took a step and hesitated. Both sides raised their weapons and lunged forward a little. Philip stopped. Both sides leaned backward again. Philip, apparently pleased in having faked the run for the pole repeated the move. This time, however, when the two sides started to back off, Philip ran for the pole. He made it three fourths of the way down the perilous aisle with hardly a blow landing on him when it happened. He fell. What tripped him up was not clear to Rebecca; but she watched in terror as the bloodthirsty mob fell upon her brother. She shrieked and ran for him. An old Indian who had been watching the challenge shouted.

"Lachenau!"

Whereupon the crown of Indians parted, leaving the motionless body of Philip face down in the dirt. Rebecca dashed for her brother and dropped down on her knees beside him. She rolled him over. His face and skull were covered with bruises and cuts. Blood oozed from the corner of his mouth. He opened his eyes and tried to smile when he saw Becky looking down at him.

"Close doesn't win anything in this game, does it?" he said. Then his eyes took on the blank stare of the dead.

"Oh, Philip," she sobbed and held her head next to his.

"He was a brave lad. We will give him a warrior's funeral." The old Indian's voice came from behind her.

She looked up, rage in her eyes.

"You, you, murder my brother and think you can make up for it by giving him a fancy funeral."

"My people call out for the blood of the whites. The whites have shed much Indian blood. Your brother's death will do much to quiet the rage within my people, for they feel the same rage as you do now toward us. Come, my braves will prepare him for entrance into the World of Spirits."

The chief then motioned to two men who took hold of Rebecca and stood her up, backing her away from the body of her brother. He then motioned to two more; who came and carried off Philip's body.

"Where are you taking him?" Rebecca demanded.

"They go to prepare him for the funeral," the chief answered. "We do this first thing in the morning. You will stay in my wigwam this night. My daughters will look after you."

The chief then motioned with his hand and two women, about Rebecca's age hastened over to the chief. He gave them some instructions in their native language. When the chief finished, the daughters each took Rebecca gently by the upper arms and led her to a small stream behind the bark-covered lodges of the village. There they removed the bonds from her hands and gestured for her to wash. After Rebecca washed her face and hands, the two Indian maidens led her back to the great lodge. There they motioned for her to sit on a log and brought her a bowl of corn soup. Rebecca devoured this. As she ate, she observed that the chief's daughters seemed to be pleased to see her eat so ravenously.

While Rebecca ate she surveyed the village around her. The Native Americans sat in various little groups around several campfires. One group in particular captured Rebecca's eye. It was a group of braves who sat, engaged in animated conversation, around the roasting hindquarter of a deer. From time to time, one of the braves would go over to the hindquarter and slice off a strip of meat with his knife. Then he would sit back down and continue in conversation with the others. The Indian who had captured her was among this group; but he was not the reason for her interest. Another Indian of the group kept looking at her.

Even sitting, this Indian bore a tall, straight posture, with a dignity Rebecca would have associated with a noble. He was hardly dressed like a noble though. His chest was bare except that a pouch hung, suspended by a rawhide cord around his neck and a cape made of raccoon shins was draped over his left shoulder. He wasn't as heavily muscled as some of the other braves; but every contour and striation of muscle was visible through the skin. He wore a breechcloth with leggings. These covered his legs, but left part of his rear exposed where neither the breechcloth nor leggings covered. Although most of the braves wore the same breechcloth and leggings, seeing this particular man dressed so sent an embarrassing sensation through Rebecca. Then there were those eyes. They seemed to penetrate Rebecca's soul although they were at a considerable distance from her. In contrast to his fellow braves, this man wore no paint on his face. Perhaps that was why his face looked almost handsome. The others had strange, multicolored symbols on their foreheads and cheeks, which Rebecca found revolting.

Realizing she was staring at him, Rebecca quickly turned her eyes away. Having done so, she was quite unaware that he had done the same. One of chief's daughters giggled. Rebecca gave her the evil eye. To Rebecca's surprise she spoke back to Rebecca.

"That one is Mamalachgook. I think he likes you." She said.

"As if I care," Rebecca answered her then asked. "How is it that you speak my language?"

"Until ten summers ago, we lived in a large village with many Lenape. It was in the land of the Miami, near the Tuscarawas River. We traded many furs with the whites. Nearly all in the village learned the language of the whites." The Indian maiden explained.

When darkness came, the chief came and told Rebecca she could sleep in the lodge that night. One of the chief's daughters took her inside and showed her to a deerskin covered bunk. Rebecca lay down on it and was soon fast asleep.

She was awakened in the morning by one of the chief's daughters and the two daughters led her to the stream again where she washed. Returning to the lodge, the two Indian maidens sat her on the log in front of the lodge while they combed her hair. Rebecca could see the people were gathering in the center of the village. In a few moments the chief came out of the lodge. He looked at Rebecca and spoke.

"We now go to bury the dead," he announced.

The chief then walked directly toward the crowd in the village. The chief's two daughters led Rebecca behind the chief. When he reached the crowd, Rebecca saw two coffins constructed of logs and bark, much like the wigwams.

The chief led the funeral procession from the village. Behind him, bearers carried the two corpses in their coffins. Rebecca and the chief's two daughters followed the coffins along with another squaw, whom Rebecca assumed was the wife of the dead Indian. Behind them it appeared that the whole village had turned out for the funeral.

The chief led them to an area in the woods where two graves had been prepared. The people of the village gathered in a semicircle around the grave. The bearers took the lids off the coffins. All sat on the ground in silence for an hour or so. At the end of this period, the bearers put the lids back on the coffins and lowered them down into the graves. As they did this, three woman mourners ran forward and began to shriek and wail, plucking at their garments snd tearing at their hair. After this demonstration, the coffin bearers laid two poles lengthwise and close together over the graves; then left. The squaw whom Rebecca assumed to be the wife of the deceased Indian, walked across her husband's grave on the poles. One of the chief's daughters gestured in the direction of the graves indicating Rebecca should do the same on her brother's grave.

Rebecca did so. Glancing down at the coffin of bark below as she passed over it.

Next a painted pole with figures on it was passed along the men at the front of the village, one to another. Then one took it to side of the grave which faced the rising sun and placed it on the coffin of the fallen warrior, holding the pole upright in place so that it rose a little ways above the ground. After this the chief turned to Rebecca.

"Do you want to place some remembrance of your brother's life on his coffin?" he asked.

Rebecca went to the forest edge and found a pole and shorter stick. Using some wild grapevine, she lashed these together in the form of a cross. Taking it to the grave, she placed it on Philip's coffin and left it there. The women of the village then filled in the graves with hoes. When they reached the original ground surface, the women took great care to cover the gravesites with twigs, branches, and leaves, so that none of the fresh ground was visible. After this some men, using poles previously prepared for the purpose, built a chest high fence around the graves.

The ceremony over, the people of the village began leaving. Rebecca knelt at the gravesite for a while, thinking about her brother and praying for him. She became so engrossed with memories of him, that she didn't notice for a while that she and the chief's two daughters were the only ones remaining at the grave site. Once she realized this, a plan of escape formed in her mind. She went to the forest edge and gathered azalea branches. She sat on the ground and began weaving them into a wreath. The two Indian maidens, seeing what she was doing, went into the woods and started to gather more branches.

When Rebecca saw that they had their backs turned, she darted for the trail they had traveled from the Indian village to the gravesites. About halfway down the trail, she ducked into the bush. She waited there a few moments until the two girls came running down the trail looking for her. As Rebecca had hoped, they ran past her toward the Indian village. She came out of the brush and headed back to the gravesites. When she reached them, she entered the woods on the far side. She saw that ground sloped down before her and then rose again, rising higher on the other side of the ravine. She chose to go that way, although she knew crossing the ravine might leave her exposed to view longer than traveling either to her left or right. Rebecca was more worried that she might accidently run into the village or one of its inhabitants if she didn't go straight ahead.

The ground on the near side of the ravine was steeper than she thought and her feet slid out from under her once as she made her way down it, causing her to slide, rather undignified, on her bottom several feet down the hill. Going up the other side also proved more difficult than she originally surmised. It was steep and the forbs covering the side of the hill still contained some dew. Rebecca had to grab branches of trees and the stems of shrubs to help pull herself up. When she finally reached the crest of the ridge, she was panting and sweating profusely. She longed to sit a moment and rest, but she had to content herself with walking up the flatter slope to her right. She decided now that she would stick to the rising ground in the hope that it would eventually lead to some vantage point where she might determine a direction to follow to safety.

Rebecca continued her uphill trek, not reaching a peak until it was dusk again. She found a flat bit of ground, concealed by switch ivy and fetterbush. She lay down. Hungry, but exhausted, she fell asleep. She was awakened the next morning by the call of the *Bobwhite*. She got up and brushed herself off. Lord! She was hungry. Never mind that, she was still free, even if she had no idea which way to go. She found her way to a clearing and discovered on the other side of it a rock outcropping that gave her a view of the land for many miles distant. She saw a variation in the vegetation with a sinuous pattern that indicated it might outline a creek. Thinking this to be Loyalhanna Creek, she decided to make for it.

After several hours she came upon the creek. It was well protected at this point by forest canopy so she decided to pause for a long drink of water and a short rest. She spotted a berry bush on the far bank and ravenously stripped it of its fruit, both ripe and not. She recalled how good the Indian corn soup tasted; but resolved that death from hunger or wild beasts would be preferable to being a slave to an Indian. She would take her chances in these woods. She was also determined to reach Fort Pitt in the hope that the commander there would send men to destroy the village of those who killed her mother, father and brother.

Renewed in purpose, she followed the creek for the rest of the day. As the shadows began to indicate daylight was waning, Rebecca was suddenly startled by a loud crunching sound in the brush. Thinking it might be an Indian war party or one searching for her, she ducked behind a large chestnut tree. Slowly, she slid around the tree until she could view the portion of forest where she heard the noise. Then she discovered what had made it. A large mother bear and her cub were ambling through the forest. The mother bear stopped, rose up on her hind legs and sniffed the air. *Would it come after her?* No, it headed away, the cub toddling along behind.

Rebecca became more and more hungry, not seeing any edible roots, finding few berries and having no weapon to secure meat. Weak and tired of wandering, she came to an area where she thought she heard the sound of rushing water. She moved toward the sound, climbing over numerous high rocks, she finally came to the edge of a great river. She followed along the bank some 15 or 20 feet above the river. Eventually this led her to a point where a high perpendicular rock formed the bank on one side of her. She continued alongside the mighty landform until the bank ended abruptly, overhanging the river. Rebecca looked up. The sheer face on the rock would be impossible to climb. She looked to the way she had come. The thought of retracing her steps to where she could get above the rock utterly depressed her. She walked to the edge of the precipice. It was a long way down; but perhaps not so far, it would be much easier following the course of the river below. She said a prayer, closed her eyes and jumped.

The free fall through the air seemed unusually long for the short distance that she traveled. She went deep, her feet striking on the river bottom. The shock of the cold water didn't hit her until she resurfaced. She stretched out on the surface of the water, being somewhat stunned from the fall, she was content to drift with the current for a while.

Rebecca then spotted a bend in the river downstream. *Good,* she thought. *The current should take me close to shore.* Rebecca lay forward on the water and began to stroke with her arms and legs in the fashion of a frog. Her mother had taught her to swim like this when she was quite young. Rebecca's water soaked dress, pockets, and petticoat tended to pull her down; but she dare not discard any of them. It was all she had in the world now. Rebecca struggled to keep her head above water as the current sped her downstream. Closer, closer, she neared the riverbank. Just as she was about to stroke crosscurrent toward shore, she noticed it– a dugout canoe!

Rebecca's first impulse was to go for the canoe, thinking she could steal it and travel downstream in it. The appearance of two figures emerging from the forest fringe dashed this hope, however, Indians! Rebecca stroked back toward midstream, desperately hoping the Indians hadn't spotted her. Luck was not with her. Shouts from the shore, followed by the two figures pulling the canoe toward the water, confirmed they had seen her.

Rebecca sized up her options. *Did she have a better chance of out running them in the water or on land? The current would give her a pretty good lead; but with two Indians paddling the canoe, how long would it be before they overtook her? If she could use her head start advantage on land, at least the forest might hide her.*

Rebecca drifted around the bend and the current now began to draw her toward the opposite bank. She rolled over in the water to glance behind her momentarily. No sign of her pursuers for the moment. They were still on the other side of the bend. She considered that the Indians being out of sight gave her a slight advantage. She swam hard toward shore. Her efforts were rewarded as her feet found the muddy ooze of the river bottom. She plodded toward shore.

As she stepped up onto the dry soil, she glanced over her shoulder. The dugout canoe was rounding the bend. The sight of the canoe provided the extra burst of energy Rebecca needed to break into a run. She darted into a stand of beech and buckeye trees. The undergrowth was thick; but Rebecca spotted a deer trail and chose to follow that for a while. Rebecca wanted to move away as fast as she could. As she scurried down the trail, rustling through the brush as she went, an idea struck. *Yes, it just might work.*

Rebecca turned and looked behind her. The impression of her shoe was clearly visible among the two-pronged deer hoof prints. *Good, that fit in with her plan.* She ran a few more paces down the trail then jumped, both feet together, into brush. Sticking to the forest understory, she began to make her way back the way she had just come.

Rebecca moved cautiously this time, stopping every dozen paces or so to listen for the sounds of Indians following her. She continued this way for some time, until she was sure she was almost back to the river. In fact, she could hear the rush of water in the distance. *Could it be they decided not to follow her?*

As if in answer to her question, she heard, she heard the swish of a branch, then another. Rebecca ducked behind a beech tree, then slowly peered around it. She could see the two Indian figures, barely visible through the brush, making their way along the trail. Her heart pounded. She backed around the tree, flattening her back against it and breathing in deeply, both to calm herself and to summon her courage for the task ahead. A moment later, she looked down the trail again. *Yes, they seemed to have disappeared again. She must move fast.* She made for the trail and ran down it toward the riverbank. Speed was most important now. She didn't worry that the Indians might hear her rustle down the trail.

When she finally broke through the brush to the riverbank, her heart stopped a moment. She didn't see the Canoe! Frantically, her eyes scanned the riverbank, both upstream and down. *Ah, there it was.* The Indians had pulled the canoe all the way up into the brush. Rebecca darted to the location of the canoe. She grabbed it and pulled. The canoe didn't budge. She set her feet and strained. It slid a little. She ran around to the other end, placed her feet against a couple of saplings and pushed with all her might. The canoe slid away and disappeared over the edge of the bank. Rebecca ran back to the other end again. Grabbing the bow she pulled it toward the water, backing up as she as she went. Fortunately the mud of the riverbank lubricated the bottom well. She moved into the cattails with it. As she moved into the shallows, the water buoyed up the canoe and made the task easier. Suddenly a surprise attack came from the water. She felt the fangs pierce her ankle and looked to see a snake with a coppery-colored head swimming away.

Rebecca's first thought was to get away from the Indians. She continued to pull the dugout canoe until she was sure it wouldn't bottom out when she got in. She rolled over the gunwale and got to her knees. She paddled the canoe through the cattails to open water. When she reached midstream she decided to inspect the bite. She reached down and tore her stocking away, revealing two puncture holes now swelling on her leg. She had no way of extracting the venom by herself, so she committed herself to Providence and continued paddling. In a little while, she passed out in her canoe and drifted, unguided, down the Monongahela River.

CHAPTER 2

CONDEMNED TO WHITE SLAVERY

As Rebecca came to, she felt a terrible shiver through her body. She looked up into a nearly cloudless blue sky and felt the gentle rocking of the canoe in the water. Something was different though. Rebecca glanced down toward her feet. The first thing which met her eyes was the bronze bare back of an Indian paddling the canoe! Rebecca then looked to her wrists. Sure enough, her hands were bound with a rawhide strap. She tilted her head back slightly and met the powerful face of the Indian brave she had watched at supper the night before.

Apparently sensing she was conscious, the Indian was staring down at her. His eyes seemed to radiate a kindly glow. This prompted Rebecca to speak:

"Where am I? How long have you been there? Where are you taking me?"

"Ah, so many questions white girl, I can answer only one at a time," the Indian answered.

For some odd reason, Rebecca reacted to the label, "white girl", first. *By what right did this man, who couldn't be more than a couple of years older than her, call her a "girl"?* Nevertheless, she posed the first the first question again, "Where am I?"

"In the canoe you stole from us," the Indian answered.

"But how did you get here?" Rebecca pressed.

"We spotted canoe. We follow it. Canoe drift near shore. It stopped by fallen tree in water. We find you in canoe. You were bitten by snake. Poison make you sleep. Mamalachgook treat you with powder from my magic bag. It Indian remedy for snakebite. It works most of the time." He answered.

"Who treated me?" Rebecca asked.

"I did. I suck poison out, then treat with powder," the Indian responded.

"So you are called Mamala, Malama…" Rebecca struggled to repeat the name.

"Mamalachgook, it means 'Spotted Snake'," Mamalachgook answered.

"I was treated for snakebite by a snake!" Rebecca gasped in irony.

"You make good joke, white eyes," Mamalachgook commented.

"How long have I been out?"

"For nearly half the time between sunrise and sunset. It will be dark soon." Mamalachgook answered, gazing at the sky as though looking for some Divine confirmation of his assessment.

"Where are you taking me?"

"We return to village. Must return you to Lenape brother who won you by conquest."

"Is it your brother who claims me as his squaw? Rebecca asked, puzzled.

"All Lenape consider themselves brothers; but he is not of my mother if that is what you mean." Mamalachgook explained.

"Do you have any brothers? That is, also born of your mother as you say?"

Rebecca wasn't sure, but did a smile form on Mamalachgook's face before he spoke?

"I have little brother. He was born ten springs ago."

"And your mother? Did she have any girls?"

Mamalachgook's face screwed up as though twisted with pain.

"Mother die seven springs ago. She have no other children. Shawnee make war on white man. White men decide to punish Shawnee. They strike our village by mistake. All warriors from village on hunt at the time. White men fire guns into village, then attack. When they enter village they find no one but squaws and little children. When warriors return to village, my mother dead. Little brother of three springs lying on her, crying."

"That's horrible!" Rebecca blurted.

"You first white who show any remorse for death of my mother," Mamalachgook said grimly.

"What's your brother's name?" Rebecca asked. She felt sorry that she had resurrected such a horrible memory and wanted to divert Mamalachgook's attention from it.

"Wyawaquacuman," he answered.

"Wyaw... That's hard to say," Rebecca responded.

"It means 'Walking Everywhere'. Perhaps those words fit the white tongue better."

"Why do call him that?" Rebecca pressed.

"He's always had a tendency to wander. I once lost him for three nights. A raccoon came into camp one night and he decided to follow it. When he finally lost the raccoon, he found he was lost. When I found him, he wasn't so much scared as hungry." Mamalachgook continued.

"You must have been quite worried, when he was missing, I mean," Rebecca offered.

"Yes, he is the only living link to my mother and father and now my responsibility. Do you understand this?" Mamalachgook asked.

"Yes, I <u>had</u> a brother too," Rebecca snipped, tears welling to her eyes; but she fought them back.

"Yes, I know. The one we buried some days ago. He had good heart. He could have become a brother to the Lenape."

The thought of Philip stirred Rebecca to sit up. Her leg throbbed; but she squirmed around until she sat, cross-legged, facing Mamalachgook. Suddenly it was important to see his face. Rebecca <u>needed</u> to see his eyes. Yes, there was sorrow in Mamalachgook's face. Could it be he really shared her loss? She studied the whiskerless face with skin stretched between cheekbones and jaw, taunt, like the head of a drum.

"Why you turn around?" Mamalachgook asked.

"I, I..I like to face the person I'm speaking to," Rebecca answered.

"Ah, vultus est index amini," Mamalachgook sighed, taking an extra-long stroke at the paddle.

"What does that mean?" Rebecca probed.

"Oh, you not recognize this language of the other white people?"

"No, what white people did you hear speak this language?"

"The ones we call the *Blackrobes*. They came with the French whom the people of your tongue took up the hatchet against."

"Was there something special about these, these *Blackrobes*?" Rebecca asked.

"Unlike most white men they not seek land or Lenape pelts. They seem to have need to share their knowledge of a Great Spirit's son whom they call Jesus Christ." Mamalachgook continued.

"On, they must have been French preachers. So what you said must be French." Rebecca proposed.

"No, it is a tongue they call Latin. The *Blackrobe* who spent several springs with us used to like to speak it much. I think he like to think of himself as a wise man. He spoke in Latin to emphasize the words were wisdom, then he tell us the meaning." Mamalachgook explained.

"So what does, well what you said mean?" Rebecca prodded.

"You mean vultus est index amini?"

"Yes."

"The eyes are the window to the soul." Mamalachgook started, then he continued. "You wished to know my heart so you felt you must look into my eyes."

Rebecca felt a blush of embarrassment. He was right, one hundred percent right; but how could a heathen, a <u>male</u> heathen, be so perceptive. Impulsively she reached to feel the neckline of her dress as though the dress had been torn open to expose her breasts. Feeling the fabric reassured her for a moment; but then she shuddered as a sense of vulnerability pulsed through her. *Could this savage know her innermost thoughts? Would he be aware of her most intimate thoughts and desires?* She looked back at the rugged, weather-cured face again. He looked back with the slightest crease of a smile.

"Is white girl worried Mamalachgook know Latin?" he asked; but before she could respond, he continued. "Or is white girl worried that Mamalachgook understand what white girl think?"

Rebecca flusher with anger. There was no way she would admit to this Indian that he could penetrate her thoughts. She couldn't bring herself to lie to him either. Instead she countered.

"My name is Rebecca. I don't like being referred to as 'white girl'. Use my real name."

"Okay, Mamalachgook understand. Re-beck-ka. What does it mean?"

"Why does it have to mean something? It's my name." Rebecca snipped.

"Did not your parents give you the name?" Mamalachgook asked.

"Yes."

"Why did they pick that name?"

"It is a biblical name. Rebecca was the wife to Isaac." Rebecca started to explain.

"Ah, the *Bible*. *Blackrobe* carried black book he call *Bible*. He said it had many stories in it. He read us some from time to time. I don't remember Isaac. Was he great chief?"

"Yes, very great. A forefather of a great tribe called the Hebrews." Rebecca explained.

"Then your father expected you marry a great chief also. That is why he give you that name." Mamalachgook said with an air of confidence.

"I, well I don't think that is why he chose that name…' Rebecca started. The image of her father's bloodied body formed and brought tears to her eyes.

"Not good to talk about your father now." Mamalachgook commented.

"What do you care?" Rebecca snarled.

"Losing parents not any different for red man. Not good to dwell on what you can't change. Let your thoughts set like sun on what has past. Rise to dawn of day ahead."

"So am I to look forward to being a slave to some savage?" Rebecca spat.

"Kshicanlenno is great warrior. True, he kill some whites; but his mother and sisters were slain by whites. That make Kshicanlenno take up the hatchet against the whites. He's a good man though. If you obey him, he will treat you well."

"Like I said, I'd be this Chicano's slave," Rebecca repeated.

"It's Kshi-can-len-no. It means 'Knifeman', perhaps the English name easier to remember." Mamalachgook corrected.

Rebecca shivered. The name chilled her very soul. She vowed to herself she would find some way to avoid the fate which lay ahead of her. Escape now dominated her thoughts. She continued the journey with Mamalachgook in silence. They moved slowly upstream. The water was getting shallower. It bubbled white as it passed over scarcely submerged stones on either side of the canoe. Mamalachgook's arms darted ever so quickly from one side of the canoe to the other as he and the other Indian struggled to keep the deeply displaced canoe from striking these submerged stations of the river bottom. Finally, they pulled into a pool formed by backwater and pointed the rough-hewn bow toward the riverbank. Just before the bow made contact with the brown earth of the shore, the Indian in the bow neatly laid his paddle on the bottom of the dugout. Grabbing both gunwales, he nimbly vaulted from the canoe into the knee-deep water. He steadied the bow and glanced at Mamalachgook.

"Your turn," Mamalachgook instructed Rebecca.

Rebecca tried to repeat the movements the Indian in the bow had made, big mistake! She failed to elevate her knees high enough. They banged against the gunwale, retarding the movement of her lower body. She couldn't check the momentum of her upper torso, however, and she sailed head first toward the water! Rebecca hadn't released her grip on the canoe, however. As her face plunged into the murky, cold liquid, she was half conscious that she was twisting the canoe toward her. In fact, she dumped Mamalachgook into the river as well as the contents of the canoe which included flintlock rifles, bullet bags, and powder horns belonging to the two Indians.

Mamalachgook, stood up, thoroughly drenched, water dribbling off the strands of his hair down the front of his chest. Rebecca thought he looked funny and let out an involuntary giggle, knowing full well she probably looked much more pathetic. The Indian on the river bank laughed robustly and said.

"Looks like white woman nearly drown Spotted Snake."

Mamalachgook's face, initially flushed with anger, quickly relaxed and broke into a smile, clearly becoming cognizant of the humor of the situation. He opened his mouth to comment; but noticed the floating powder horns. Mamalachgook lunged toward them and snatched up before the current could carry them away downstream. He tossed the powder horns on the riverbank and dove underwater for the rifles and bullet bags. When he surfaced he'd recovered the weapons and bags. Of course the rifles would be too wet to fire– even if they were loaded.

Rebecca edged toward them nonetheless, thinking she could use one as a club. She hesitated a moment. While she had no scruples about smacking one of her two captors on the head with a rifle; the thought of bloodying Mamalachgook repulsed her. She summoned her resolve. It might be her best chance for escape. Rebecca started to reach for the closest rifle. As she bent over Mamalachgook looked toward her. She seized the rifle and started to stand up; but Mamalachgook, at a dead run, met her as she straightened up. He threw both his arms around her waist and hauled her to the ground, forcing her to drop the weapon. She tried to squirm out of his clutch; but he released the grip he had on her waist and grabbed Rebecca's wrists instead, forcing her onto her back and pinning her wrists to the ground.

Mamalachgook then straddled her thighs with his legs, effectively immobilizing any part of her body which might do him damage.

Rebecca looked up at the face hovering over her. Mamalachgook wore a broad smile, obviously pleased he had control over her.

"What you plan to do with rifle, Rebecca?" he asked.

At the sound of her name, a sense of calm coursed through her body. Mamalachgook spoke with an affectionate tone. "Rebecca," as he spoke it, hung in the air like the sweetness of a wren's song. She let her muscles relax.

"I was going to hit you with it," she answered him truthfully.

"Looks like we have to keep your hands bound," Mamalachgook responded; then he continued, "You plenty audacious girl."

The word "audacious" stunned Rebecca. Where did a savage pick up words like that? The presence of Mamalachgook sitting on her thighs was now also having another effect on her– one that gave her simultaneous feelings of guilt and pleasure.

"Will you let me up now?" she asked.

Mamalachgook neither spoke nor acted for a moment. He was staring at her in a way no one had ever looked at her before.

"Please," she added.

As though being awakened from a trance, Mamalachgook released his grip on her wrists and stood up, not taking his eyes from her. *There was something about that look. It was not the look of a hunter afraid of losing his prey. It was the look of, no, that was silly, but it appeared to be a look of adoration.* Mamalachgook extended a hand to her. Rebecca took the offered hand. He pulled her to her feet. The other Indian now came up behind Mamalachgook and said something in their native tongue.

"My brother here asks if we should bind you again," Mamalachgook translated, then continued, "We're not far from village here, I think that unnecessary. You follow brother."

Mamalachgook then said something to the other Indian. That one picked up the other rifle and started into the woods. Rebecca turned and followed him. There was little else she could do. Mamalachgook followed her. Rebecca was grateful, however, they hadn't bound her hands again.

Mamalachgook was right. The trip to the village was very short indeed. It must not have been more than half to three quarters of a mile from the river. Oh, how she wished she'd known that before! She could have spent the last couple of days following the river instead of exhausting herself trekking over hills and down ravines.

As they entered the village, the braves gave the returning warriors a cheer when they saw Rebecca. She felt as though she belonged suspended from a pole between the warriors like some deer killed on the hunt. Rebecca then noticed one of the chief's daughters was sitting on a log grinding corn. The daughter looked up. When she saw Rebecca, she set her wooden bowl of corn down and rushed to her.

"Oh, you are soaking wet. Come to our wigwam. I will find you some dry clothes," she said. Then she took Rebecca by the arm and led her away from the others to the hut Rebecca had slept in before.

Inside, the Indian woman went to one of the skin covered log platforms, which Rebecca recognized as a bed from her previous night in the wigwam. The young Indian maiden pulled a large bear skin bundle from underneath the bed and untied it. She stood up holding a deer skin cut and sown in the shape of a petticoat. As Rebecca watched, the young Indian lady unrolled the petticoat by stretching out her arms; then explained.

"It wraps around you, so one size fits all."

"But will it be long enough?" Rebecca asked.

A frown formed in the face before Rebecca.

"Yes, I am shorter than you," the Indian girl started; but then she broke into a smile again. "I have very fine leggings you can wear."

With this last statement, the girl dove back into the bearskin bundle and surfaced again holding what appeared to be two leather stockings without feet.

"Very nice; but can you afford to do without, ah what is your name?" Rebecca asked.

"I am called Taskemus. It is Lenape name for a bird. The one the whites call Mocking bird." Taskemus answered.

Then she continued, "I don't wear these. I was saving them for when I marry."

"Oh, Taskemus, I couldn't wear your trousseau!"

"No need to worry, I have no prospects for marriage," Taskemus responded, casting her glance toward the floor.

Rebecca immediately read in the gesture a sense of shame and sought to comfort her.

"I'm sure some brave has his eye on you. Is there no one you would like to marry in your tribe?" Rebecca asked.

"There is one," Taskemus began sheepishly.

"Who is that?" Rebecca asked. She was delighted to be engaged in some 'girl talk'.

"His name is Kshicanlenno, the one who takes you as his squaw," Taskemus answered.

"Him! You can have him. I haven't the least desire to marry him."

"I'm afraid you have no say," Taskemus started. Then she continued to explain. "Kshicanlenno is proud warrior. He looks on you as a living trophy. The story of your capture will be told around campfires for many winters from now. If anyone doubts him, he has only to bring you forth to show them."

"But surely he'd want a wife to be more than a trophy," Rebecca protested.

"I think pride guides Kshicanlenno more than love. Although, I'd like to see him love me." Taskemus responded.

"Maybe we can divert his interest from me to you," Rebecca suggested.

"How?"

"Give me a little time to think about it. Believe me, if we can get him to marry you, both of us will be happy." Rebecca answered.

"Very well, but now you must wear the clothes I offer you so we may clean and mend yours."

With that statement Taskemus dug into her bearskin bundle and withdrew an indigo and white striped line shortgown. She held it by the shoulders, sizing up Rebecca.

"I think this will fit. You are not so much tall from neck to waist as from waist to ground."

"Where did you get this?" Rebecca asked, not sure she wanted to know the answer.

"Morovian missionary live with Lenape for a while. They give some of us cloth. I make from their cloth." Taskemus explained.

"Do you know of a place where I can bathe without the men of the village watching? I'd like to clean up before I change."

"There is a small pool in the stream, not far from wigwam. If I go with you, no one will follow. Here I carry clean clothes and we go." Taskemus said. Then she threw the skirt leggings and shortgown over her arm. She headed for the flap of the wigwam, then, turned suddenly.

"Oh, almost forget, you need moccasins to complete outfit."

With that, Taskemus bent over and reached under one of the log and deerskin cots. She retrieved a pair of rather worn looking moccasins.

"These see many moons wear; but should last for a couple more. I teach you how to make new ones."

"I'm sure they will do." Rebecca answered. She looked at her shoes. Her dad had made them for her. She had no intention of parting with them; but the trials of the past few days had taken their toll. The leather was splitting from the alternate wet and dry cycles as well as encounters with thorns and rocks. The moccasins were indeed, welcome.

Taskemus darted through the deerskin-covered exit from the wigwam and Rebecca followed. As Rebecca walked alongside Taskemus on the way to the creek, she felt an urge to forget about the bath and head back to the wigwam to change. Taskemus seemed to sense Rebecca's apprehension.

"Don't worry, once we reach place to bathe, no one will bother us. Being daughter of chief does have some privilege."

Taskemus was right. The pool was well concealed by oak trees and spiraea, Rebecca stripped naked and sat in the cool water. The water was cold, causing her to shiver, but it was so clear. It felt so cleansing. Rebecca lay back and let the water course over her body. She took her shift and soaked it. Using it as a wash rag she scrubbed and scrubbed, washing away the silt, sweat, mud and blood accumulated over the past days. When she finally felt clean again, she stepped to the bank and put on the clothes Taskemus provided. Taskemus assisted her by adjusting, straightening, and showing her how to lace the leggings.

Rebecca felt strange not to have her usual under garments; but the deerskin skirt and linen blouse caressed her skin as well as her usual clothes. She felt embarrassed by the skirt. It was too short, ending almost six inches above her knees. She hadn't worn anything that exposed that much leg since she was five or six years old. The leggings only reached to the bottom of her knees. Rebecca compared herself with Taskemus. Taskemus wore no leggings; but her skirt terminated nearly halfway down her shapely caves. Rebecca recalled this was typical of the other women in the camp. Rebecca felt strangely indecent. She resolved she must clean and repair her own clothes as soon as possible.

"It is getting dark now. We wash your clothes after sun up." Taskemus announced.

Taskemus was right. It was getting too dark to see. Rebecca gathered up her clothes and walked back to the camp with Taskemus. When she arrived, to her relief, most of the men were engaged in some sort of dance around a great fire. Taskemus' sister, upon seeing them return, went to a crock with two earthen bowls. She ladled some of the contents into each of the bowls. She brought the bowls to Taskemus and Rebecca. In each of the bowls was a spoon fashioned from animal bone.

"Thank you," Rebecca said as she took a bowl from Taskemus' sister.

Taskemus' sister just smiled and walked off to join the crowd of children and squaws beginning to collect around the dancers at the big fire.

Rebecca and Taskemus sat on a log near the small campfire. They ate in silence. Rebecca was famished and quickly emptied her bowl. She wasn't sure what she ate. It was some sort of stew or soup with corn in it. There was also meat which Rebecca assumed was venison; but the other ingredients were unidentifiable. After her first bowl, she asked Taskemus if she could refill hers. Taskemus nodded her approval. Rebecca then went to the large point-bottom clay pot held upright by supporting stone. To her surprise, the pot was nearly half full. Rebecca sunk the ladle deep, deliberately trying to capture as many meat morsels as possible.

By the time Rebecca had finished her second bowl, she was feeling a little bloated from eating too fast, and quite sleepy. She looked at Taskemus, then asked, "Do you mind if I go to sleep now?"

"You do not want to join in the dance?" Taskemus asked. Then, before Rebecca could answer, she continued. "Come on. I will show you where to sleep."

Taskemus then led Rebecca to one of the cots. As Rebecca stretched out on the taunt deer hide, Taskemus brought Rebecca a blanket of woven feathers.

"Use this if you get cold," Taskemus instructed.

Rebecca pulled the blanket over her. She closed her eyes for a moment, listening to the sounds of the drums and chanting outside. The next thing she knew all was quiet and Taskemus' hand was shaking her shoulder.

"Wake up, Rebecca, the sun is almost to its highest point in the sky," she said.

Rebecca opened her eyes. Sure enough, daylight streamed in from the giant hole in the roof over the fire place and the single entrance to the wigwam. Rebecca longed to close her eyes again. Her body felt like a sack of lead rifle shot.

"Come on, we have much to do," Taskemus prodded.

Reluctantly, Rebecca swung around and sat up. She felt as though she aged 20 years during the night. After pulling on her moccasins, she stood and stretched. Taskemus headed for the opening and Rebecca followed. Outside, Taskemus handed her a clay pot, not unlike the one which contained the stew the night before. Rebecca watched as Taskemus grabbed a second one and instructed.

"We go to fetch water, you can wash at creek."

The creek was just the stimulant Rebecca needed. After washing her face and arms, she felt greatly refreshed. Had she not been a captive, she might have said it was the best she had ever felt.

They filled the pots and returned with the water. After a breakfast of grits and cornbread, they set about doing the laundry, which was mostly Rebecca's clothing. The shift and pockets washed up well and were intact; but her stockings badly needed darning and her petticoat was torn in at least a dozen places. When Rebecca placed the garments on several bushes so they could dry in the sun, Taskemus surveyed them alongside her.

"We must go plant corn now. Later, when these are dry, I will help you repair them."

Taskemus was true to her word. After a day in the corn patch and supper, Taskemus produced a couple of spools of white thread and a couple of needles. When she handed a spool to Rebecca she explained. "I'm afraid white is the only color I have; but it will seal the rips."

"Where did you get these?" Rebecca asked.

Taskemus looked at the ground, the she answered, "It, it was among the belongings taken during a raid on a white cabin."

Rebecca was suddenly repulsed with the thought that the blood of another woman had probably been spilled while acquiring the sewing materials. She had the urge to throw the spool back at Taskemus in disgust. When she looked on her though, Rebecca saw a woman who humbly lived day to day. The thread and needles were undoubtedly highly prized by Taskemus as finery, yet she was sharing them freely. Rebecca couldn't insult this woman. She said nothing and started to darn one of her stockings. Taskemus said nothing more. She picked up Rebecca's petticoat and began to work on it.

A blood curdling scalp-yell startled Rebecca to her feet. *Warriors returning from another raid no doubt*, she thought. This was the same sound they made when they brought her and her brother into the village. She stood still as the rest of the village, including Taskemus ran to greet the returning party of braves. Suddenly a different sound began. This was a sound of wailing, not unlike the Indian women at the funeral. That sound piqued Rebecca's interest. She edged toward the crowd that had formed around the path of the returning warriors. At first the crowd obscured Rebecca's sight of the returning party, but, presently, the spectators parted to allow the single file of Indian men to pass between them.

A young male carried a scalp pole with two scalps on it. Behind him followed two warriors transporting a litter upon which lay a motionless body with the unmistakable scalp lock of a Delaware. Behind and a little to the side of the litter staggered Taskemus, tears streaming down her cheeks, but making no sound. Rebecca suddenly felt compelled to go to her, as though some great invisible hand had pushed her from behind. She threw her arm around Taskemus who now sobbing into Rebecca's petticoat.

"Did you know him well?" Rebecca asked.

"Don't, don't you recognize him?" she sobbed.

Rebecca strained to try to see the face of the slain man; but, by now, he was too far away.

"No, who is it?" she asked Taskemus.

Taskemus gave Rebecca a look of contempt. Then she answered, "It is Kshicanlenno!"

A feeling of delight overcame Rebecca. She could no longer be forced to marry him. Nevertheless, she fought to conceal this emotion. The loss of the young warrior devastated Taskemus, and Rebecca dare not show the elation she felt.

"I'm sorry." Rebecca muttered.

Taskemus responded by burying her head in Rebecca's shoulder. Then Taskemus sobbed at length. Afterward, Taskemus pulled away and straightened up, wiping her eyes dry with Rebecca's petticoat. She looked at the petticoat then handed it to Rebecca.

"Here, I'm afraid you may need to dry this again. I must go now to help prepare Kshicanlenno for burial." Taskemus said.

"Oh, don't worry about the petticoat. Can I help you with the funeral preparations?" Rebecca asked, hoping in her heart Taskemus would decline.

"No, this is something that Lenape must do. Please see my sister if you need anything. She will see to your needs."

Rebecca stood and watched as Taskemus joined the train of mourners trailing the corpse. When the body was taken into one of the wigwams, Rebecca looked at the petticoat she held in her hand. *Well she would finish working on it*, she thought. Just then she heard a familiar voice behind her.

"Re-beck-ah."

She turned to face the chief. "Yes?" she answered.

"As you can see, Kshicanlenno is dead. He no longer has a claim on you." The chief spoke.

Rebecca's heart leapt in her chest. *Did this mean she would be freed?*

"Since he no longer can claim you, it falls upon me to decide your fate."

The chief paused for a moment as though pondering her reaction before continuing. Rebecca remained silent. She was afraid to say anything that might jeopardize her chance of release. The chief continued.

"There is a chief in another village of the Lenape. I owe him many favors. His wife die several summers ago. He grows old with no one to serve him. I will make you a present to him."

Rebecca fought back the urge to scream. *How could she be handed over to someone as though she were a cow or pig to be his slave?*

The chief continued. "Tomorrow I will have a brave take you to my brother sachem at this village. Be prepared to leave after the funeral."

The chief then left to go to the wigwam which held Kshicanlenno. Rebecca's first impulse was to run, far and fast, the direction didn't matter. She slowly turned around a full 360 degrees. Running wasn't an option right now. There were Indians everywhere she looked, some braves here a few squaws there. Sure, she could probably get by the squaws; but all they had to do was shout and she would probably have warriors hot on her heels. She hadn't been very outrunning warriors.

Rebecca went to the log in front of the chief's wigwam to content herself with sewing the rents in her petticoat. The chief's other daughter was there also and they ate together; but mostly in silence as Rebecca's mind was preoccupied with the coming day. When darkness forced her to stop sewing, Rebecca entered the wigwam and went to bed. She fell asleep instantly.

The next morning Rebecca attended the funeral with the rest of the village. The ceremony was so much like the one when Philip was laid to rest, that it brought tears to her eyes, even though she bore no feelings for the slain Indian. When the funeral concluded, Rebecca thought to console Taskemus; but decided it was wiser to leave her to mourn with the other women of the tribe. As Rebecca left the gravesite with the other members of the village, she sensed the presence of someone walking alongside her. She looked to her left and discovered it was Mamalachgook. As she looked up to the now familiar face, he spoke.

"The sachem says for me to take you to the camp of Maghingua Tscholens. I will walk with you to your wigwam. You get belongings and make ready for journey. We must leave soon."

Despair seized Rebecca. Taskemus was the closest thing she had to a friend and now she had to leave her.

"May I go back and bid Farewell to Taskemus?" Rebecca asked.

"Yes, but I must with you. You are my responsibility until I deliver you to Maghingua Tscholens; and I know you are like a captive hare, always looking for a chance to escape!"

When Mamalachgook made this statement, he gave Rebecca a smile, which, to her disbelief, she found rather charming. Perhaps it was the fact that Mamalachgook thought of her as a challenge. Nonetheless, a feeling of comfort began to displace the despair she felt earlier. Rebecca was suddenly glad the chief had assigned Mamalachgook as her escort. With Mamalachgook at her side, she returned to the gravesite. There Rebecca found Taskemus, her sister and two other women covering the grave with trigs, branches and leaves.

"Taskemus," Rebecca called out.

Taskemus rose from her knees and walked toward Rebecca. Taskemus' cheeks were streaked from the tears she had shed.

"What is it you want?" she asked, clearly distressed.

"I must go now, Rebecca answered.

Taskemus looked from Rebecca to Mamalachgook and back to Rebecca again.

"Where is it you go?" she asked.

"Your father sends me as a present to a chief in another village," Rebecca answered.

"Ah, yes. He wants an alliance with Maghingua Tscholens, so he wants to get on his good side."

"Well I think it is disgusting for him to give me as a slave to win political influence," Rebecca spat.

"I'm sorry, Rebecca, I wish I could persuade father to keep you here; but when he decides something, there's no changing his mind," Taskemus answered her. Then she rushed to Rebecca, threw her arms around her, and gave Rebecca a hug. "I'll miss you," Taskemus continued.

"And I'll miss you," Rebecca responded. She could feel the rush of emotion bring tears to her eyes. "Oh, I will leave your clothes in the wigwam," Rebecca blurted out. She suddenly realized all she had on belonged to Taskemus.

"No you keep," Taskemus began, then continued. "I not need them for wedding. I can make new ones. You need to have more than one set of clothes."

Rebecca embraced Taskemus.

"Thank you."

Rebecca didn't want to let Taskemus go; but she knew the longer she held on the tougher it would be to leave her only friend in the world behind. Taskemus must have felt the same way because she released her hug at almost the same time. Taskemus then turned and ran back to the gravesite, Rebecca watched sadly as Taskemus departed. Then she felt the weight of a male hand on her shoulder.

"We go now," Mamalachgook commanded.

"All right," Rebecca said and headed for the wigwam. She gathered her underclothes from the bushes where they had been drying; and took them and rolled them into her petticoat. Then she ducked into the wigwam to find something to fasten the bundle. After looking under the deerskin cots, and finding nothing, she spied a bow hanging from a peg above the entrance to the wigwam. The bowstring was just the thing she needed; but the bow belonged to the chief. Rebecca hesitated to take it; but then she recalled the chief was giving her, having been born to free parents, to someone as a slave! *Serves him right*, she thought, and took the bowstring. She tied her bundle so it would sling easily over her shoulder with most of the weight resting on her back. When she exited the wigwam, Rebecca found Mamalachgook waiting, musket in hand, with powder horn, and bullet bag strapped across his chest and a small pack on his back.

"This way," he ordered, pointing to a path leading into the woods from the village.

Rebecca looked to the sky, trying to assess the direction they would be traveling by the position of the sun. As near as she could figure, the path seemed to head toward the southwest.

Rebecca headed toward the path, with Mamalachgook following. They had just begun to enter the woods when Rebecca heard a woman's voice shout, "Mamalachgook."

Rebecca turned at the sound of the voice to see Mamalachgook had done the same. A woman Rebecca did not recognize was running toward them.

"What is it?" Mamalachgook asked.

"It's Wyawaquacuman. You must come quick," she gasped, obviously winded in her rush to overtake them.

"What about Wyawaquacuman?" Mamalachgook asked.

"He has taken sick. He calls for you," she answered.

Mamalachgook looked back to Rebecca. "We must go to Wyawaquacuman. "

"Of course," Rebecca answered, inwardly grateful for the interruption and delay.

The woman turned to lead the way. Mamalachgook motioned for Rebecca to follow, which she did. The woman led them to a large wigwam. Rebecca wondered how a young boy lived in a wigwam larger than the chief's. When she followed the woman leading them inside the wigwam, she understood why. This one was obviously occupied by more than one family as there other women retrieving some corn hanging from the roof.

Mamalachgook pushed passed them and rushed to the lashed cot that served as a bed for Wyawaquacuman. Mamalachgook's mighty body obscured Rebecca's view of the sick bed. She moved around to get a better view as Mamalachgook spoke to his brother.

"What is the matter, Wyawaquacuman?"

"I shiver and my stomach won't hold food," Wyawaquacuman said feebly.

Rebecca watched as Mamalachgook put his cheek against Wyawaquacuman's forehead.

"You have fever. We must prepare a sweat oven," Mamalachgook announced.

"Can I help?" Rebecca asked him.

"Yes, come," Mamalachgook commanded.

Rebecca followed Mamalachgook out of the wigwam. She noticed the women who had been retrieving the corn were following also– without the corn. Mamalachgook led them to the side of a hill on the outskirts of the village. What Rebecca saw was an odd sight. To Rebecca, it appeared as though someone had tried to build a hut there; but only had enough tree limbs to make half of it, so they dug the rest into the side of a hill. In front of the entrance, on either side of it, were piles of stones, about the size of a large turnip. A little way out from the entrance was a spot where the earth had been blackened in the past, indicating there had been a fire. Mamalachgook hastily constructed a fire with dried grass and twigs. As the spark from a piece of flint struck against his knife grew into a flame. He turned to Rebecca and barked.

"Bring wood, quick."

Rebecca scrambled to the edge of the forest. She quickly collected an armful of branches. When she brought these back to Mamalachgook, she noticed the women who had followed her were dismantling the piles of stones and placing them near the fire. Mamalachgook took the wood from Rebecca and commanded again.

"More wood, bigger this time, must make many coals."

Rebecca searched the woods. While there were downed trees and many with dead branches, she had no axe to cut them. She finally found a branch with a thick base. Struggling, she was able to pull it from the woods. When she reached Mamalachgook, he looked up at her and said.

"You must break that up."

"And just how do you expect me to do that?" Rebecca challenged.

A sheepish look formed on Mamalachgook's face as he realized the irrationality of his expectations.

"Go to my hut where Wyawaquacuman lies. You will find my tomahawk there."

Rebecca ran into the village. As she hurried for Mamalachgook's wigwam, it coursed through her head how much easier it was to run in the short skirt of Taskemus. *It would be nice if it were the fashion for all women to wear.* "Perish the thought," she said to herself. "No self-respecting woman could expose so much leg in public." Still, she savored the freedom of movement she now enjoyed.

She arrived at the wigwam. When she entered, the sight of Wyawaquacuman languishing on the cot immediately caught her attention. He squirmed, tossed and turned on his cot, desperate to be free of the illness that gripped him. Rebecca had never seen anyone so sick before. Living in the wilderness, she had not been exposed to much disease. There was the occasional distemper, which her mother cured with a mixture of whiskey, honey, and hot water. Her father and brother had contracted infections from time to time; but these her mother took care of by lancing the swollen area and soaking it liberally in whiskey. Rebecca wished she had some whiskey right now. She detested the taste of it; but full believed in its curative powers. She could make it. She's helped her father often enough. He liked keeping the amount he made secret from her mother. As Rebecca's father had put it.

"Your mama frets that I'll drink too much of the mash squeezin's, so let's not be worrying her by telling her the details of how much and how often."

Rebecca pictured the twinkle in his eye as he said this. She fought back the tears beginning to well up inside her. The memory hurt, because it would never be more than a memory again. At the same time, the memory gave her an idea. She needed to talk to Mamalachgook.

CHAPTER 3

YELLOW FEVER

Rebecca snatched the tomahawk from the peg where it hung on the wall. She paused for a moment. Next to the tomahawk hung Mamalachgook's powder horn and bullet bag; and, leaning against the wall, was his musket! With these and a good lead, she really would have a "fighting" chance to escape. Her father had taught her to shoot also. As he'd put it.

"In these wild parts, they's no telling when a woman might be called on to provide meat for the table or defend her honor against redskins, or white men for that matter."

The thought dissolved as Wyawaquacuman groaned in agony again. She looked back to him again. *First things first*, she thought and headed back to cut wood.

It seemed like the whole village had gathered at the site where she last left Mamalachgook. Some were busy cutting wood and feeding the fire. Others were placing stones where they could be heated. A couple of squaws worked around a kettle, cutting some roots and dropping them into the kettle. Mamalachgook struggled with a tree limb, trying to pull it from the woods. He spotted Rebecca.

"Rebecca, bring me the tomahawk," he ordered.

Rebecca hastened to Mamalachgook, who took the tomahawk and began using it to strip branches from the tree limb.

"What are preparing here?" she asked.

"We are preparing a sweat house. I will enter with Wyawaquacuman. The steam from the hot stones and water will make us sweat. The women are also preparing a special medicine to promote sweat. We will stay in the house until the sweat comes no more." Mamalachgook explained.

"Do you think that will cure the fever?" Rebecca asked.

"Have you a better idea?" Mamalachgook snarled.

"Well, maybe not a better idea; but there is a potion my father used to make when we were ailing," Rebecca started. She was reluctant to use the word whiskey. She'd heard that Indians were easily intoxicated and preferred they didn't know that she could provide them with the liquor.

"What is this, this potion?" Mamalachgook asked.

"It is made from corn, but takes 4 to 5 days to prepare, and I need a special pot to prepare it."

"What sort of pot?"

"A special copper one with a coil like a snake," Rebecca explained.

"We have no such pot in the village. Nor do we have copper or one who can work with copper," Mamalachgook protested.

"Yes, but there is one at the cabin where I lived; before you destroyed our farmstead."

"It can do us little good there," Mamalachgook countered.

"But I could prepare the corn mash and we could retrieve the pot. The mash must sit for about four days before it is ready for the pot."

"I will consider your way as last resort. We will try Lenape way first. If it doesn't work, we'll see." Mamalachgook answered. "Here, put this wood on fire."

Rebecca took the branches Mamalachgook had reduced to four-foot long logs with his tomahawk. She carried them to the fire. She continued at this task as the hours passed. As she worked, she saw Mamalachgook go back to the village and return carrying Wyawaquacuman in his arms. The boy was coughing and wincing with pain. Mamalachgook entered the sweat house and moments later discarded the clothing he and Wyawaquacuman had been wearing through the opening; although they remained out of sight within. The village medicine man took bowls of the liquid from the kettle on the fire to the two within. Rebecca continued to tend the fire as the hours passed. Finally, Mamalachgook shouted something and two young boys took blankets to the entrance of the sweathouse. In a few moments Mamalachgook reappeared, a blanket wrapped around his chest and extending the remaining length of his body. He was carrying Wyawaquacuman again, who was also wrapped in a blanket. Rebecca caught only a glimpse of the young lad before Mamalachgook's back obscured him. Wyawaquacuman didn't appear to be any better.

Rebecca followed the medicine man who, in turn, followed Mamalachgook, chanting something incomprehensible. A few others of the village were following also. The boys who brought the blankets carried the clothes of Mamalachgook and Wyawaquacuman. When they got to the wigwam, Rebecca waited outside as the others entered. She paced back and forth nervously until a familiar voice spoke behind her.

"He shows no improvement," Mamalachgook said.

"Is there anything I can do?" Rebecca asked.

"Our medicine is not working. We will try yours. I will get one of the warriors who was in on the attack of your father's farm to lead me there. You must tell me where to find this, this copper pot."

"Take me with you and I will show you," Rebecca pleaded. She thought of the corpses of her parents.

"No, two warriors can travel much faster. A woman would slow us down." Mamalachgook answered.

"Please, I want to bury my parents," Rebecca protested.

"We will do that. You must stay here and prepare the corn so it will be ready when we return."

"I could do that before we leave. It must ferment for several days. It should be ready upon our return." Rebecca proposed.

"Waiting for you to prepare the corn will delay our departure; besides I would like you to look in on Wyawaquacuman from time to time to see if he needs food or water." Mamalachgook continued.

"But can't one of the other women in the village do that?" Rebecca asked.

"They are afraid to get too close. This fever is strange to them. Wyawaquacuman's skin turns a strange color. They fear he has caught a new white man's disease."

"I will stay then."

Rebecca then picked up a stick. "I will show you how to locate the copper pot."

She drew a map of her farmstead in the dirt, showing how to get to the location on the creek where her father kept his still. Then she drew a picture of the still itself, carefully explaining to Mamalachgook that she required all the parts to make it work. Rebecca also instructed him to look for one of her father's jugs; but as she put it, "Do not tarry long at this task. When the jugs had liquid in them, father kept them well hidden."

"Why was that?" Mamalachgook asked.

"He liked to take a little of the medicine even though he was not sick. My mother thought this to be a wasteful practice." Rebecca lied a little. Actually her mother didn't approve of her father drinking whiskey. Nevertheless, her mother valued the liquor for medicinal purposes. Her father made great sport of hiding his whiskey and imbibing only at such times and places when he could be reasonably assured his wife wouldn't find out. Of course Rebecca's mother knew her dad drank with some regularity because his breath betrayed him. Since, however, her father didn't drink to excess, Rebecca's mother tolerated his drinking. As her mother put it.

"As long as father believes I don't know he sips from the jug, he takes great labor to do it in moderation. If I were to pester him about it, he'd likely increase his consumption to compensate for being nagged about it."

"Anyway, father hid his jugs to avoid arguing with my mother about how much of the medicine he consumed," Rebecca explained.

Mamalachgook shrugged and gave Rebecca a puzzled look. She couldn't tell if she had convinced him, but he seemed more anxious to get on with the task ahead.

"I must talk to the sachem now. Go to Wyawaquacuman and wait." Mamalachgook ordered.

Rebecca entered the wigwam. Wyawaquacuman was in a fitful sleep. His eyes were closed, but he squirmed and twisted on his cot as though wrestling with some invisible being. His skin had turned from bronze like the other members of the tribe into a sickly yellow-brown much like the oak leaf turns before it drops from the tree in the fall. Rebecca, looking on the suffering youth, felt a strong impulse to take his hand or touch his face in some sign of compassion. She hesitated. *Would she contract the mysterious disease if she made contact with him? In fact, she had heard her mother say that "bad air" could convey disease. Perhaps she was already exposed because she breathed the air within the wigwam which was rather foul smelling from when she was last inside. Well, if the air bore the disease, it was already too late.* This element of despair, coupled with her empathy for the pain the lad bore, impelled her to his side. She laid her hand on his forehead. It was hot. She then touched her cheek to his forehead. He was burning up!

"How is he?" the low masculine voice of Mamalachgook came from behind her.

"Not good," Rebecca answered. "I think we should get him into the open air; but shade him from the sun."

"Why's that?" Mamalachgook asked.

"My mother once spoke of a disease caused by bad air. This may be it."

"Very well. The sachem is sending Taskemus to assist you. As she is the sachem's daughter she can obtain any assistance you require. Just tell her of your needs. I must be off if I'm to return within four sunrises."

Mamalachgook then came forward and grasped Wyawaquacuman's forearm with his left forearm.

"Sleep well my brother, and may the Great Spirit heal you before I return," he said.

At the same time he put his right hand on Rebecca's shoulder. She enjoyed the gentle pressure of this powerful hand, and turned to look into Mamalachgook's tearful eyes.

"Care for him as you would your own brother," he pleaded.

"I will," Rebecca answered. Then on impulse she wrapped her arms around Mamalachgook and hugged him.

"Hurry," she implored and released him.

"I'm off then," Mamalachgook answered. He grabbed his rifle, bullet bag and powder horn and disappeared through the entrance to the wigwam.

Rebecca looked back at the contorted body of Wyawaquacuman. *Would he survive until Mamalachgook returned?*

⁂

The next several days actually passed quickly. Most of the time she spent tending to Wyawaquacuman. He brought up black vomit, which she constantly washed off of him. She tried to bring the fever down by continuously applying a strip of deerskin soaked in water. In order to ensure the deerskin stayed cool, Rebecca had to make repeated trips to the creek to get fresh water. In addition to caring for Wyawaquacuman, Rebecca prepared the corn mash and stored it in a special hole she dug inside and stored in a special hole she dug inside Mamalachgook's wigwam. With Wyawaquacuman sick, she felt confident there'd be no "busy-bodies" snooping about. She worried that one of the Lenape might recognize that she was preparing to distill whiskey. Her mother had told her stories of the behavior of Indians in the cities when they'd obtained whiskey to drink.

It was now halfway through the fourth day. Rebecca longed to see Mamalachgook again. No matter how hard she toiled, Wyawaquacuman seemed to be slipping away. She was afraid he would die before Mamalachgook return. Rebecca, busy with the task of bathing down the feverish body of Wyawaquacuman, didn't notice the subdued commotion accompanying Mamalachgook's return. It wasn't until his shadow fell on

Wyawaquacuman's body that she noticed his presence. Rebecca turned to see Mamalachgook, hands crossed at his waist. His face bore a severe look. Beads of sweat dropped from his cheeks.

"How is he?" Mamalachgook gasped, the rapid and deep breaths that followed betrayed the fact that he'd probably been running for some time.

"Not good," Rebecca began; then she continued. "There's no sign of the fever breaking. He's been delirious since you left. All I've been able to do is keep him clean and cool."

Mamalachgook said nothing more. He rushed forward and dropped on his knees beside Wyawaquacuman's cot. He took his brother by the arm and mumbled something in Delaware.

Rebecca backed off. She wanted to leave and let Mamalachgook alone with his brother; and there was the matter of the whiskey to prepare. After a few moments, she prodded. "Did you find the copper I spoke of?" she asked.

"Yes, we left it by the stream. It is heavy with liquid in it. Does it require much water? Is that why your father kept it near the stream instead of by the cabin?"

"Yes," Rebecca answered. She really didn't want to tell Mamalachgook any more about the distillation process lest he ask too many probing questions. Fortunately Wyawaquacuman mumbled a few words in his delirium, drawing Mamalachgook's attention back to him. Rebecca took this opportunity to slip away and recover the pot of corn mash she'd stored in the wigwam.

By sundown Rebecca had the distillation process underway. She now sat alongside the still by the stream. She tended the fire under the still and watched as the first drops of the precious liquid dropped into the collecting jar. To get as much liquor as soon as possible, Rebecca had decided to tend the still throughout the night. Sitting on a flat stone and listening to the gentle rush of the water as it passed her, her mind drifted into a daydream. She imagined riding into the Indian camp at the head of an armed militia and seizing the remaining warriors who had made the raid on her house. *Justice would demand that she take them to Fort Pitt to stand trial; but she thought it would do more good to hang them here, where the noose might deter other warriors from following the same course.* Then her thoughts drifted to Mamalachgook.

How would he take the sight of his "brothers" as he called them dangling by their necks from the end of a rope? Why should she care? After all, he could just as easily have been on that death party who murdered her parents? Still there was something about Mamalachgook that convinced her he couldn't be a cold-blooded killer.

"When will your medicine be ready? Mamalachgook's voice broke into her thoughts.

Rebecca looked up and to her right. The evening sun was at his back and low on the horizon. Against the sun, the figure of Mamalachgook was little more than a silhouette; but the voice was unmistakable. In spite of the fact that he'd interrupted her thoughts, Rebecca felt glad for the company.

"There will be enough for the first dose by the time the village beds down for the night," Rebecca answered him.

"How many times will he have to take this medicine before it works?"

"Mamalachgook, I don't know if it will work," Rebecca protested as she rose to her feet to face him.

"We try anyway," he answered; then reached out and put his hand on her right shoulder.

"My brothers in the village tell me you tend Wyawaquacuman night and day while I was away. I thank you for that," Mamalachgook continued.

"I don't like to see anyone suffer," she replied. Then she asked the question she'd wanted to ask earlier. "What can you tell me of the bodies of my parents?"

"We took the time to bury them," Mamalachgook answered.

"Thank you," Rebecca answered as tears welled into her eyes.

"Is this something I can look after?" Mamalachgook asked, pointing to the still.

"I suppose... all you have to do is keep enough heat under the pot to produce a little vapor. The cold water around the copper tubing causes the vapor to condense into the liquid we want. As long as the pot's hot and the tube's cold everything should come out all right. Why do you ask?"

"You look awful. You'd better get some sleep."

"Well thanks for the compliment," Rebecca sneered.

"It was not an insult, just a statement of fact. You have a much more appealing presence when you are rested." Mamalachgook countered.

"What do you mean by appealing?"

"Go to wigwam and sleep," Mamalachgook responded, then added. "Before I take back my offer to tend the fire under the medicine pot. I will wake you when I need sleep."

Rebecca said no more. Tonight she decided to sleep in the Sachem's wigwam instead of on the ground by Wyawaquacuman. She desperately needed sleep and Mamalachgook was back to look to his brother if necessary. She dropped on the cot and stretched back lacing her fingers behind her head. Was Mamalachgook's comment about her "appeal" an attempt to flirt with her? With that thought in mind, she drifted off to sleep. As she slept she dreamed. It was a strange dream. She was running through a forest of hickory and beech. Strangely there was no understory. Just a carpet of brown leaves– even though the tree branches were full of green leaves. She looked over her shoulder, a band of the Lenape were in pursuit. They were screaming and waving tomahawks and war clubs. She ran on. They were closing on her. She picked up her pace. She looked back again. The war party sprinted toward her. She turned and impacted with a bare-breasted warrior. She screamed in terror. The warrior took hold of her shoulders and shook her, shouting in Mamalachgook's voice.

"Rebecca, Rebecca."

"What?" She shouted back. "Rebecca, Rebecca" Mamalachgook's voice answered.

"What do you want?" she demanded. "Wake up, Rebecca, I need you," came the answer.

Rebecca opened her eyes to discover she was staring into the worried face of Mamalachgook. His hands gripped her shoulders tightly, conveying a sense of desperation. As the cognizance of reality overtook the vision of the dream world, Rebecca realized she was safe within the hands that held her.

"What is it?" Rebecca asked.

"The fever burns Wyawaquacuman. He is hotter than he has ever been. Will you see if we have enough of your medicine yet?"

"Of course, get Wyawaquacuman and dunk him in the steam, keep him there until the fever shows a little improvement. Then dry him and return him to his bed." Rebecca ordered, then added: "I'll check the medicine."

Mamalachgook said nothing more, just dashed out of the wigwam. Rebecca got up and hurried to the still. The sun was above the horizon and the sound of the Bobwhites announced the beginning of a new day. Mamalachgook had done well tending the still throughout the night. Rebecca reckoned there must have been at least a pint of whiskey in the jar the Lenapes had provided to collect the liquid. She poured a little of the liquid into an earthen cup and took a sip. The fumes inflamed her sinuses and the liquid burned her throat. She involuntarily coughed. It was nasty stuff indeed! If it didn't cure Wyawaquacuman, it would likely kill him. Rebecca recalled how her father told her that aging mellowed the raw whiskey taking off the rough edge; but that took a lot of time, time Wyawaquacuman didn't have. What she had would have to do. If she could just get him to sleep, nature might take care of the rest. She filled the cup half full of whiskey and added water. Then she placed the cup next to the fire to heat the contents. When the liquid was as hot as "a proper cup of tea", Rebecca picked up the cup and headed for the creek.

When she reached the stream, she could see Mamalachgook standing thigh deep in water. All she could see of Wyawaquacuman was his head bobbing above the water surface.

"The medicine's ready. Bring Wyawaquacuman to the shelter," she shouted.

Without waiting for a reply, Rebecca walked toward the shelter. By the time she got there, Mamalachgook caught up to her. He held Wyawaquacuman wrapped in a bearskin robe. Mamalachgook lay his brother on the cot. Wyawaquacuman started to sit up and speak; but fell back on his cot. Rebecca rushed to him and put her cheek to his forehead. It was still hot, although his hair was still damp with the cool creek water.

"Hold him up for me, Mamalachgook," Rebecca ordered. Mamalachgook knelt down and put his arm behind Wyawaquacuman, gently inching him into a sitting position. Rebecca offered the cup to Wyawaquacuman.

"Here, drink this," she urged.

Wyawaquacuman fixed his eyes on the cup, then took it with both hands. He raised it to his lips and took a long draw of the liquid. Involuntarily he coughed and much of the fluid sprayed from his mouth again, some hitting Rebecca in the face. She wiped her face with her sleeve and responded.

"Whoa, take it easy. Sip it a little at a time."

Mamalachgook repeated her orders in the Lenape language. Wyawaquacuman said something to Mamalachgook and Mamalachgook repeated the words he said before. "What did he say?" Rebecca asked. "He said the medicine must be the Devil's brew for it burns his mouth. He wanted no more of it."

"It is important he drink all the contents of the cup while it is still hot," Rebecca instructed.

Mamalachgook spoke to Wyawaquacuman again. Reluctantly, the young lad began sipping from the cup again. He struggled to force down the liquid, stopping several times as a coughing fit seized him. When he'd consumed the last swallow. Mamalachgook laid him back on the cot.

"It's best he rest now. The medicine should help him sleep." Rebecca explained.

"When can we expect improvement?" Mamalachgook asked.

"I don't know for sure that he will improve." Rebecca began.

When she saw the Mamalachgook's face screw up in a grimace of anger, she continued: "It's the only other thing I know to do."

Mamalachgook stepped close to her and placed both of his palms on her shoulders. "I'm sorry. There is no reason for me to expect your medicine to be stronger than the Lenape. I have watched you. Your heart is one with Wyawaquacuman. He will not die as long as your heart beats strong."

Mamalachgook's expression of faith shocked Rebecca. She felt the urge to hug him in a gesture of comfort; but decided it better that she give him some task to occupy him while they waited to see if the whiskey would affect a cure.

"I think when Wyawaquacuman awakes, he will be hungry. Fresh venison would be best."

"Will you attend to him while I hunt the deer?" Mamalachgook asked.

"Of course."

"Then I will go," Mamalachgook replied.

He withdrew his hands from her shoulders. Rebecca watched as he turned and went for the wigwam. Mamalachgook was in and out of the wigwam in a flash. In a moment he was jogging into the woods, rifle in hand. Rebecca returned her attention to Wyawaquacuman. He was asleep now. Rebecca noted that it seemed a deeper sleep than she had seen since he first took ill. She knelt down and put her cheek to his forehead again– still very hot. Rebecca said a silent prayer, then she got up to check the still.

Rebecca spent the rest of the day going between the still and Wyawaquacuman's sick bed. By the end of the day she had collected nearly a gallon of whiskey. She took the earthen jar and put it in Mamalachgook's wigwam, putting it under his cot where it was not likely to be seen. She worried that the other Indians would discover she was making whiskey and feared the consequences of such a discovery.

Wyawaquacuman slept sound the rest of the day. As the sun began to set, she noticed something different. He now had beads of sweat on his forehead. She dropped down to feel the forehead. It was wet, but cool. The fever had broken at last! With a sigh of relief, Rebecca lay on the ground, stretching out on her back and gazed unfocused into the dimly light sky. She whispered a prayer of thanks. She didn't know whether to credit God or the whiskey for the improvement in Wyawaquacuman's condition. The whiskey, yes, it was time to dismantle the still. She'd better not make any more now. The less available, the less the likelihood the Indian's would discover that her "medicine" was whiskey.

Rebecca went first to the wigwam to retrieve her jar of whiskey, then to the still. She transferred the contents of the jar collecting the newly distilled liquid into the nearly full one for storage and returned the whiskey to the wigwam. Then she cleaned the still of mash and rinsed it thoroughly in the stream. Afterwards, she dug a pit in the wigwam to store the still. With this chore completed, Rebecca noticed she was famished. She decided to see if Taskemus might provide something to eat. When she stepped outside the wigwam; however, she nearly ran into Mamalachgook, returning from the hunt with a young buck on his shoulders.

"How is Wyawaquacuman?" Mamalachgook asked, not bothering to remove the deer from his shoulders.

"The fever broke not long ago, he sleeps peacefully now." Rebecca answered.

"Mamalachgook," Wyawaquacuman's voice called from the darkness.

Mamalachgook dropped the deer from his shoulders, and ran to him. Rebecca followed. When she caught up with him he was hugging his brother who now sat up on the cot. Rebecca heard them say a few words to each other in the Lenape language. Then, apparently, Mamalachgook told his brother to lay down again. Mamalachgook rose to his feet and came towards Rebecca, smiling broadly.

"Wyawaquacuman is hungry. Let us go prepare him something to eat." He said.

"He's not the only one," Rebecca commented.

As they turned to retrieve the deer, Rebecca felt Mamalachgook's hand on her shoulder.

"You know, Wyawaquacuman said he had a dream of a princess who came from the spirit world to care for him." He said.

"An angel?" Rebecca asked.

"Yes, that is what the whites call them, I think."

"The medicine I made often causes delusions- dreaming of strange things," Rebecca explained.

"From his description, I think he spoke of you."

"I don't know why he'd mistake me for a spirit. I think he has had his eyes closed all the time I've been tending him." Rebecca responded, perplexed.

"Ah, but he could easily mistake you for an angel, for I think you are one too."

With the last statement, Mamalachgook exerted a gentle pressure on her shoulder, pulling her close to him momentarily. Rebecca delighted in the sensation of pleasure, which pulsed through her body. She glanced up at his face over her left shoulder. He smiled down at her as if to reinforce his statement with gesture. He then released his hand from her shoulder.

"Ah, here we are," Mamalachgook continued. They were back at the spot where he'd earlier dropped the deer. Mamalachgook knelt down and rolled the carcass back on his shoulders again. "Come we must prepare the meat."

To Rebecca's relief, Taskemus and her sister assisted them with preparing the deer. One hindquarter was set to roasting over a fire. When it was ready to eat, Taskemus bid Rebecca and Mamalachgook take portions for themselves and Wyawaquacuman and eat while she finished dressing the deer. Rebecca and Mamalachgook didn't need a second entreaty. They took the roasted hindquarter and dined with Wyawaquacuman. To their surprise, the lad seemed as hungry as them, for he ate nearly as much. After eating, drowsiness overcame Rebecca, and, sensing that Mamalachgook longed to talk privately to his brother, she went to her cot in the chief's wigwam and slept.

She awoke to Mamalachgook's gentle shaking again the next morning.

"Rebecca, arise," he ordered, then repeated "Rebecca, arise."

"Why, what is wrong? Is Wyawaquacuman..." she started to ask.

"No, he is quite well this morning, but the sachem has ordered me to deliver you to Maghingua Tscholens again, now that my brother is well again."

Startled, Rebecca bolted to the sitting position, nearly kicking Mamalachgook as she did so.

"What?" she shouted, throwing her hair back away from her eyes. Then she noticed her deerskin skirt was nearly to the top of her thighs. She quickly pulled the skirt back toward her knees.

"I must continue the task the sachem gave me before my brother took sick and take you to the other chief." Mamalachgook explained.

Rebecca rose to her feet. Yes, the thought had been in her mind these past several days; but, as her attention became more and more focused on caring for Wyawaquacuman, the thought became buried in her subconscious. Now the horror of being presented as a "gift" for a strange savage interested in wiving seized her.

"But, I thought, well, I hoped making medicine for Wyawaquacuman might have changed the sachem's heart." Rebecca protested.

"I'm sorry, Rebecca. It will hurt me to lose you. You saved my brother and I am in your debt for this."

"But you will still deliver me to the other chief!" Rebecca protested tears welling up in her eyes.

Mamalachgook's eyes met hers. They had a glassy look as though he shared her emotion.

"I'm afraid, Rebecca, I must obey my sachem." He explained.

"And if you refuse?"

"He will only assign someone else the task."

Rebecca shuddered at the idea that anyone but Mamalachgook should be alone with her in the woods.

"Very well, then," she answered, "When do we leave?"

"Now I go for my rifle. When I return, we will leave." Mamalachgook answered, then darted from the wigwam.

Rebecca took her dress and other personal belongings and rolled them into a bundle. She arranged everything into a pack she could carry on her back. She had little to call her own, so the pack wasn't heavy. She exited from the wigwam only to find Mamalachgook waiting outside for her.

"Shall we eat before we leave?" he entreated.

"I,.. I'm not very hungry," she answered. The dread of the journey ahead, and, more so, the life she faced at its conclusion, tightened and twisted the bowels of her stomach, leaving her little appetite.

"We eat now," Mamalachgook ordered. "We will walk far this day. If we eat well now, we will not need to eat again till sundown and we will need to carry less corn and meat."

Rebecca didn't try to argue. If nothing else, having breakfast first delayed the journey. Mamalachgook led her to a communal fire where Taskemus surprised the both of them with a treat. She had prepared flapjacks of corn meal and served them with syrup made of maple sugar. The taste of the maple syrup delighted Rebecca. She hadn't had any since last spring. Her previous aversion to food disappeared and she ate until she felt as though she would burst.

Mamalachgook, astonished at her new found appetite, commented: "If that is how woman who is not hungry eats, the Sachem is wise to send you to another tribe."

This comment offended Rebecca. First the comment on how much she ate, but more so Mamalachgook's comment on the "wisdom" of sending her to the other chief. Taskemus giggled at the comment, conveying a sense of betrayal. Surely Taskemus should empathize with her, or did not Taskemus consider being presented as a chattel to a chief as a dehumanizing act?

Rebecca sprung to her feet. She pulled on her pack.

"Let's go," Rebecca snarled.

Taskemus ran to her and threw her arms around Rebecca. When her eyes looked up to Rebecca, Rebecca could see Taskemus' eyes were watering.

"K'dahoel," she said in Delaware, then, followed it up with "May the Great Spirit go with you," in English.

Rebecca could feel her own eyes welling up with tears as she choked a weak "Thank you, and also with you." The two friends hugged each other tightly, then, broke the embrace. Mamalachgook had taken the time to strap on his power horn; bullet bag and another deerskin bag, which Rebecca assumed contained food for the journey. He came up to Rebecca and announced sternly.

"Just one more thing."

"What is that?" Rebecca asked.

"I must bind your hands," he announced.

"Why?" Rebecca shouted. She looked around. It looked like everyone in the camp had their eyes on her.

Mamalachgook glanced around at the staring faces, the answered. "One reason is that I must assure the Sachem and the others watching us I have you under control."

"And what other reasons?" Rebecca spat.

"To save me much trouble. I think that you would give me much grief on the journey ahead if I don't have some means to restrict your movements." Mamalachgook answered.

"Sure, I'm going to overpower a savage brute like you and escape!" Rebecca protested.

"You have the spirit of the panther. Mamalachgook thinks you will only being to look for the opportunity to strike or make an escape." He answered.

With this last statement, Mamalachgook pulled a strap made of braided deerskin from the pouch he carried and bound Rebecca's hands in front of her. Rebecca noticed that he took care not to fasten the bindings so tight as to constrict the circulation in her wrists. Sufficient excess strap remained after the bindings to provide Mamalachgook a long tether with which to lead her. This he did walking very quickly through the village, forcing her to nearly run to keep up. The people of the village, apparently pleased to see Mamalachgook leading off the white woman, shouted words of praise.

Mamalachgook continued the fast pace, forcing Rebecca to sweat as she tried to keep up, until they were into the woods, well beyond the camp. He finally slowed down and Rebecca drew up alongside him.

"Think we put on a good show?" He asked.

"Is that what that was all about?" Rebecca gasped, still trying to catch her breath.

"My people like to see whites suffer. It gives many of my village pleasure to see you hauled away like that."

"I suppose it gives you pleasure too? Rebecca snarled.

"It gives me pleasure to see the red color that running brings to your cheeks," Mamalachgook answered. Rebecca blushed. From any other man she would take those words to be a compliment. *Could it be Mamalachgook meant them in the same way? If so, perhaps she could win her freedom by charming him to release her. But what if that approach only enticed him to take her as his squaw?* She decided to take the risk. "Why does the red in my cheeks, pleasure you?" Rebecca asked, trying to maintain only a hint of coyness.

"It seems to radiate your inner spirit," Mamalachgook answered.

Rebecca wasn't sure, but it appeared as though he was blushing. "Since we no longer have an audience, would you unbind my hands?" Rebecca asked.

Mamalachgook reflected for a moment, then responded. Without saying anything he stopped, drew her hands to his and untied the leather strap. As he put the braided strap back in his pouch, Rebecca rubbed her wrists. To her surprised, Mamalachgook took both of her hands in his. He looked first at the back of her wrists then turned her palms up to look at the insides.

"I see no damage. Do they hurt?" he asked.

"They did a little when you were pulling me," Rebecca responded, then, continued. "They're fine now. Thank you for removing the binding."

Mamalachgook still held her hands, rubbing them gently with his thumbs. "Such soft hands. I trust you will not use them against me if I leave them free?" He asked.

"I promise." When Mamalachgook failed to release her hands right away, she added. "Could I have them back now?"

With an embarrassed look, he released her hands. Then he pointed toward the trail. "Let's go," he said.

Rebecca started forward, then, slipped her left hand in his right. She smiled up at him and said: "Perhaps you'd better hold on to this one, just in case I have an inclination to escape."

Mamalachgook smiled back down at her. They started walking down the trail. The gentle pressure of Mamalachgook's hand on hers gave Rebecca a rather unladylike sensation. She realized that she was enjoying walking with this young warrior, despite the fact he was bent on killing any of her people who might get in his way. With this thought in mind, Rebecca asked: "Do you think you might live in peace with us some day?"

"I don't think so." He answered.

"Why?"

The white people only want peace when the Lenape and other tribes fight to defend their land. The white peoples thirst for land is great. Even now, whites fight whites over land which belongs to neither of them." Mamalachgook explained.

"You mean the Revolutionary War? That war is about whether a king who cares little about the people on this side of the great ocean should continue to rule, or whether we shall have our own government?" Rebecca answered him.

"What does this mean, have your own government?" Mamalachgook asked.

"I, I'm not sure." Rebecca searched her mind for the answer. "I guess it means we will be ruled by our governor instead of a king."

"Will that stop the whites from continuing to sail across the great sea to take our land?" He asked. "I don't know; but it seems there is land enough for us all." Rebecca protested.

"Then why do your leaders continue to pressure us to move farther and farther to the west? My tribe once lived not far from the great sea;

but now there is a thing called a treaty, which says we can no longer live or hunt east of the mountains. Most of the Lenape have moved to lands on the other side of the Ohio River. Our Sachem has decided to return to the land of his birth where he has decided to remain until he dies. My brothers are with him."

"And you?" Rebecca asked.

"I am with my brothers." "Would you kill me also?" Rebecca asked.

"You are alive are you not? I would not wish to kill you."

"But why did your people kill my mother yet spared my life?"

"Your mother attacked the warriors. She was probably killed in the passion of the moment. The warrior who claimed you and who is now dead, thought you to be a treasure like the other spoils they took from your house." Mamalachgook explained.

"If you had been there, what would you have done with me?"

"If I'd captured you, I would have claimed you." Mamalachgook answered.

"And then?" Rebecca pressed. "You would have the choice to be my wife?"

"And if I refused?"

"You would be my servant. You would do my bidding and, if I wished, I might trade you at some future time?"

"What if I agreed to marry you; but only if you left that band of renegades?" Rebecca proposed.

"You must have a high opinion of yourself if you think I would abandon my people for you." Mamalachgook answered. Rebecca saw a smile and thought she saw a twinkle in his eye when he delivered the answer. She decided to test him a little more.

"Don't you think I would be worth it?" She pressed.

"You have some nice features, but I am not ready to take a wife and prefer to take time to choose. Perhaps I will meet a woman I like better in the future, maybe at the Sachem's camp we journey to." Mamalachgook responded.

"So you do like me," Rebecca cooed, tugging at his arm.

"Did I ever say otherwise?"

"No, but you are delivering me to an uncertain fate as though you care not for my happiness." Rebecca sneered.

"So you think because you have a pretty face and a fair set of limbs, I am supposed to disobey my Sachem and run off with his gift to an ally?"

Rebecca relished the comment about her face; but his reference to her legs brought mixed feelings. While she delighted that they attracted his attention, she felt a sense of shame.

Proper women did not display their naked knees in public. She tugged at her skirt in a desperate attempt to restore proper modesty; but realized the skirt was just too short.

"You could just allow me to leave you," Rebecca suggested.

"And how could I face the Sachem?" Mamalachgook countered.

"You could say I escaped?"

"I will not lie to my chief."

"Is their nothing I can do to convince you," Rebecca responded as she pulled Mamalachgook to a stop. She reached up and pulled his head toward her until their lips met.

CHAPTER 4

ELOPING

Mamalachgook did not resist. Rebecca could feel his left hand move across her shoulder blade to the middle of her back. His right hand cradled her head gently. He pressed her to him until her breasts touched his chest. As Mamalachgook stroked her back with his hand, she tingled as the blood rushed through her body. The pleasure of Mamalachgook's lips transformed her to a state of euphoria. Rebecca was aware of nothing else but Mamalachgook and the sweet sensation of pleasure, which pulsed through her. Hers was an experience like none she ever had felt before. Rebecca found her hands running up and down the hard muscles of Mamalachgook's back. She instinctively felt that this man had the power to protect her– to keep her safe.

As desire swelled within her, a sense of shame suddenly gripped her. What was she doing? What was it she wanted to do? The strange arousal of her private most being shocked her. She pushed herself away from Mamalachgook, panting heavily.

"I, I... well it's the first time I," Rebecca tried to speak.

She looked at Mamalachgook. He looked as though he were flushed, in spite of the bronze tone of his body. Strangely enough, Rebecca noticed he was panting. *Did she have the same effect on him as he had on her?* The thought that she might have such power over him filled her with pride. Mamalachgook now held her by the hands. Her fingers could feel his calloused palms.

"I liked that very much," Mamalachgook spoke.

"As did I," Rebecca confessed. Mamalachgook said nothing more. Instead he began to pull Rebecca toward him again. She began to float toward him, mesmerized by those dark native eyes. The feeling of shame took over this time. She pulled away.

"No, Mamalachgook, it's not right," she protested.

"What's not right?" Mamalachgook responded.

"To kiss each other, to be intimate as we just were," Rebecca explained.

"Why?" The single word question stung Rebecca.

"My mother taught me it is not right to kiss a man unless I be betrothed to him."

"What does this 'betrothed' mean?" "It means that he has asked me to marry him and I have accepted. That we have entered an engagement period." Rebecca explained.

"You are right. You are promised to another." Mamalachgook answered, as he releases her hands and straightened up.

Still feeling the bliss of the past few moments, Rebecca blurted out: "But if I were to marry you…"

"What are you talking about? I cannot take you as a wife. I must take you to the sachem. Come, let's go." Mamalachgook responded gruffly taking Rebecca by the upper arm and shoving her in the direction of their destination.

Rebecca picked up her bundle and turned toward the trail. Mamalachgook's sudden roughness convinced her— *he wanted her.* Intuitively, Rebecca felt her destiny lay with this man. As she walked along the trail she began to visualize what a life with Mamalachgook might entail. *Could she marry him? How? Would it be an Indian ceremony or a proper church wedding? No, she couldn't marry him. He was a heathen. Surely, God would not bless the union of a Christian and a nonbeliever.*

Her thoughts then turned to what lay ahead. *What would become of her if Mamalachgook delivered her to the sachem? Would he torture her until she submitted to him? Then what? Would she be forced to bear his children?* Rebecca looked back at Mamalachgook. Right now, the view behind looked infinitely more desirable than what she envisioned ahead. The trail widened for a time and Mamalachgook came up abreast of her. Rebecca reached over and took his hand.

"Mamalachgook," she began.

"Yes?"

"Why don't we become betrothed?" Rebecca suggested.

"You mean that I should take you as my wife?"

Mamalachgook responded. Rebecca could feel the palm of his hand began to sweat. She squeezed it to reassure him.

"Well we would have to have a proper period of engagement," Rebecca continued.

Mamalachgook stared at her sternly but remained silent. Then he turned back and stared blankly down the trail as though wishing to ignore the words he'd just heard.

"Am I an unpleasant companion?" Rebecca probed.

"No."

"Ugly?"

"No."

"Do you like me?"

"Very much."

"Then why not ask me?"

"Ask you what?"

"If I will marry you?"

"Because I must do my duty to my sachem, or I cannot return to my people." Mamalachgook explained.

"We could go to Fort Pitt– just the two of us. After a proper engagement we could get married by a minister there."

Rebecca, although uncertain whether she should really marry Mamalachgook, hoped she could convince him to abandon the journey they now undertook. She decided to use her feminine whiles to help convince Mamalachgook. Stopping, she tugged on his hand. When Mamalachgook turned to face her, Rebecca threw both her arms around his neck and pulled him to her kissing him hard on the lips. As Rebecca released her grip, Mamalachgook staggered back and nearly fell. Then he put one hand to his head in a thoughtful gesture.

"I suppose I could ask the sachem if I could take you for my wife," he said.

"Would you?" Rebecca responded, then quickly kissed him again as though trying to seal that thought in his head.

"Alright, we shall return to the village." Mamalachgook answered.

The trip back to the village seemed to take no time at all. Along the way back, Mamalachgook talked of nature and hunting. He spoke the Lenape names for the plants and birds they encountered and Rebecca did her best to repeat the words after him. Mamalachgook laughed as Rebecca butchered his language; but seemed not at all offended.

The sun had disappeared into the trees by the time they came upon the camp. At the outskirts Rebecca could see the squaws busy with preparing the evening meal and a group of men were erecting a new hut. By the time they had gone twenty paces within the camp, however, they had drawn a crowd of curious spectators. Ahead, the Chief was coming out of his hut, apparently to see what the commotion was about. When the chief glanced their direction his face scowled and pace quickened. He made straight for Mamalachgook.

"Why have you returned with the woman?" he asked.

"I would like to take her as my own." Mamalachgook answered.

"And what do you propose to give me for her?" the chief asked.

"I have some 12 beaver skins from the hunt last winter," Mamalachgook answered.

Rebecca could tell from the tone of Mamalachgook's voice that he knew the gift would be inadequate. Then the chief answered and confirmed her suspicion.

"This will not do." The chief countered.

"I would promise to provide you two dozen more by this time next year." Mamalachgook offered anxiously.

"If you now had the three dozen beaver skins would you trade them for a white woman of child bearing age to be taken captive by this time next year?" The sachem proposed.

Rebecca could see Mamalachgook struggle to respond to the chief's logic. He scratched at the sheave of hair on his scalp. After a long pause he spoke again.

"But it is this woman I seek. If I cannot provide the sachem with a suitable gift at this time, could we not keep her in our village until this time next year when I can produce the additional skins?" Mamalachgook asked.

The sachem stepped forward and put his hand on Mamalachgook's shoulder. "Ah, my young man," he started. "I see your desire for this woman is great. However, we are engaged in a struggle for survival against the white man. Right now the whites fight among themselves– mostly in the east; but it weakens their ability to resist us here. If we can get our brothers in other tribes to join with us, we might be able to drive the whites from the lands of our fathers. The woman you desire is a healthy one. Strong of limb and appealing to the eye."

The chief glanced at Rebecca as he said this before continuing. She didn't know whether to take that description as a complement or the words of a lecher. She listened as he continued,

"She will make the sachem of the other tribe a good present. We hope he will reciprocate by committing his warriors to join with ours when we must battle the whites. We need this alliance now for we know not how long the war among the whites will last. The sooner we can strike in force against the remaining soldiers in the western part of this land they call Pennsylvania, the more likely we will be successful."

"But Sachem…" Mamalachgook started to protest; but the chief interrupted.

"I can see you have too much passion for this woman to undertake the task I have assigned you. I will have another deliver her."

"But," Mamalachgook started again.

"I have decided." The chief said firmly. "Since it is late, she will stay in my lodge tonight and I will assign another as her escort tomorrow."

The sachem then took Rebecca by the upper arm and turned toward his lodge. She looked back over her shoulder and saw Mamalachgook shuffling away. The chief led her to the campfire outside his hut where his daughters busied themselves with cooking. Rebecca saw Taskemus smile as Rebecca approached. Taskemus then dipped a bone ladle in a pot and ladled its contents into a bowl. This she brought over and presented to Rebecca. Rebecca took it. The stew had a sublime aroma and suddenly she was ravenous.

"What is this?" the sachem addressed his daughter.

"You serve this white woman before your sachem and father?"

"Are not guests served first, father?" Taskemus asked.

"Guests, yes," the chief started; but before he could continue Taskemus interrupted.

"Now, father, Rebecca may be a prisoner to you; but she is a guest to me. Please let me treat her that way this last night we will have together."

"Harrrruummph," the sachem answered, then walked to the fire where his other daughter drew him some stew.

"Thank you, Taskemus, you are very kind to me; but won't your father be angry with you?" Rebecca asked.

"Don't worry about that. He knows that we have become friends and I think he feels guilty about depriving me of you."

"Then why does he do it?" Rebecca asked. "The sachem of the tribe he is sending you to is a very powerful man. He commands many warriors. My father wants an alliance with him very badly; but that sachem does not seek an alliance with father." Taskemus explained.

"Why is that?" Rebecca asked. "The other sachem doesn't think he needs the assistance of my father's warriors. My father seeks to win his support by giving him a gift of great value."

"Oh, so what would your father do if he didn't need the other sachem's support?"

"He would probably give you to whichever brave in our village could offer him the best present in exchange." Taskemus explained.

"So I'm mere chattel no matter what!" Rebecca snorted. "Well at least then Mamalachgook would have a chance," she muttered.

"So you seek him as a husband now?" Taskemus asked, a smirk clearly visible on her face.

"Well it's preferable to having to serve as some sachem's slave," Rebecca spat.

"Ah, but I think there is more than that. Do you not love Mamalachgook also?"

"I don't know, Taskemus. It's just that…"

"That you always planned to marry a white man?" Taskemus offered.

Rebecca studied Taskemus' face. Her eyes stared back at Rebecca, as if in anticipation that Rebecca's answer would wound her. Rebecca seized both of Taskemus' hands in a gesture of reassurance.

"Well, yes; but it is more than Mamalachgook being Lenape and I being white."

"What then?" Taskemus pressed. "I've always dream of having my own house with my own cow and a horse to ride– one of those fine horses that the gentry ride. Mamalachgook seems to content to live by the chase, hunting deer and elk. Would he be content to live in one place? Then there's the problem of where to live. We would have to leave you and the village for us to be together. My people might not accept us as neighbors either." Rebecca explained.

"You are probably correct," Taskemus answered. "In the past, white captives have become content to live among us; but I know little of how we are treated among your people."

"Do you think there is any hope?" Rebecca asked as she squeezed Taskemus' hands.

"There is always hope."

Taskemus then stepped forward and hugged Rebecca. Then she slid her arm around Rebecca's back.

"Come, let's get some sleep. Things always look better in the morning." Taskemus said as she led Rebecca toward the wigwam.

࿄

It seemed to Rebecca that she had barely closed her eyes when it happened. She awoke in the darkness feeling the force of a male hand on her mouth. A shiver of fright pulsed through her in reaction to the rude awakening.

"It is I, Mamalachgook," the familiar voice reassured her, then went on to say: "You must be very quiet. If you want to leave the village with me, merely nod your head."

Rebecca nodded affirmatively. "Then quietly get your things and meet me just outside the entrance to the wigwam. Go no further than that. Do you understand?"

Rebecca felt the pressure of Mamalachgook's hand lift from her mouth. Then sensed nothing else. Apparently he had slipped out silently in the darkness. She felt under her cot. Her bundle of belongings was still there. She had not opened it since they returned to camp. There was little light to guide her out of the wigwam. She inched forward, trusting to memory the location of potential obstacles that lay before her. She was particularly scared of crashing into the Sachem's cot. She felt her way forward, on hands and knees, feeling first the way in front of her then dragging her bundle behind on the dirt floor.

Once outside, she breathed a sigh of relief. Then Mamalachgook whispered so close to her ear she could feel his breath.

"Do you know the trail out of the camp to the south?"

"Yes," Rebecca whispered back.

"Now do exactly as I say. Remember if we are caught we may well be tortured. There is a guard on both the north and south entrances to the camp. I will go and distract the guard on the south entrance. Wait until you hear me say N'tschu, then swiftly and silently leave camp by the trail to the south. Once out of the village, keep walking. Don't stop. I will follow and overtake when I can get away without my brothers' knowledge. Do you understand what you are to do?"

"Yes," Rebecca answered.

"What is the word you are to wait for?"

"N'tschu," Rebecca answered.

"Spoken like a true Lenape," Mamalachgook whispered back.

Rebecca knelt in the shadow of the wigwam as Mamalachgook walked toward the south trail. A dying fire from the common area of the village, with the assistance of a risen half-moon, provided just enough illumination, for Rebecca to see Mamalachgook's silhouette as he walked away from her. When the darkness swallowed him up, Rebecca scanned that part of the village she could see, looking for any other signs of activity. Saw nothing but a few sparks rise now and then from the well burned embers in the fire pit. The only noise she heard was that of mosquitoes buzzing about her ears combined with the occasional sounds of crickets chirping and bellow of bullfrogs. Rebecca was reassured by the night sounds, all seemed normal. She wondered what time of night it was. *How long had she slept? More importantly, perhaps, how long would it be before she would sleep again?*

"N'tschu," Mamalachgook's powerful voice interrupted her thoughts.

Rebecca was off. She scurried toward the darkness into which Mamalachgook had disappeared. Soon she could see and hear two figures in the darkness. One had his back toward her. As she hurried to pass them, she noted that the other figure kept moving while talking so that the first figure always kept his back to her. Mamalachgook certainly knew how to maneuver the guard.

Before long, Rebecca was on the narrow trail leaving the village. Fortunately the trail was well enough worn and that the illumination of the half moon was sufficient for Rebecca to stay on the trail. From time to time though, she would stumble on an exposed root or stone protruding from the ground. As the night wore on, Rebecca began to become more anxious. She began to worry that Mamalachgook had been caught and she was now on her own. Now on her own– wasn't it ironic? Not long ago she would have been more than happy to be free of those redskins; now she worried whether she would ever see Mamalachgook again.

Thinking about him, Rebecca had become nearly oblivious to the environment around her. Suddenly she re-entered the real world. Simultaneously she became aware of two things. She no longer heard the usual night noises. At the same time she became aware of a crashing in the bushes on her left. Fear gripped her. *Was it a bear or a panther? Worse, could it be another Indian?*

Rebecca pushed on. The animal/person seemed to be following her. The longer the noise continued, the more she became convinced that it wasn't an Indian. An Indian would have grabbed her by now and probably wouldn't be making quite so much noise. That left the possibility it was an animal. *Oh where was Mamalachgook? Why wasn't he here when she needed him?* There she was, no weapon, and something was stalking her. Rebecca's heart began to pound harder. There was a large crash behind on the left. Rebecca turned to see if she could see anything. While doing so, she continued to walk backwards, unconscious of her direction of travel. Her right heel hit something and the next thing she knew was falling backwards. The pack of belongings on her back cushioned her fall so that she fell flat on her back without injury. As she stared into the starry sky, a huge dark object sailed over her and into the brush on the opposite side of the trail. It remained aloft long enough for Rebecca to notice it had a large rack of antlers. *A deer, only a deer,"* Rebecca thought. *The thing that had scared her half out of her wits was only a deer*!

Rebecca picked herself up and brushed herself off. At the moment she was glad Mamalachgook wasn't there. He would probably have teased her mercilessly about being scared by a deer. As she resumed her journey down the trail, Rebecca noticed it was getting easier to see her way. She started to marvel at the amount of light the moon emitted, when she realized that the day was dawning. She glanced back down the trail, no sign of Mamalachgook. She was starting to worry. It seemed so long now since she left camp. What if they found him out and took him prisoner? Well he, himself, had told her to keep on going. She would do just that. She knew not where the current trail led; but chances were good that it might eventually lead her to civilization, although this now bore only secondary importance to being reunited with Mamalachgook.

Rebecca began to pass through a forest of hickory and chestnut. Hunger began overtake her. Perhaps it was the sight of the chestnut trees. She thought back to gathering them in the fall. It would be good to have a bunch of them now; but it was the wrong time of year and she didn't have the time if it were. Pondering the taste of chestnuts led to pondering some of her other favorite foods like pumpkin pie and hasty pudding. As her thoughts turned to these earthly delights, she thought she could smell the fragrance of some delectable victual. Instinctively she breathed deeper, forcing her inner senses to analyze this fragrance. Goose! Somewhere, someone was roasting a goose! Curiosity and hunger seduced her to seek out the source of the smell. Cautiously she wormed her way through the brush trying to locate the source of the delightful smell. As the smell grew stronger, and Rebecca inched toward it, reason began to exert its influence. Surely if she discovered the location of that luscious meal she would be in mortal danger. Sadly she turned back in the direction of the trail from which she had strayed. Standing not far away was the dark figure of a male Indian! The sun had now arisen in the sky to a high enough altitude that it formed a brilliant disc of light behind the man, blinding her to most of his features although there was no mistaking that hair standing like a sheath of grain on top his head.

Although startled at first, some instinct in Rebecca told her she had no reason to fear anything from this man. As he moved towards her, she realized why. It was Mamalachgook. Rebecca felt the urge to rush toward him; but realized any sudden move in the surrounding brush might betray their presence to whomever was cooking that delicious goose behind her. It didn't matter, swiftly and silently, Mamalachgook glided through the distance between them until he was able to lean down and whisper.

"Why do you depart from the trail?" he asked. "I, I was attracted by the smell of goose," Rebecca confessed. "I haven't had roast goose since last Christmas. I guess I just had the hope there might be some way of getting some. I guess that was rather silly wasn't it?"

"Yes," Mamalachgook started, then went on to explain. "We are close to the camp of that chief whom our sachem wanted to give you too. You realize it would be very easy for me to march you into that camp and turn you over to the chief. I would regain the favor of my sachem and probably a generous portion of the goose besides."

Mamalachgook smiled at Rebecca and she didn't like the mischievous look in his eyes. "You wouldn't," she stamped.

Mamalachgook's grin broadened. "Well I wouldn't leave you there; but that could be a good way for us both to get a taste of that goose. What do you think?"

"If you think I wish to risk a life as chief's sex slave for a taste of roast goose, you are a Lenape lunatic!"

"I'd help you escape. It might even work." Mamalachgook teased.

When Rebecca realized he wasn't serious, she sighed. "You enjoy vexing me, don't you sir?"

"It brings such a lovely color to your cheeks." Mamalachgook answered.

"You're dreadful," Rebecca answered. She could not, however, avoid the sense of pleasure she felt knowing that she delighted Mamalachgook in that way.

"I have an alternate idea," Mamalachgook proposed.

"What's that?" "Perhaps I can persuade them to part with some of their goose for a hungry traveler." Mamalachgook explained.

"Can you do that?"

"Sure. We practice hospitality. One tribe will willingly share their meals with a traveler."

"Then we can just walk right in?" Rebecca asked.

"I don't think it wise we go into together." Mamalachgook answered her.

"Why?"

"A white woman attracts inquisitors like flies to manure— too many questions to answer. Too many suspicions aroused." Mamalachgook explained.

Rebecca felt quite offended at being compared to manure; but she got the point.

"What's the plan then?" she asked.

"You stay right here. Have a good rest. I will go see what food I can obtain. It make take a while. Travelers are always pressed for news they might carry. This often means much talk."

"Very well," Rebecca said with a pout. She resented having to stay here, famished and alone while Mamalachgook feasted on food and company. As he disappeared into the shrubbery in the direction of that delicious smell, Rebecca removed the load she carried and placed it on the ground. She found a soft spot on the bundle to place her head and lay down. Normally she would find it impossible to sleep in the bright sunshine that was steadily ascending in the sky. Having spent much of the night traveling; however, she soon was fast asleep.

The next thing she knew a voice whispered so close to her ear that she could feel his breath. She opened her eyes, then being nearly blinded by the sun that was now directly overhead, promptly shut them again. A strong arm drew her to her feet. Standing, she now opened her eyes to see Mamalachgook's grinning face.

"Only lazy squaw sleep this time of day. Come, we must be on our way."

"What about food? I'm starved." Rebecca pleaded.

"They were most generous about feeding their guest," Mamalachgook answered, patting his stomach. "But it would have been rude to take away more than I could eat." He continued.

"So I'm to starve then. Is that the way of it?" Rebecca spat. Anger pulsed through her body.

"I think you more handsome if you stay a little hungry."

"Are you saying I'm FAT?" Rebecca exploded. She followed with an emphatic blow to Mamalachgook's solar plexus, which caused him to gasp for breath.

"No I think you quire comely, and I which to keep it that way." Mamalachgook answered.

For a moment Rebecca wasn't sure she liked the way he eyed her. She involuntarily looked down to her breasts and below to ensure she wasn't indecently exposing too much. *Was it the fact that the deerskin skirt she wore exposed too much leg?* At the same time, in some sense she felt aroused at the compliment. Hunger, however, suppressed any other biological urges.

"And it doesn't matter that I am faint from lack of nourishment, while you look lustfully at me with your belly full? She snarled.

"Ah, yes, I would not like for you to swoon on me during our journey. I don't want an extra burden to carry"

With this statement, Mamalachgook reached into his bullet bag, which Rebecca had failed to notice was swollen to nearly twice its normal size. He drew out nearly half a goose, roasted to a lovely brown with only a few streaks of black where the flesh had been burned.

"Will this put a more respectful tongue in your head?" Mamalachgook tantalized her.

"For me?" Rebecca demurred. "All of it, if you like." Mamalachgook beamed then he continued "But I think it best you eat while we walk. It would be best if we didn't remain here too long."

Rebecca pulled on her makeshift pack then took the bird from Mamalachgook. Before taking her first bite she just had to ask.

"If you are worried about warriors from your village overtaking us, why did you stay in this camp and feast until midday?"

"Actually, I'm a little more worried about someone from this camp discovering I made off with the extra goose."

"You mean you stole it?" Rebecca asked.

"It is possible they might look on it that way," Mamalachgook answered.

"Oh you're a darling," Rebecca responded, impulsively kissing him on the cheek. "Let's be off."

Rebecca motioned for Mamalachgook to lead the way. As he started to work his way back toward the trail, Rebecca bit into the breast of the goose and savored the succulent flesh.

Before they had walked a quarter mile, she'd devoured the last morsel of roast goose and cast away the skeleton. She was satisfied but not feeling overstuffed. *"My God,"* she thought to herself, *"I've never eaten that much before in my life!"* Just then, Mamalachgook glanced back at her. Embarrassed that she had portrayed such a gluttonous behavior, she turned her eyes from his.

"So you ate the whole thing," Mamalachgook teased. "Yes, I was famished," Rebecca replied defensively.

"If you continue to eat like that, you'll likely lose that comely figure."

Rebecca spied a stone on the ground, picked it up, and flung it at Mamalachgook. Of course, she didn't really mean to hurt him, so the projectile didn't carry the velocity she was capable of producing. Mamalachgook easily deflected the stone with his wrist.

"It isn't proper for a man to take such notice of a woman's body," Rebecca sneered.

"But I am a savage," Mamalachgook smirked. He turned and resumed his trek along his trail. Irritated by his smugness, but delighted that he found her figure "comely", Rebecca followed close behind.

They traveled along the trail in silence for what must have been many hours. They traveled in silence because Rebecca had to struggle to keep up behind Mamalachgook. He moved at a rapid place. She found herself breathing hard to keep up and certainly had no air to spare in idle conversation. As the afternoon lead to evening they came upon a small stream with a low gradient as it snaked through the woods in a sinuous pattern like a giant snake.

"We'll camp here tonight," Mamalachgook announced.

Rebecca looked around. *Yes, it looked inviting.* The ground was fairly level and free of noxious plant life. What really drew Rebecca's attention was the apparently deep pool of water before her. Following the face-paced Mamalachgook, she had sweat profusely and now felt quite uncomfortable. She longed to bathe in the pool before her.

"I will see what I can find for dinner. You gather wood for a fire." Mamalachgook commanded.

As Mamalachgook disappeared into the woods, Rebecca quickly set about gathering firewood. It didn't take long. Dead branches littered the forest floor all about her. In a very short time she had accumulated a pile of well-graded branches she thought would easily last through the night. Considering that Mamalachgook would probably be delayed for some time, Rebecca decided to bathe in the deep pool. Just in case Mamalachgook should make an unexpected early return, she decided to go a little distance where she could easily duck into reeds along the bank if necessary to maintain modesty. She found a suitable site where foliage was dense enough that she couldn't see her wood pile. Since she couldn't see it, it was unlikely that Mamalachgook could observe her from that point she reasoned.

She removed her moccasins and leggings first followed by the skirt and deerskin tunic. These she hung the clothes on some branches close enough, out of the water. Now naked, she entered the cool water, shivering at first until submerged to her neck and her body established quasi-equilibrium with the chilly waters of the creek. It felt so delightful. The luscious cool liquid soothed every bruise and fatigued muscle in her body. She ducked under the surface and came up to feel face washed of the sweat and grime of the journey. She wished she had some soap to scrub herself thoroughly, but this was better than spending the night surrounded by her own sweat.

Rebecca ducked under time and time again. Then, thinking she'd been in there for quite some time, Rebecca headed for the spot on the shore where she'd left her clothes. Immediately she knew something was wrong. She could see the leggings suspended as where she left them but her skirt and tunic were gone!

Mamalachgook, surely he had returned and snatched them, she thought. *That devious man probably just stole them to force her to expose herself to him for his own lustful delight!* The thought angered her; but she intuitively she felt he wouldn't press his advantage any further than that. Confident he would return her clothes on demand, she covered her breasts with her forearm and waded only close enough to the shore that she remained submerged from the waist down. At first she saw nothing. This prodded her to call out in a low voice, "Mamalachgook?" She could see some movement in the reeds; but heard nothing but the accompanying rustling of the brush.

"Mamalachgook?" Rebecca called a little louder. Almost immediately she regretted calling out the second time. *Suppose it wasn't Mamalachgook;*

but some other savage. She would be better served to keep quiet. Rebecca eased over to the edge of the reeds and sat down on the muddy streambed. She would be quiet in the hope that she might see whoever it was before they spotted her. After the refreshing bath in the deep water, Rebecca squirmed and the mud oozed around her.

She didn't have to wait long. Presently she saw a creature emerge from the reeds and into a clearing on the shore. With a head and face like a cat, Rebecca immediately identified this grey, reddish skinned creature as a panther. She had never seen one before herself; but her father had told her stories of encountering them before. She tried to remember if they could swim; but couldn't recall her dad ever speaking of that ability. Next she noticed that the panther had something in its mouth. She had to observe quietly for a few minutes before she identified the object. It was either her skirt or tunic and the panther was busy ripping it to shreds!

The goose, that must have been it, the revelation struck Rebecca. Yes, she had been quite sloppy eating the goose, and likely spilled grease and juice from it over both the tunic and skirt. The panther then picked the item up and shook his wildly from side to side as though trying to shake it to death. Then, he dropped it on the ground and stared straight at Rebecca.

Rebecca's first impulse was to scream; but two thoughts held her back. *First, she didn't want to attract any hostile Indians and she wasn't sure she wanted Mamalachgook to come while she was indecent. Second, intuitively she felt that if she made her inner fear known to the panther, the panther would perceive her as defenseless and attack.* Rebecca slowly backed away from the stream bank and into the deeper water. As she backed away, she kept her eyes fixed on the panther. She desperately hoped that the panther couldn't swim or at least wouldn't try to attack her in the water. As she backed away, the panther paced restlessly back and forth on the bank. Rebecca could feel the water rise until it covered her breasts and began to approach her neck. Then it stopped. She moved about from side to side searching for a deeper spot; but the water only got shallower in any direction. Rebecca decided to stay put and wait. The panther stopped pacing and lay back down on the bank, apparently temporarily content to lick any residual left by the goose off Rebecca's garments.

Rebecca, submerged nearly to her neck, was content to wait. She hoped the panther would satisfy itself with whatever nourishment it might glean from her clothes and move on before Mamalachgook returned. The panther seemed in no hurry, however, and Rebecca slowly swam in circles to try to keep warm. She kept this up; but as time waned on, she began to grow impatient. Perhaps she might shock it into a retreat and she could recover what was left of her clothes.

Rebecca strode toward the shore. As her body emerged from the water, she straightened up. She needed to move in closer if she were going to make a dash for the bank. Gradually the water receded from her body. A mild breeze chilled her as it hit her exposed flesh. The panther stopped and rose to its paws. The creature snarled and stared at Rebecca as though preparing to attack. Rebecca, nonetheless, was determined to follow through with her plan. The water now was only knee deep. A few more steps and she would be able to run at it. Although her body involuntarily shook with fear, she forced one shivering limb after another to advance toward the shore. One step, then another, then another, she deliberately stepped forward.

Summing up all her courage, she dashed toward the panther, then, caught up in the moment, screamed at the top of her lungs, "Aieeeugh".

The panther, startled, ducked into the bush. Rebecca spied her shredded clothing and snatched it up. She put them on; but both the skirt and tunic were shredded so bad there was no way she could be considered "decent" wearing them. Rebecca went to where she'd left her makeshift bundle. She quickly undid it, hoping she could change back into her own clothes before Mamalachgook returned. She'd just untied the bundle when she heard the familiar voice.

"Are you alright?" he asked.

Rebecca instinctively grabbed her dress and held it in front of her, positioned to cover any exposed skin.

"Yes, there, there was a panther," she explained.

"I saw, you did a very brave thing charging it like that," Mamalachgook commented.

Rebecca clutched her dress tight to her bosom. "What? You saw me?" she cried.

"Yes, I spotted the panther tracks in the woods and saw they were headed this way. Unfortunately, I'd only just arrived as you screamed and dashed for the creature."

"You mean you saw me…..undressed?" Rebecca gasped.

"Well… yes," Mamalachgook answered. "Does that bother you?" he continued.

Rebecca wasn't sure how to respond. *She was glad to know he'd come to help her; but she was so embarrassed he'd seen her naked.*

"Yes, I mean I am a woman. It isn't right for a Christian woman to be seen naked before her wedding night." Rebecca explained. Then she continued: "Turn around so I can get properly dressed."

"Does it matter, since I've pretty well seen everything?" Mamalachgook smirked.

Rebecca picked up a stick and hurled it at him. Mamalachgook parried it away with his forearm then obediently turned around. Rebecca chuckled inwardly. *What else was she to expect from a man?* She quickly snuggled into her clothes. It felt good to feel the comfort of homespun linen against her body once more. When she felt everything was in place, she spoke.

"You may turn around now," she addressed Mamalachgook.

He turned slowly, as though expecting Rebecca to rebuke him for some undefined discretion. He stared at her for a long time in silence. Rebecca felt uncomfortable. What was he looking at? This led her ask:

"What?"

"You, you look so beautiful," Mamalachgook responded.

"Thank you," Rebecca answered. Her cheeks flushed from embarrassment.

"But, your hair," Mamalachgook continued. "You look like a drenched muskrat."

Rebecca looked for another stick to hurl at him; but then though better of it.

"I supposed I do," she smiled. I'll have to work on it."

"Okay, you do that. I will prepare us some dinner."

"What did you find to eat?" Rebecca asked.

"Someone was good enough to trap us a beaver," Mamalachgook answered.

"Beaver?" Rebecca responded. She tried to recall if she'd ever eaten that. It didn't sound particularly appetizing; but there was the time her mother had made stew and refused to describe the ingredients. Perhaps she had eaten beaver one of those times. Nevertheless she was hungry enough that beaver would have to be pretty repulsive for her to refuse it.

Mamalachgook set about building a fire, then preparing and roasting his catch. Rebecca dug out her comb and went to work on her hair. She watched as Mamalachgook efficiently skinned and gutted the animal. He noticed her observation and commented.

"You should watch close. All Lenape women can prepare an appetizing meal from any creature of these woods."

"Well I am not Lenape, or have you noticed?" Rebecca sneered.

"Ah, but you must learn how to please the Lenape man if wish to please me," Mamalachgook countered.

"And what makes you so sure I want to please you?" Rebecca teased.

"I have seen the desire in your eyes."

"And you can tell this by looking in my eyes?"

"Yes"

"And where do you get this power to divine one's thoughts by looking into their eyes?" Rebecca prodded. She felt uneasy at his self-confidence.

"From my mother, I think." Mamalachgook answered. "She had the same power over me," he continued.

"All mothers are like that with their children," Rebecca commented, then she continued. "MY mother had the same power. Who else's thoughts can you read?"

Mamalachgook looked thoughtfully at the ground, then to Rebecca and smiled.

"Actually, only you."

"Why only me?" Rebecca asked, agitated.

"There is something special about you. When I look into your eyes, I feel I share your soul."

"I think, sir, you overestimated your ability," Rebecca answered. *The thought of Mamalachgook having insight into her soul, made her nervous, yet she somehow felt glad it was so.*

"I believe we can eat some of the beaver now," Mamalachgook answered. Apparently he wasn't pleased with the direction the conversation was going.

Rebecca took several strips of the beaver meat from Mamalachgook. While it didn't taste nearly as good as the duck she had earlier, it was palatable. They ate and talked until the last of the beaver was consumed. Then, drowsy from a fulfilling meal, Rebecca yawned.

"You are tired, no?" Mamalachgook asked.

"Yes, I am." Rebecca responded.

"Sleep now, then," Mamalachgook entreated. "We will try to make much distance tomorrow."

Rebecca sought out a spot near the fire as the mosquitoes were quite plentiful as nightfall came. She missed having the bundle of her dress and undergarments for a pillow. She tried to use the shredded buckskin tunic and skirt for the same purpose; but it just wasn't quite the same. She lay for a long time gazing at Mamalachgook slowly feeding the fire just enough wood fuel to keep it smoldering. The mosquitoes continued to annoy her by buzzing about her ears; but fatigue finally won out and she drifted off into sleep. As she slept, she dreamed of being in a canoe, on the river, very similar to the time Mamalachgook and the other Indian captured her for the second time. Only this was different. It was night and the sky must have been cloudless because when she stared into it she saw stars everywhere. There were single stars and great clouds of stars. She realized she was lying down in the canoe and from somewhere came a deep masculine voice singing song. The song seemed so familiar but yet she couldn't understand any of the words. Her gaze went from the sky to the rear of the canoe where she encountered the rugged face of Mamalachgook. He knelt back on his heels in the rear of the canoe, gently stroking on the paddle. He was looking at her and singing as he paddled. She thought to ask him what the words of the song meant; but dare not break the mood of the sweet melody. After a time he came to the end of his song. This prompted Rebecca to cry out:

"Oh, Mamalachgook that was beautiful and you are so wonderful!"

"Praise won't get you anymore sleep." Mamalachgook's voice shot back.

Nearly simultaneously she felt hands shaking her shoulders, the night vision vanished, and found herself looking into Mamalachgook's face now illuminated by daylight.

"You must rise now, Rebecca. We must eat and be on our way."

Rebecca sat up and brushed her hair back with both hands. She felt numerous swollen lumps where the mosquitoes had feasted on her. Mamalachgook backed off and went to tend the fire. She could see four fish, scaled and cleaned roasting on sticks over the fire.

"Were you up all night?" she asked.

"No, I sleep some. Nature hard to fight, and I finally dropped off. You sleep deep. Did you dream too?"

"Yes, I did," Rebecca responded, feeling flush with embarrassment.

"It must have been a pleasant one, since you call Mamalachgook 'wonderful,'" Mamalachgook commented, apparently pleased with himself.

"It was a nightmare," Rebecca snarled. She didn't like Mamalachgook's smugness.

"Proper ladies shouldn't tell lies," Mamalachgook responded. "Come have some fish."

Rebecca stripped a little of the white flesh from the fish's back and plopped it in her mouth. It was delectable.

"What kind of fish is this?" she asked.

"The whites call it white perch I believe. It is very good is it not?" Mamalachgook replied.

"Vury goob," Rebecca mumbled her mouth full of fish.

"I thought white ladies taught not to speak with mouth full."

Rebecca threw the stripped fish bone at Mamalachgook. He adroitly ducked to one side and the bone sailed past his ear without making contact. Mamalachgook first smiled but quickly his face became grim. Rebecca quickly sensed something was wrong.

"What is it?"

Mamalachgook said nothing but put his forefinger to his lips. He stood up, crossed over to her and grasped her arm, pulling to her feet. He started to usher her toward the rushes. Too late, for directly ahead they found themselves looking at the barrel of a Kentucky long rifle with a squirrel's tail hanging from it!

CHAPTER 5

CONFRONTATION

At the other end of the rifle was a short grizzly-looking man. He wore a coonskin cap, deerskin tunic with fox fur around the sleeves, buckskin leggings and moccasins. Rebecca guessed that the quantity of gray hair mixed with the walnut brown of his beard made him to be about 50 years old. They soon found out he was not alone. Out from behind this man followed some 8 or 9 others. They rapidly moved to surround Rebecca and Mamalachgook. Both Rebecca and Mamalachgook couldn't help but follow the newcomers as they moved into the big circle. Then the grizzly man spoke:

"Sam McCain at your service, missy. Anymore of his kind about?"

Rebecca nodded, "no". Then she thought she might regret that as she feared these men.

"Who might you be?" the grizzly man asked.

"I'm Rebecca Walker. I was living on my father's homestead; but Indians raided us and they killed my mother, father, and brother."

"Aye, I thought it might be something like that. Don't worry missy, we'll see you safe to Fort Pitt after we deal with this Injun."

"Mamalachgook? Please Mr. McCain, don't harm him. He helped me escape from the others of his village who captured me."

"That so?" Sam McCain rubbed his beard in a thoughtful gesture. "These Delawares have taken to raid'n up and down the territory west of the mountains. We've been trying to make retribution; but we's not inclined to take prisoners. What d'you say boys?"

"Lynch him," they shouted in unison.

"Please, Mr. McCain, I would be a slave to the Delaware if it were not for Mamalachgook here. He was taking me to Fort Pitt at great personal risk to himself. He defied his own sachem and people. I owe my freedom to him." Rebecca pleaded.

Sam McCain stroked his beard again, as though perplexed. After a moment he spoke again.

"Well missy, this kind of puts a snag in our mission; but we don't want to turn him loose, lessen he tries to rejoin his clan. You know many settlers have been killed by his kin?"

"Yes, but Mamalachgook isn't one of them. Can't you do something for him? Rebecca pleaded.

"Well, if we get a move on, we can make Fort Pitt by nightfall. We'll turn this redskin over to the commander there. He can decide what to do with him." Sam answered

"Is the commander a just man?" Rebecca asked.

"Well he's known for liking to hold court a lot. So's I reckon he'll get as fair a trial and any Injun would." Sam McCain answered. "The ways folks are feeling about injuns in these parts nowadays though he might not make it to trial."

"Please, Mr. McCain," Rebecca pleaded. "Mamalachgook isn't like the others. I told you before members of his village killed my father, mother and brother. Don't you think I would be just as anxious to see him hang if he were like them? Can't you just release us?"

Sam McCain, apparently touched by Rebecca's plea, contemplated a moment. With this slight hesitation, other members of McCain's party began to grumble. McCain's eyes scanned around the circle of men then returned to meet Rebecca's.

"Sorry Missy, it's either Fort Pitt or the rope for him. You make the choice."

"Let's go to the fort then," Rebecca sighed.

"Okay, a couple you boys bind up his hands," McCain ordered.

One man produced a strip of rawhide. Two others forced Mamalachgook's hands behind his back and a third bound them. One of the men noticed the last fish roasting on the fire, bent down and picked it up.

"Guess he won't be needing this." The man said and started nibbling on the fish.

Rebecca started to tell him that was her fish; but she no longer felt very hungry. She began to feel apprehensive that only trouble lay ahead. She gathered up the scraps of her belongings.

"Follow me, missy," Sam McCain ordered.

Rebecca followed him into the woods where they soon came on a well-worn path. She looked back over her shoulder to see Mamalachgook in the middle of the column She thought to go back and keep him company. The path was pretty narrow though, and it would be difficult to walk abreast of him. In addition, she didn't want these men to overhear anything she might say to Mamalachgook.

Instead Rebecca listened intently to what scraps of conversation she could catch from the men escorting her and Mamalachgook. As the day wore on she began to be more and more concerned. The men began to boast among themselves about how many Indian scalps they had obtained. They also began to brag about their prowess among women. They described in indecent detail various trysts among women of Indian villages and various taverns. From time to time she thought she heard one or more of the make comments about her "comely" appearance and how "after being with a savage" she should appreciate the "comfort" of a white man. Then came an unusual request. As the sun began to go lower in the western sky, one of the men in back of Rebecca requested they stop and camp for the night. Sam McCain turned and argued to continue the journey.

"Why, camp now, if we continue to push on we should make Fort Pitt an hour or two beyond sundown?" He asked.

Immediately the men began to grumble.

"We've been on the march 12 hours of every day for the last fortnight." One complained.

"Yeah, we have no reason to hurry," said another.

"If we stop now, we'll have time to hunt a proper meal," argued another.

"All right then," Sam conceded. "We'll make camp here this night; but there'll be no more belly ach'n till we reach Fort Pitt."

The men set about building a fire and clearing a place to settle for the night. They had Mamalachgook sit near the fire, his hands bound, where they could keep an eye on him. As a further precaution they drove a wooded stake into the ground and bound his right ankle to it by means of a piece of rawhide which was just long enough to allow him a short radius of movement. The men seemed to have their own provisions. Several of them offered jerky and a biscuit they called "hardtack" to Rebecca but offered Mamalachgook nothing. Rebecca took the food they offered and slipped some into her pockets when they weren't looking. She planned to try to get it to Mamalachgook after dark.

One of the men produced a bottle of whiskey, which he passed around to his comrades. They then began to tell stories of their adventures while trapping or Indian fighting. Rebecca politely excused herself and sought a comfortable spot in the shadows where she might sleep. Her shredded deerskin garments didn't make as soft a pillow as her dress would have; but it was adequate. Rebecca hoped she might wake up sometime later when most of the men were asleep and slip the food she'd secreted to Mamalachgook. Exhausted, Rebecca quickly drifted off.

She was awakened abruptly by the force of hands on her mouth and on her shoulders. Just enough residual light from the fire provides the vision of two scraggly men from the party over her.

"Get up," one of them commanded, "But be quiet."

The man holding her mouth removed his hand from her mouth but neither released their grip on her arms. Instead they assisted her to her feet. Both men reeked with the distinctive smell of homemade whiskey.

"What do you want?" she asked.

"Well me and Burt here ain't enjoyed the company of a woman in quite a spell. We thought you might afford us the pleasure of your womanly charms."

A chill pulsed through Rebecca. She wasn't sure what they were talking about; but the fact that they woke her up in the middle of the night, coupled with the fact that they both maintained a firm grip on her had an ominous portent.

"Come on. Let's go back into the woods a piece," the one called Burt urged.

Rebecca was convinced these men were up to no good. *What should she do? Should she scream? Would that help?* Suddenly all she wanted was to get away from this group of men, but how? Then there was Mamalachgook. *If she somehow could get away, what would become of him?* They would hang him for sure.

Rebecca glanced at the man who held her on the right. A buckskinner's knife was suspended from his belt on his left side. If she moved just right…

"Why are you holding me so tight?" she cooed to the man on her left.

"Well, I guess if you coming with us quietly, t'aint no real reason," he answered. With that, he nodded to his companion who released his grip on her other arm. They passed Mamalachgook who was sleeping, with wrists bound in front and one foot bound to a stake. Apparently the two men she was with were supposed to be guarding him so he hadn't been secured any further. This was good. She managed to kick Mamalachgook's ankle as she passed without being noticed. She hoped it would be enough to rouse him from his sleep. When Rebecca and her two escorts were about ten paces past him, Rebecca decided to make her move. She sauntered up alongside the man on her right. With a delicate move she managed to slip his knife from its sheath. To her surprise he didn't notice it. She took a few more steps forward, then turned abruptly and said: "Oh, I forgot something."

The two men were stunned just long enough for Rebecca to get a good head start. She dashed back to where Mamalachgook lay. Swooping down in an almost curtsy-like fashion she slashed the bond fastening his wrist. Then she dropped the knife on his chest. As she had hoped, he was already awake. Mamalachgook grabbed the knife and cut himself free of the stake that bound his foot. He sprung to his feet, just in time to confront the two men who pursued Rebecca. Facing Mamalachgook poised with the knife ready to battle, the men were taken aback.

Both Mamalachgook and Rebecca knew that all these men had to do was shout and the rest of the men encamped could overpower them. Strangely enough, the two men stood in silence as though wondering what to do next. This gave Rebecca an idea.

"I know you two had plans to do something with me you didn't want the others to know about. Now, if I told Sam and the others about that what do you think they would do to you?" Rebecca asked.

Neither man answered; but both looked at the ground in shame.

"Here's what I propose. You let Mamalachgook and I leave. Give us a good head start, say when daylight begins to overpower the darkness, then arouse the rest. Tell them we've escaped."

"But what if they ask us how?" The man called Burt asked.

"Just tell them the truth. I stole your knife without your knowledge. I set Mamalachgook free and we escaped. The only difference will be <u>when</u> it all occurred."

Both men looked at each other.

"Fair enough," the man named Burt said.

Mamalachgook, still holding the knife as though to defend against the two men, eased around them. Both men made no sound as Mamalachgook, with Rebecca behind him, slipped away into the darkness.

Once away from the encampment, Mamalachgook, with Rebecca at his heels, asked.

"What were they doing with you?"

"I don't know for sure; but I sense they had evil on their minds." Rebecca answered.

"Do you think they will give us till dawn before awaking the others?" Mamalachgook asked.

"I think so. I think they will want to do the most to save face now. I don't think they'll be wanting me to tell what really happened." Rebecca answered.

"What really happened?" Mamalachgook asked.

"They were taking me into the woods for some purpose which I sensed was evil." Rebecca answered.

"Those maggots," Mamalachgook hissed.

"Never mind now," Rebecca responded. "I think we should make for Fort Pitt with all haste."

"Why there?" Mamalachgook asked.

"I fear it is the only place we may be treated justly. Your people may be searching for us because you defied your Sachem. Likewise, those whites we just left might want to kill you for revenge or just so no one learns what happened this night."

"And you think I will be treated fairly at Fort Pitt?" Mamalachgook asked.

"I think so," Rebecca started, then she continued. " With me to vouch for you I'm sure the commander will give us sanctuary."

"I trust you are right," Mamalachgook responded. "But I'm leery of trusting what the white's call justice. Nevertheless, we will make for Fort Pitt."

In the darkness of the night, Rebecca followed Mamalachgook into the woods. He seemed to know the direction so she followed without question. As they moved through the woods, Rebecca began to feel a mild headache. As they pressed on, the muscles in her body began to ache also. The further they went, the worse it got. Before long, she began to feel chills throughout her body. Something was wrong. She'd never felt like this before. She couldn't stop. It was too important. She must keep going. Then she fell. Mamalachgook turned around.

"Rebecca, what is it?" he asked.

"I, I,…" Rebecca started to answer him. Then she succumbed to an uncontrollable spell of vomiting.

"You are sick," she heard Mamalachgook say.

Rebecca was semi-conscious as Mamalachgook picked her up in his arms. She felt herself being transported and then things went blank. Later she felt the cool sensation of water on her forehead and Mamalachgook speaking to her. She couldn't make out what he was saying; but the words gave her a sense of comfort.

Rebecca lost all sense of time. She could remember eating some soup or stew then later vomiting. Then there was the cool sensation of the water on her forehead and the comforting voice of Mamalachgook. She dreamed. She and Mamalachgook were going to see her parents. He brother Philip came to greet them and told Rebecca not to bring Mamalachgook to meet her parents. "They won't understand," Philip insisted. Rebecca pressed on nonetheless. Then the dream ended. Rebecca awoke to find the sun in her eyes. Then she saw the silhouette of a head. It was all black at first; but had long hair. She tried to sit up; but felt extremely weak.

"How are you doing, my little one?" Mamalachgook asked.

Rebecca struggled to push herself to a sitting position. She could feel Mamalachgook's strong arm assist her. With the sun now out of her eyes, she recognized his familiar face.

"What happened?" Rebecca spoke.

"You've been out many days," Mamalachgook answered.

"My body feels exhausted. Why is that?"

"You sleep much; but very restless. You throw up much. Act much like my brother did. You must have same sickness."

Rebecca was suddenly aware she smelled and desperately need a bath.

"Where are we?" she asked.

"We are across the river from Fort Pitt."

"What river would that be?" Rebecca asked.

"The Monongahela," Mamalachgook answered.

"Oh, good, we made it, Mamalachgook. Are you ready to cross?"

"We'll have to swim. Do you feel up to it?" Mamalachgook asked.

Rebecca wanted to strip naked and wash every inch of her body; but she was with Mamalachgook and that was out of question. Still, she longed to be cleansed by the waters.

"I, I think so. Can you help me if I should weaken?" Rebecca asked.

"I have an idea," he answered.

He led Rebecca to the water's edge. There was a log half washed up on shore.

"Come," Mamalachgook entreated.

He led Rebecca to the riverbank. With a little effort, Mamalachgook managed to get the log to float.

"Come, sit on this. I will push you across." He said.

Rebecca staggered to the log. She entered the water and managed to get on the log, straddling it with her legs and resting her forehead on her hands. She still felt quite weak, but longed for the cool refreshment of the water. Mamalachgook got behind and began to propel the log across the water with powerful kick of his legs. As they entered the current, things slowed down. Mamalachgook apparently was finding it hard to make progress against the powerful cross current. Rebecca, anxious to have a bath anyway, slid into the water and began to kick to assist him. Nevertheless, she hung desperately to the log so as to maintain her bouncy, and so she could keep her head above water and breathe. The cold water felt delightful! Although the crossing was strenuous work, she felt her strength returning.

Rebecca looked up. The fort was now rapidly arising before them as reached the far bank. She could see the heads of soldiers moving back and forth above the ramparts. She also heard shouts; but couldn't make out what they were saying. When their feet finally touched the muddy bottom on the shore below the fort, Rebecca could see a small group of soldiers coming toward them from the direction of the fort. As she and

Mamalachgook lumbered up on the beach, they were confronted by a man in a blue and white uniform who couldn't have been more than a few years her senior. He snapped his heels together and saluted.

"Ensign Butler at your service ma'am. Who are you and who would this be?" he asked as he pointed to Mamalachgook.

"I am Rebecca Walker. My parents were homesteaders recently slain by Indians. This is Mamalachgook. He helped me to escape captivity."

"Come with us please," the young ensign ordered.

The ensign then motioned to the group of men with him. They immediately formed lines on each side and to the rear of Mamalachgook and Rebecca, as though to fence them from moving any direction but forward.

"Squad, forward march," the ensign commanded.

Mamalachgook and Rebecca moved forwarded with the group of soldiers. They crossed marshland and then the ground began to rise, becoming firmer and much drier. They were led to a great wooden gate made of poles with ends sharpened and pointing to the sky. The bi-parting leaves of the gate were partially open and a soldier manned each leaf. These gate guards opened the gates a little wider on their approach, then closed it once they were inside. They were marched to a small log building, where the ensign ordered the soldiers to halt.

"Miss Walker, you will come with me," the ensign ordered. Then he continued. "Corporal, take this man to the stockade. Lock him up until we receive further orders. Then dismiss the squad."

"Where are you taking him? He's with me." Rebecca protested.

"Sorry, ma'am, General Brodhead's orders. He's ordered all hostiles brought into the compound to the stockade."

"But Mamalachgook isn't hostile," Rebecca protested. "He defied his own chief, and escorted me here himself. He even nursed me through a bout of fever."

"Ma'am I only follow orders, and, until I receive orders to the contrary, he must be locked up." The ensign replied, then turned to his men and barked: "Proceed."

For a moment Rebecca did nothing but stare in disbelief as the small contingent of soldiers marched away with Mamalachgook in the middle.

"Ma'am," the ensign's voice broke in. "The General likes to debrief any captives who have escaped from the hostiles. Would you please come with me?"

"Now?" she replied. Rebecca very much wanted to talk to the General; but she'd suddenly became self-conscious of her appearance. Lord, she must look a fright.

"Yes ma'am. The general doesn't like to be kept waiting."

"Couldn't I clean up a bit? My appearance can hardly be suitable to meet your commander." Rebecca responded.

"You look quite beaut–," the ensign caught himself, then continued. "Harumph, I mean the general will think none the less of you on account of your present appearance."

Rebecca blushed. *She knew what the young ensign intended to say. He wasn't a bad looking chap; but didn't possess the allure of Mamalachgook.* She brushed her ragged dress off and straightened up.

"Very well," Rebecca said, "let's be off."

"Would you care to take my arm?" the ensign offered. He extended his forearm toward Rebecca.

"I'm quite capable of walking unassisted," Rebecca snapped back.

"Very well then. This way," the ensign snorted and strode rapidly across the grounds of the compound.

The ensign led Rebecca to a small log building that had an elevated porch in front of the door. The porch was constructed of split logs and had a rough-hewn bench on either side of a door in the center. On the right side of the door stood a young man, clad in buckskin, wearing a fur cap, which looked to be made from the hide of a skunk. Upon the ensign's approach, he snapped to a rigid stance drawing his rifle to a position diagonal across his chest.

"Good day, sir" the sentry greeted.

"Is the general available?" the ensign asked.

"Yes, sir," the sentry answered, then he continued. "I'll see if he will see you."

The sentry then entered, closing the door. Rebecca heard mumbled voices from within, and then the sentry reappeared.

"The general will see you, sir."

"You may return to your duties, the general's voice boomed from within.

"Yes sir," the ensign answered, then he turned toward Rebecca. "Go on in."

Rebecca took several steps forward then heard the door close behind her. The general sat at an unfinished, but well sanded table. The two candles placed in pewter holders illuminated the small room quite well. Behind the general suspended from a peg on the wall, hung a curved sword with polished brass handle in a well-oiled leather scabbard. The general was busy attacking a leathery slice of meat with his knife and fork. He tore off a small piece and plopped it into mouth. The movement of his muscular jowls indicated that his molars were working as hard to break down the meat as his massive hands had to work to separate the morsel from the slice remaining on his plate.

Rebecca approached cautiously. She tried to size up the man. He wore the blue coat of a Continental Army officer with linen shirt underneath. His silver-lined walnut colored hair was tied back into a ponytail with a black strip of rawhide. The wrinkles of his forehead told of endless hours in the field and that he bore the burden of responsibility for many people.

"My Lord," Rebecca spoke to get his attention.

The general looked up from his meal. When his dark, bloodshot eyes focused on Rebecca, he stood up, and bowed to her. It was a short stiff bow, the general's upper torso scarcely leaning forward.

"A simple, Sir, mademoiselle, will suffice. I am not royalty; but a commander of patriots who seek to eliminate royal positions. I am General Brodhead."

Rebecca curtsied and answered: "Yes, Sir."

General Brodhead responded: "I am told you arrived with one of the Delawares who now have been terrorizing the settlers; yet you are clearly white. Why have you come to Fort Pitt?"

"Well, sir, some time back, Indians raided the home of my family. They killed my mother and father, then they took my brother Philip and I prisoner."

"And what became of your brother?" General Brodhead interrupted.

"He was killed later, at their village. They made him run between two lines of people with tomahawks and clubs. He fell and they beat him to death." Recalling the scene made Rebecca sob and she found it hard to speak. General Brodhead put his arm around her shoulder and gave a gentle squeeze. Simultaneously he snatched a chair, from where Rebecca couldn't tell and set it in front of his desk. He nudged her to it. She sat down.

"Take a moment to calm yourself. I must ask you more questions; but it can wait for a bit."

The general then walked to the door and stepped out. Rebecca was conscious of the general saying something to someone outside, and then he came back in. He strode to the chair behind his desk and sat down.

"I've sent for a clerk to record my interview with you. I've also sent for a few refreshments. You look as though you could use something to eat."

Rebecca was reassured by these words; but before she could answer, there was a knock on the door.

"Enter," the general bellowed.

A young man came in. He wore the same uniform as the general; but the material appeared to be of a much poorer quality and lacked many of the ornate embroideries of the general's uniform. He carried a leather pouch suspended from his shoulder about the size of a saddlebag. The man saluted the General; but as he opened his mouth to speak, a second rap on the door interrupted him.

"See who that is," the general ordered.

"Yes sir," the young man replied and opened the door.

A portly man dressed in working clothes, carrying a small table burst into the room, followed by a lad, Rebecca guessed was about Philip's age, struggling to keep from dropping a tray loaded with foodstuffs and drink.

"Where do ye want this, guvnor?" the portly man asked.

"Set it before the lady, Mr. Peele, and, good God, see to your apprentice before he falls and ruins the lot!" General Brodhead scolded.

Mr. Peele set the table in front of Rebecca, then began unloading the articles from the tray. He set before her a plate containing several slices of cheese and corn pone. It also had a scoop of some sort of stew. The delectable aroma assailed her senses. Rebecca picked up the wooden spoon and reached for a bite of the stew. Mr. Peele, however interrupted.

"What would the missus like to drink?" he asked. He gestured to the tray with a palm up to present three different containers, a jug, a mug and bottle.

"I have whiskey, ale, and rum. Which be your pleasure?" Mr. Peele asked.

"Are you daft man?" General Brodhead broke in. "Do you expect a young lady to imbibe in spirits?"

"My humble apologies, sir; but I was told to provide food and drink for a woman much distressed."

"I would like the ale, sir," Rebecca broke in. "My father used to brew some now and again. We often drank it with meals when times were rough and we were forced to eat hominy for long spells of time. It helped make the meal more palatable."

"Very well, then," the general started, then continued. "Serve the lady the ale, and take the whiskey and rum away."

"Sir, it wouldn't bother me if Mr. Poole left the whiskey for you," Rebecca chimed in.

General Brodhead looked at Mr. Poole, who appeared bewildered.

"You heard the lady. Leave the jug and be off with you."

Mr. Poole bowed, took the jug from the tray, and set it on the general's desk. Then he grabbed his apprentice's shoulder and hustled him out the door. Rebecca watched as General Brodhead opened a drawer and produces two glasses. She had never seen anything so beautiful. You could see clear through them!

"Ensign, let's have a drink while the lady enjoys her meal." The general entreated the other soldier. "If you'll do the honors?" The general continued, extending the hand with the two glasses.

"Thank you very much, sir," the young soldier answered.

Taking the glasses from the general, he filled both about half full. The general motioned with his hand to fill them. The soldier set the jug on the desk and handed one of the glasses to General Brodhead. The ensign then took a short drink and broke into a short spell of coughing. The general took a sip, consuming at least the same amount as the ensign. He leaned back and sighed.

"Not bad, but Mr. Poole certainly didn't bring the quality liquor. He has much better spirits in his establishment. Now, young lady, let's start with your name."

"Rebecca Walker, sir."

"And what prompted you to suggest the tavern owner leave the jug?"

"My father, he used to have some from time to time. I know it pleasured him greatly." Rebecca answered.

"And how did your father procure spirits?"

"He made his own; mostly from corn."

"Please tell me more of your father," General Brodhead entreated. Then he turned to the ensign. "Time to start recording. We have much to learn from this woman."

Rebecca told the whole story of the attack and everything that happened afterward. She noted that the general kept asking her questions involving numbers. How many braves in the village? How long did it take to travel to Fort Pitt? How long ago did her captivity start? By the time the general was through, she had completely drained the mug of its contents and was wishing for another.

"Well that should be all the information we require from you," General Brodhead addressed her. Then he turned to the ensign. "Get me the quartermaster."

The ensign saluted and left. The general then looked back toward Rebecca.

"We'll see if the quartermaster can find you accommodations for a few days while you seek suitable employment. Is there anything you wish while we wait for the quartermaster?"

"Yes, sir, there are a couple of things." Rebecca began.

"Such as?"

"First, might I have a little of the whiskey?"

"Harrumph," was the general's first reply; but he pointed toward the jug with the palm of his hand in an entreating gesture.

Rebecca took the jug from his desk and filled her mug about one-quarter full. She took a sip. Yes, the whiskey was pretty raw; but not as bad as some of that of her father's. General Brodhead looked astonished that she didn't break into a coughing spell like the ensign had earlier. Rebecca was amused.

"How long have you imbibed in such strong spirits?" He asked.

"Well, sir, out of curiosity I once sneaked a taste of my father's. Since it deadened my feelings, I would sneak a little more now and then when I was hurting." Rebecca answered.

"And he never caught you?" The general pressed.

"No, sir. I was lucky he didn't. He once caught my brother, Philip tasting his jug and wailed the tar out of him."

"I guess you were lucky, young lady. What other requests did you have?"

"Will you release Mamalachgook?"

"I'm sorry, Miss Walker; but that I cannot do."

"But why?" Rebecca protested.

"There are many here who have lost family because of the recent rash of raids by renegades. He must stand trial." The general said gravely.

"Why? I've just told you how Mamalachgook freed me at the cost of alienation from his people. Surely he can't be guilty of anything?"

"That you know of anyway. There is, however, another reason he should remain our prisoner."

"What's that?" Rebecca asked.

"He is safer in our guardhouse." General Brodhead began. "Among those in these parts who have lost family to the Indians are many who would try to kill your friend just because he is an Indian. Mamalachgook will be safest in our custody."

"Oh, I hadn't thought of that, perhaps it would be best if we left Fort Pitt?" Rebecca offered.

"To go where?"

As Rebecca pondered the General's question, he continued.

"Why would you wish to leave with this Indian?"

The general's question confronted her. *She would be a white woman running around with a redskin. Certainly such behavior was forbidden in proper society. Why was she considering going with him? Was it because she felt she owed him for saving her from a fate worse than death? After all, if the general could see to it that Mamalachgook was safely returned to the wilderness, he would be fine on his own. On his own, perhaps that was the key phrase. Mamalachgook would likely be on his own for the rest of his life. He wouldn't be able to return to his own village or likely any of his tribe. Perhaps that was what was bothering her. Because of her, Mamalachgook would be condemned to spend his life alone.*

"I guess I feel responsible for him. I asked him to bring me here. He can't go back to his village. I'd hate to see him spend the rest of his life alone."

"But it would hardly be proper for an <u>unmarried</u> woman to be accompanying an <u>unmarried</u> man thus. What would you do for him?" General Brodhead asked.

Rebecca suddenly realized how her relationship with Mamalachgook must be viewed by others. She felt a flush of embarrassment and sought a suitable answer for the general's question.

"I guess I figure if I was with him at least none of our people would harm him."

"But didn't you say you already had one such encounter?" General Brodhead reminded her.

"That's true," Rebecca answered, shuddering at the thought of her encounter with Sam McCain and his group. Then she continued: "Isn't there something I could do to help Mamalachgook?"

"It would help if you could procure the services of a good lawyer," General Brodhead suggested. "I could assign an officer to defend him at trial; but I'm afraid my officers only have experience in defending soldiers accused of things like drunkenness and brawling. Your friend will likely be on trial for his life."

"Where could I find such a man?" Rebecca asked.

"Aye, that may be tough. Most of the few men west of the mountains that have any legal training are Tories and not likely inclined to assist you. Perhaps Nate the publican can help you find one. I'll have to have a word with him." General Brodhead proposed.

"Who is Nate the publican?"

"Ah, he is the one that provided the meager meal you just ate. He owns and operates the pub on Fort Pitt. It is quite a thorn in my side since scarcely a fortnight goes by without one of my soldiers becoming entangled in a drunken brawl."

"Then, sir, why don't you just close the place down?"

"Ah, that sounds simple enough; but my men they work hard and are asked to march against the renegades knowing some will not return. They need some sort of diversion. In the long run, it helps me maintain discipline. The men need to enjoy some pleasure…oh, that reminds me."

"What's that, sir?" Rebecca broke in.

"A pretty young wench, such as yourself, could be in some danger here. I'd best find some family to look after you." The General explained.

"Why should I be in danger?" Rebecca asked.

"Harrumph," the General responded. He pulled at his collar with a finger, indicating he was uncomfortable discussing the matter; but continued. "You are a very pretty woman, and of prime marrying age." The General struggled as though the words were within; but he couldn't force them out.

Rebecca blushed, it gave her a warm feeling to be described so by the General; but it made her nervous also. Nevertheless, she interrupted.

"I'm quite flattered by the General's compliments sir; but to what purpose are they made?"

"I guess I'm trying to tell you that some of my men, or other men you may chance upon within Fort Pitt could be less than gentlemen."

The General coughed and cleared his voice, then looked toward the ceiling as though seeking Divine inspiration. Rebecca pressed.

"What are you trying to say sir?"

"Well some men might try to induce you to partake in activities not appropriate for an unmarried woman."

A chill pulsed through Rebecca. Although the General was not specific, she knew he was trying to warn her of something hideous.

"Thank you for your concern, sir; but what do you propose?"

"There is a Quaker family. The wife has been ill much and could use help with the household chores. I think that they would welcome your assistance."

"Very well," Rebecca answered. "How do I find this family?"

"Sentry," the general shouted.

Rebecca involuntary jumped backward at the sound of his voice. The sentry easily heard him and entered, snapping a salute to his chest with his rifle at his side.

"Yes, sir," he shouted.

"See if Mister or Missus Easton is available and tell them the Commanding General requests their immediate counsel." General Brodhead ordered.

"Yes sir," the young soldier responded. Then he clicked the heels of his boots together and did a smart turnabout. A moment later he was out the door.

General Brodhead looked toward Rebecca. "Well we may have a bit of a wait. What more can you tell me of yourself? Have you any cultural upbringing?"

"What do you mean, sir?" Rebecca asked.

"Can you read or write, for instance?" the general asked.

"Well sir, my mother taught me to read the Bible; but we didn't have much call for writing there in the woods. I suppose I could copy words if I had a Bible to work from and things to write with and on." Rebecca answered.

"Well I'm sure the Eastons can help you with that. They are both literate. What sort of skills do you have?"

"I can tend a vegetable garden. I know most plants you'd find in the woods that can be used for victuals. I can weave cloth from flax and make garments from different animal skins."

"Well I'm sure you can be of assistance to the Easton's also. They have several small children and Mrs. Easton hasn't fully regained her strength from the birth of the last one." General Brodhead offered.

"What does Mr. Easton do at Fort Pitt?" Rebecca asked.

"He's a blacksmith. He makes all manner all manner of implements from iron, horseshoes, knives, tools... almost anything you can name."

"I take it his skills are quite in demand."

"Yes, I don't know what my soldiers would do without him. He often casts new parts for my men's muskets and makes new tires for our wagons."

A series of loud raps on the door interrupted their conversation.

"What is it?" the general shouted.

"I have returned with the Eastons sir, permission to enter?" the young sentry's voice called from outside the door.

"Enter," the general bellowed.

The door swung open. Rebecca then encountered a scene that took her quite by surprise!

CHAPTER 6

AT FORT PITT

Entering first was a woman carrying a baby with two others holding fast to her petticoats as though they were afraid of being swept away by some imaginary wind. The woman, Rebecca thought, couldn't have been a day older than herself– if any older. Following the young lady with a pale, but pretty face, was a massive man. He looked to be almost twice the height of the woman. His shoulders, stretching a calico shirt were so broad that he had to turn a little sideways to enter the door to General Brodhead's office. The most unusual thing, however, was the polished oak limb where his lower leg should have been. He entered on two crutches, which appeared to be made from the same oak tree. Rebecca couldn't take her eyes from him, as she had never seen such a man before. He seemed to sense her curiosity as he strode in on the crutches with the grace of a man who long ago had mastered their use. Once inside, he offered his hand to Rebecca. She extended hers and he took in his. To Rebecca it was huge, hairy, and she could see scars from a multitude of previous injuries. To Rebecca's astonishment, he lifted her hand slightly, then gently bent over and kissed the back of it.

"Henry Easton's, the name miss, would you be good enough to tell me yours?"

"Rebecca Walker, sir," she said as she withdrew her hand from his.

"You look rather surprised, miss." Henry Easton continued. "Is it my wooden leg which perplexes thee?"

Rebecca blushed from embarrassment; but she answered nevertheless. "Yes sir, I don't believe I've ever see a man without two feet before."

"Aye, I thought as much. I lost it during the battle of Harlem Heights in New York. A British cannon I believe. Anyway, I woke up and it was gone. The surgeon must have cut the old leg off while I was still unconscious from the blow. I made the peg leg me self. Nice piece of work don't you think?"

"Hank, no need to be embarrassing the woman," the young lady with the children interrupted.

"Yes dear," he responded, then continued. "I'd like to present my wife, Hanna, and our children, Faith, Hope, and the littlest, Charity."

Hanna did a short courtesy, then spoke.

"We are pleased to meet you," she said to Rebecca, then turned to the General. "For what purpose have you summoned us here?"

General Brodhead walked a few paces and strokes his chin in a thoughtful gesture.

"Rebecca here had just been through a rather harrowing ordeal, having lost her parents and brother to a group of marauding renegades. I was wondering if you might take her in until such time as she might find a suitable husband.'

"We would be glad to share our humble home with her," said the young Quaker wife. "I hope she won't mind living with the little ones."

"Oh, no missus, missus, Easton," Rebecca replied.

"Thee may call me Hanna," the woman answered.

"Well, that being settled, I will bid you all good day," the general said frankly.

Rebecca looked at Hanna. "May I carry the baby for you?" she asked.

"I am fine with the baby, thanks, but if you could take the hands of Faith and Hope, it would be a great help."

Rebecca crouched down to eye level with the two toddlers. "Can Becky have your hands?" she asked, holding hers out towards them. They pulled tighter on their mother's petticoat, trying to bury themselves within it.

"Faith, Hope, thee will take Miss Becky's hand," Hanna ordered.

To Rebecca's surprise, both girls released their grip on their mother's petticoat and shuffled to her. Rebecca gave both a hug, then took their little hands in hers. Meanwhile, Hanna strode toward the door. Rebecca followed with both children in tow. As she followed Henry and Hanna back toward their residence, Rebecca was delighted to see the two little girls support themselves on her hands as they skipped and jumped alongside her. Henry Easton led them across the parade field of the fort to a building that shared a common wall with one of the fortress walls of the fort. Rebecca was surprised to learn how swiftly Henry Easton moved along on his crutches. Both Hanna and herself, burdened with the children, found it hard to keep up with him.

As they drew close to the building, Rebecca could see it was divided into two sections. One had a large opening with a great stone fireplace in the center. The fireplace was made of stone with a large bellows to blow air into one end. Between knee and waist high Rebecca could see a flat table top of the stone edifice. On it were some half a dozen metal tools of some sort. Rising from one corner of the fireplace was a stone chimney with a rectangular opening. A fire smoldered in the opening.

Henry Easton, apparently sensing her curiosity, hobbled over and touched Rebecca on the shoulder.

"Let Hanna look after the children a moment and I will give thee a tour of my shop." He said.

Rebecca released the children's hands. They dashed for their mother and held fast to her petticoat.

"Come," Mr. Easton entreated. He led Rebecca to the bellows near the fireplace.

"Take hold of that ring there," he ordered.

Rebecca spotted a large iron ring attached to a rope, which, in turn, was attached to the bellows. She stepped up and grasped it.

"Pull," Mr. Easton ordered.

Rebecca pulled. She heard a large "whoosh". The fire suddenly sprung to life. Fascinated, Rebecca pulled the ring again several times in rapid succession.

"That is how I heat the metal so that it might be workable," Mr. Easton explained.

"How do you tell when it is workable?" Rebecca asked.

"Usually once it becomes red hot."

"Then what do you do?" Rebecca asked.

"Then I remove it with these pair of tongs," Mr. Easton explained.

Rebecca noted he held up an object that looked something like a pair of scissors except they had funny curves where the scissor blades should be. She listened while he continued.

"I take the piece to the anvil here and pound it into the required shape."

Rebecca saw he pointed to a large iron object sitting on an old tree stump. The anvil had a flat top and a pointed cone protruding from one end.

"When I have the desired shape, I quench the metal in this bucket of water to set the form and cool the iron."

"What sort of things do you make?" Rebecca asked.

"Horseshoes and wheel tires constitute the bulk of my business. But with the militia at the fort I often repair firearms. I also make domestic utensils like gridirons and frying pans." Mr. Easton answered.

Just then, Mrs. Easton came back into the shop. "Rebecca, will thee take Faith and Hope? I just got the baby down for a nap."

"Of course Mrs. Easton."

"Hanna," Mrs. Easton corrected.

"Hanna," Rebecca repeated. Then she continued: "Would you mind if I take them on a walk around the fort?"

"Not at all," Hanna answered, then she added: "But walk not too close to the tavern."

"Why is that?"

"Many who frequent there are not God fearing, and when they've imbibed in spirits, they use the most vulgar words. I would not like the children to hear them." Hanna Easton explained.

"I will be careful to give that a wide berth," Rebecca reassured her.

Rebecca followed Hanna to the door leading to the living quarters. She didn't actually get to see inside as Faith and Hope were standing in the doorframe.

"Come take a walk with me," Rebecca entreated.

Although they spoke not a word, the children rushed to take Rebecca's hands, Hope on the left and Faith on the right. Rebecca led them back out onto the grounds of the enclosed fort. The fort was bustling with activity. In one area, a group of about 30 men were marching back and forth. A single man in a soldier's uniform was barking at them. The 30 men were not in uniform; but wore homemade clothes; predominately made of buckskin. They all carried rifles; but these seemed to vary in length and design as much as their clothes. Rebecca stopped to watch them for a while. She was amused to see a couple of them run into each other when the group reversed direction. The man shouting orders wasn't much amused, however as he ran up alongside the men and shouted at them even louder.

As Rebecca walked further on she saw a group of four soldiers working on an object that looked like a hollow log made of iron, mounted on a carriage with wheels. This item aroused her curiosity. She looked down at Faith, who appeared to be the older of the two.

"Do you know what that is?" she asked.

Faith just shook her head to indicate "No".

Rebecca was so curious she decided to venture forth and ask what this strange object was. She led the two children over to the group of four. One man, dressed in a smart blue uniform with stripes on his sleeve, seemed to be giving all the orders, she walked up to him.

"Sir, what is that object?" Rebecca asked, pointing at it.

"Why it is a cannon, wench," the man answered. "Have you never seen one before?"

"I'm afraid not, sir," Rebecca answered. "I was raised in the woods," she continued.

Rebecca noticed the man broke into a smile, which made her feel uneasy. It didn't help that he was eyeing her from head to foot as though sizing up prime livestock. The soldier asked:

"Is your husband within the fort?"

"I'm not married," Rebecca answered. Then, realizing she had two children in hand, continued: "I am assisting Mr. Easton's wife."

Then the soldier asked: "Might I call on you this evening?"

Rebecca, taken by surprise wasn't sure what to say. Something within her sent a chill down her spine. She didn't enjoy the attention this man was giving her. She had no idea why, but she felt she should leave.

"I'm afraid I have obligations this evening," she answered, glancing down at the two children. The intent was to suggest she had to mind them. It might, in fact, be true. Mrs. Easton's had not delineated when she expected Rebecca to be available to look after the children.

Before the soldier could ask another question, Rebecca scurried off with Faith and Hope in tow. She moved so rapidly, that the two children just pulled on her arms to elevate themselves off the ground. They sort of skipped along this way, their feet only occasionally touching the ground. She heard the soldier yell something after her; but she pretended not to hear. After she'd felt she'd moved a comfortable distance away she slowed her pace again. She was now coming up on a structure, built of logs, but with a grid of cast iron plates located where the windows would normally be. In front of the door, a solder marched, first ten paces in one direction, then ten paces in the opposite direction. As Rebecca approached, the soldier stopped in front of the door. He smartly removed his musket from his shoulder and held it diagonally across his chest.

"Sorry, ma'am, but you must come no further," he said.

The soldier's eyes stared of into the distance as though he were addressing someone behind Rebecca. She turned to see if anyone was there. Seeing no one within earshot, Rebecca queried the soldier:

"What is this place?"

"This is the stockade," the guard answered.

"What's the stockade?" Rebecca asked.

"It's a place where we keep prisoners," the guard answered.

"Do you have an Indian, named Mamalachgook, in there?" Rebecca asked.

"We have an Indian. I know not his name," the sentry answered.

"Might I speak with him?"

"Sorry, Miss, I have my orders. I'm to allow no one near the prisoner."

"How can I get to see him?"

"You'll have to talk to the Corporal of the Guard. He'll have to arrange for escort for you. Why would you care to see this renegade anyway? Rumor is he is responsible for many deaths." The sentry spat.

"He is a friend of mine. He risked everything to see me here safely. Any rumors of him killing have to be false." Rebecca protested.

"Well you still need to see the Corporal of the Guard to get in here." The sentry said curtly.

"Where would I find him?" Rebecca asked.

"He'll most likely be inspect'n the other posts. If you follow the wall of the fort, you'll like as not run into him."

"How will I know who he is?"

"He is one of the few here who has the regular blue uniform of the Continental Army. He'll be wear'n two stripes on his sleeves."

"Thank you," Rebecca smiled, then walked off. As she strode away she called back over her shoulder: "Mamalachgook, I'll be back to see you later."

Rebecca tried to scurry along the wall of the fort to find the Corporal of the Guard; but the children soon started to complain that she was moving too fast for them. Rebecca suddenly realized she'd been nearly dragging them along the ground. She realized seeing Mamalachgook would have to wait until later, perhaps even tomorrow.

"Sorry, Faith and Hope, I'm sorry, what would you like to do?" Rebecca asked them.

"Can we look over the wall?" Faith asked.

"Me too," Hope followed.

"Okay, we'll see what I can do," Rebecca agreed.

A little further on they came across a ladder leading to a walkway about 5 feet below the top of the pointed logs that formed the wall. A sentry dressed in buckskin, with a cap, which, in life, must have once been a skunk. Walked back and forth along the wall. Rebecca shouted up to him:

"May we come up?"

The soldier stopped. He was a grisly looking character. He had a black beard with streaks of gray embedded in it. As he turned to face her, she also noticed the index and middle finger of his right hand were missing.

"Now why would you be want'n to so that, lass?" he asked.

"The children would like to see over the wall."

"Aye, well it probably wouldn't hurt for the wee ones to have a quick peek. Come on up; but you'll have to quick about it. The Corporal of the Guard might give me hell for having civilians up here. Oh, and take care you don't fall climbing the ladder." The sentry answered.

Pleased, Rebecca helped the children up the ladder. Faith was able to scale it pretty much on her own; but Hope, being the younger of the two, needed an assist. Rebecca essentially hauled her up, holding Hope in her right arm while she used her left hand to help her climb the ladder. Once on top she took both children's hands and led them to the wall. Rebecca had to lift both children so they could see. Rebecca took in the sights below also. Below she could see two rivers converging a short distance away.

"What are the names of those rivers?" Rebecca asked the guard.

"The one on your right is called the Allegheny, the one on your left, the Monongahela. After they come together they form the river called the Ohio." The sentry answered.

"So the Monongahela and Allegheny flow into the Ohio?"

"That's right miss," the sentry answered.

"Where does the Ohio go?" Rebecca asked.

"I've heard tell it flows into still a greater river called the Mississippi which ends in the ocean somewheres in Spanish territory. Never been down it far myself, but I've a hanker'n to follow it someday. I think when the war's over and my enlistment's up I jest might do that."

"Sounds exciting, I think it might be good to explore new territory."

"Ah, Missus that's no place for a woman by herself, especially a woman with children. Have you no husband to look after you?"

"I'm not married. I am only looking after these children for a Quaker woman who has taken me in. Indians killed my parents and brother. I am alone now except for the Quaker family that has taken me in and an Indian friend who is imprisoned here." Rebecca answered.

"Ah, the renegade, I heard of him. A Delaware isn't he? How did you get linked up with him?"

"It's a long story; but I was captured by men of his village and he helped me to escape."

"I'm surprised he didn't lift your scalp, or worse?" the sentry commented.

"Mamalachgook, is an honorable man, more so than some whites I've encountered," Rebecca answered.

"Well I'll take your word for it ma'am; but you best get back down now. I could get in trouble for letting you up here."

"Thanks, sir," Rebecca said as ushered the children to the ladder.

"Don't mention it. If you want to visit again, especially if you want to come on your own, I'd welcome it."

"Perhaps," was all Rebecca said.

She saw the sun was near to setting. She led the children back to the dwelling of the Easton's. When she arrived, Mrs. Easton beckoned her into the residence. As Rebecca entered the room, she saw that everything was ready for dinner. Before her was a wooden table with benches on either side. It had been set with places for them all. At each place was a wooden bowl of soup, a large pewter plate and pewter eating utensils. This was the first time Rebecca had seen such finery in dinnerware.

"Come take your place here, "Hanna Easton entreated as she motioned to a place at the table.

Rebecca sat down. Faith and Hope took their places opposite Rebecca. Rebecca was pleased to see Hanna chose to sit beside her. Mr. Easton sat at the end of the table.

"Would thee say the blessing?" Mr. Easton addressed his wife.

Hanna said a short prayer of thanksgiving. After this they started on a delicious supper of venison stew, biscuits, hominy grits, and apple cider.

"This taste is so good, and where did you get such fancy dinnerware?" Rebecca asked.

Hanna looked at her husband. "Does thee want to tell her?"

Mister Easton appeared nervous. Rebecca noticed a red flush wash over his face; but he spoke nevertheless,

"During one of our campaigns against the British, we managed to overrun their encampment. A couple of companions came and I across an officer's tent. It was set for supper with these fine pewter pieces. While the two soldiers with me scavenged through the officer's belongings, I collected up the dinnerware." Mr. Easton related.

"Well that is before he became a member of the friends." Mrs. Easton interrupted. Then she continued: "Since it would now be impossible to return these things to the rightful owners, we've chosen to put them to good use. We do, pray for those we deprived of their property."

"Oh," was all the answer Rebecca cared to give.

After supper, Hanna read the children some stories from the Bible while Rebecca busied herself with scrubbing the dinnerware. When bedtime arrived Rebecca helped Hanna dress Faith and Hope in their nightshirts and settle them in their beds under the loft. The baby woke up and Hanna had to nurse her briefly; but then the baby fell off to sleep again. After putting the baby back in her crib, Hanna led Rebecca to her quarters. This turned out to be a bed Mr. Easton had built in the shop. It was like nothing Rebecca had ever seen before. Curious, she lifted the mattress from the wood frame and discovered a rope matrix underneath that supported the mattress. The mattress itself was very soft, which prompted Rebecca to ask: "How did you get something as soft as this?"

"It is stuffed with goose feathers. I collect them whenever I can for just such a purpose." Hanna responded.

"It looks so wonderful," Rebecca answered. "I can't wait to try it out."

"I think thee will need a nightgown," Hanna interjected.

"Oh, I can sleep in my shift," Rebecca responded.

"I have a spare one thee can use. It may be a little short since thee are so tall; but it will do until we can make thee a new one."

Hanna then disappeared into the house before Rebecca could respond. She promptly reappeared with the garment in her hand. It had the smell of lime indicating it had been freshly laundered.

"Come, I will help thee out of your clothes," Hanna ordered.

Rebecca made no attempt to argue. The thought of having clean cloth next to her skin was far too tempting to resist. She soon was wearing nothing but the shift Hanna had provided. Hanna was right. The body only reached to the tops of her knees and the sleeves ended halfway up her forearms. She could see Hanna suppressing a giggle.

"I guess I do look a little silly; but the clean fabric feels so good." Rebecca commented.

"Sit on the bed and throw the quilt over you to keep warm. Let's have a look at the condition of your other garments."

Rebecca did as Hanna ordered and watched as Hanna inspected each item under light of the betty lamp.

"Tsk, Tsk, Thee could really use a new wardrobe, Rebecca," Hanna commented. "These have been patched and repaired so much there is hardly a scrap of original cloth to attach to. You have no other clothes?"

"I had deerskin clothes, an Indian woman gave me; but a panther set upon them and rent them beyond use while I was bathing in a stream." Rebecca explained.

"You poor dear!" Hanna sighed. "The Friends collect clothing donated from the congregation for redistribution to the poor. We don't usually have a lot; but tomorrow we can see if there is anything that fits you."

"Oh, I mustn't take clothing destined for the poor," Rebecca answered, feeling quite embarrassed.

"Thee should not feel ashamed. We are all ultimately dependent on the Almighty for the necessities of life. He just provides for each of us in different ways."

"I guess I never quite thought of it that way. Until the Indians attacked our homestead, we were pretty self-sufficient." Rebecca answered.

"Care to tell me about the attack?" Hanna asked.

Rebecca spent the next hour or two relating the story of the attack, her capture and escape, right up to her arrival at Fort Pitt. To Rebecca's surprise, Hanna was sympathetic to Rebecca's relationship with Mamalachgook. Hanna explained that the Friends tried to bear no malice toward the Indians; but that too many of those who attended Meeting had lost loved ones to their attacks. Those who were not Friends were openly hostile toward any Indian. As Hanna put it: "Mamalachgook will find it very difficult to find justice here."

"Oh, I must find some way to help him," Rebecca gushed.

Hanna reached out and took both of Rebecca's hands. "Tomorrow thee should go see Colonel Brodhead again, perhaps he can suggest something," Hanna continued.

"But I talked to him about it already, he said to talk to Nate the Publican" Rebecca started.

"Well if you must, we will find thee the time to see him. Thee should get some rest now."

Hanna then left and went back into residence. Rebecca blew out the lamp and snuggled under the cover of the quilt. In an instant she was asleep.

Clang, clang, clang, the sound of metal hitting metal awoke Rebecca the next day. For a moment she was confused, but then remembered where she was. She leaned up on one elbow. Henry Easton was busily occupied with hammering something on the rim of a large iron hoop. Rebecca drew the quilt around her in a modest gesture, and sat up. She looked for her clothes. Seeing none, she remembered that Hanna had them last before she went to sleep. *How could Hanna have left her in a room with a man and nothing to wear– and her husband to boot?* She looked back towards Mr. Easton. He was still busy with his work, his attention devoted to the hot metal he was working. Rebecca thought of wrapping the quilt about her and running to find Hanna, but, before she could act, Henry Easton glanced to her. Noticing that Rebecca was awake, he spoke:

"Ah, I finally woke thee up. I hate to disturb your slumber, but I promised to have this tire ready by noon. Give me a few more moments here and I'll fetch Hanna. Gotta strike while the iron is hot."

Rebecca sat nervously as Mr. Easton went about his work. He was true to his word, though. A little more hammering, the he lifted the iron rim and quenched the part he'd been working on in water. After setting it down, he smiled, then walked passed her into the residence. A moment later Hanna appeared, carrying a bundle of clothes. She dumped the lot on the bed beside Rebecca.

"I've told Henry to stay inside until I return so you can dress now. I think you'll find everything you need here."

Rebecca held each article up and examined them. Yes, there was a complete set, even stockings. As Rebecca dressed she inspected them more closely. They looked as though they had scarcely been worn.

"Where did you get these?" Rebecca asked?

"I'm afraid a member of our Meeting died during childbirth some weeks ago. Her husband donated the things she left behind to the Meeting." Hanna explained.

"What of the child?" Rebecca asked.

"The child, a boy, survived the birth; but died several days later. We don't know for sure why. The woman looking after him is very conscientious. She has nursed a couple of healthy children of her own." Hanna answered.

Rebecca, now finished dressing, stood up. She pivoted about in front of Hanna and asked: "How do I look?"

"You look fine; but would thee like me to help you fix your hair?"

"Thank you, I guess it is quite a mess. I haven't had a comb to use on it for several days." Rebecca answered.

"Good. Let us go inside. Henry must get about his work again and I need to be where I can observe the children."

Rebecca followed Hanna into the house. She sat in a chair at the table while Hanna went to work on her hair. She looked about the room. All the children were still asleep. She decided to ask Hanna a question that had been in the back of her mind.

"Do you think Nate the publican would assist me in finding a lawyer to defend Mamalachgook?"

"If the price were right, he would. He's not likely to assist anyone unless there is some profit in it for him." Hanna answered.

"Is there anyone else who would help me find a lawyer?"

Hanna chuckled, "I'm afraid Nate's the one most likely one to associate with lawyers."

"What's so funny?" Rebecca asked.

"Any lawyers to be found in these parts are likely ones who gotten into trouble with the law themselves. I would expect if you found one, he would be just as big a scoundrel as Nate himself."

Rebecca wasn't amused. Getting assistance for Mamalachgook seemed impossible. Nevertheless, she had to do something. She resolved that she would see Nate the Publican.

"May I enquire about the matter this morning?" Rebecca asked.

"Sure, but take care. You should conduct any conservation with men in public view."

"Why is that?" Rebecca asked.

"Many around here would brand you as a harlot if you had private dealings with men?"

"Thank you for the advice, I will be careful." Rebecca reassured her.

Hanna not only combed her hair; but also braided it so it would stay upon her head. Afterwards she gave Rebecca a bonnet.

"I think I'll be off then." Rebecca said and made her way outside. Outside, she headed straight for the pub of Nate the Publican. It wasn't hard to find, even though it was on the far side of the fort. Rebecca had actually spotted it on her walk the day before.

The building differed from the other structures within the fort in that most of it was built of limestone. The doors and windows, however, were framed with neatly whitewashed lumber— a rarity on the Western frontier. In front of the building there was a long hitching post made consisting of a single rail and a watering trough. Rebecca thought it could accommodate twenty horses or more. Right now, however, only one horse was tied to it. Hanging above the front door, suspended from a wrought iron support was a wooden sign. The sign, primarily a wood carving, but with paint to enhance the image, bore the image of a smiling beaver with a foaming mug in his hands. Lettering identified the establishment as *The Thirsty Beaver*. Rebecca sighed, then reached for the door handle and entered.

She found herself under a great roof. It looked like the kitchen at home but many times at large. There must have been at least a dozen tables, some round, some square. Rough-hewn chairs with seats that looked as though they'd been worn to a polished state surrounded each table, four to eight, depending on the size of the table. The ceiling above consisted of oak planks, supported by massive, squared beams, spaced about a man's height apart. On one side she could see a large chimney with fireplace. The same stone she'd seen on the outside formed the chimney and fireplace. Sitting on the hearth, an old woman slowly turned the hindquarter of some sizeable animal on a spit as the fire roasted the flesh. Along the intersecting wall was a different sort of structure. It rose to about the height of a man's chest. It was made of the prettiest dark wood, Rebecca had ever seen. Furthermore, it was polished to a shine so brilliant, Rebecca thought she might be able to use it as a mirror. Behind it, a set of shelves bore a few bottles, a large number of jugs, and a couple of barrels. The barrels lay on their sided, with small tubes with corks in the end.

Behind the walnut structure, the man whom had brought food and drink to Colonel Brodhead the day before busied himself filling a pewter tankard. When a dome of foam appeared on top of the tankard, the man, whom Rebecca assumed was Nate, lifted a section of top of the polished counter and strode over to a table where a single man busied himself with a plate of meat and scrambled eggs, occasionally taking a bite from a small bread loaf.

Rebecca waited for the publican to serve the customer. The publican then glanced toward Rebecca.

"An what would you be want'n wench?" He asked.

"Sir, I've been told you know a great many people, hereabouts," Rebecca began.

Nate the Publican straightened up. Rebecca thought she saw his chest swell a little, and then he answered her. "Aye, it seems most everyone hereabouts visits Nate the Publican at some time or t'other. Not many Quakers though, and the Colonel'd have me flogged and shut down if I served the redskins."

"Would you know of any lawyers?" Rebecca asked.

"Lawyers, eh," Nate started as he stroked his chin in a thoughtful gesture.

"Well, there's been a few stop here who professed to be lawyers; but they usually headed for somewheres else. If you're look'n for lawyers, ye'd best go to Hannastown."

"And where would I find this Hannastown?" Rebecca asked.

"It is about 30 mile east of here– as the crow flies," Nate began. Then he continued, "But I hope yer not thinking about going there alone."

"Why's that?" Rebecca asked.

"Oh, miss the forest is full of renegades these days. Yer likely to lose your scalp or worse."

"I'll worry about that," Rebecca mumbled.

"What's that miss?" Nate asked.

"Nothing,... Nothing," Rebecca answered as she backed toward the door of the tavern.

Outside she felt confused. She felt she owed some service to Hanna and Henry; yet Mamalachgook's life might very well depend on her being able to get him legal assistance. She made up her mind. She would present her problem to Hanna and hope Hanna would understand.

"Of course you must go," Hanna implored.

Much to Rebecca's surprise, Hanna fully supported her.

"But what about the children?" Rebecca asked.

"Oh, I managed before you came here. I can manage during your absence," Hanna smiled at her.

"Thank you very much. You know I wouldn't go if it weren't a life and death matter." Rebecca replied.

"You think it is that serious?" Hanna asked.

"I don't know for sure. But it seems like enough people around here would like to hang an Indian– any Indian."

"You rest tonight," Hanna began. "I will prepare some things for your trip. How many days do you think you'll be gone?" She continued.

"About four. I figure 2 days there and 2 days back. Hopefully, I will be able to get a lawyer as soon as I arrive. If not, I may be a little longer." Rebecca responded.

"I'll pack you a week's provisions, just in case," Hanna answered.

"Oh, I don't know how to thank you!"

"No need to. There are times when we women must do what we need to do. Still, I will worry about you with so many hostilities about," Hanna mumbled.

"Thank you," Rebecca responded, rushing to Hanna to give her a hug. She noticed Hanna's eyes were tearing.

"Well you best be getting some rest, you have a long journey ahead," Hanna answered as she pulled away.

The next morning Rebecca was up at first light. She had slept well; but was anxious to be on her way.

CHAPTER 7

THE SHOOTING MATCH

R ebecca dressed and went to assist Hanna with morning breakfast. After a breakfast of porridge, johnnycakes with jam, and some sort of herbal tea, Rebecca helped clean the dishes. When the chores were completed she looked at Hanna and announced:

"I'd better be on my way."

Hanna responded by going to the pantry and extracting a deerskin bag. Rebecca noticed it had two straps on it that would allow her to wear the bag on her back.

"I've made you some provisions for the trail, deer jerky, sea biscuit, and some fruit preserves. There's a blanket for the night, a scissors, thread, needles, and some rawhide thong for sewing repairs. I think I have everything you will absolutely need. I didn't want to make the burden too heavy." Hanna explained.

"Thank you so much," Rebecca responded.

After hugging Hanna she knelt down and hugged Faith and Hope. They said nothing; but Rebecca could see their eyes were watery, as though on the brink of crying.

"Now, then," Rebecca consoled, "I plan to be back here in a few days."

The two children hugged Rebecca harder, and it hurt her to break the embrace. Standing up again, she slung the pack on her shoulders and left. Rebecca strode rapidly across the fort grounds toward General Brodhead's office. To Rebecca's amazement he sentry outside the door looked as though wasn't more than a year older than Phillip. Nevertheless, he demanded:

"State your business."

"I'm here to see General Brodhead."

"He's busy conferring with another officer. My orders are he's not to be disturbed." The sentry responded.

Rebecca resented being talked down to by a boy trying to act the soldier; but she just responded, "I'll wait." Then she took off the pack she was wearing and sat down on the wooden planking outside the office. The wait wasn't long. She was pleased to hear door open and military courtesies being exchanged. Rebecca turned to see the young ensign whom she first met on her arrival at Fort Pitt. Behind him, coming out of the office, was the buckskin-clad man who had helped the children look over the fort wall. Both men tipped their hats at Rebecca, then proceeded across the compound. Rebecca turned toward the sentry.

"Will you ask the general if he will see me now?"

"Yes, ma'am," the sentry answered. He disappeared through the door but returned only seconds later.

"You may enter," he announced.

Rebecca left her pack on the porch and walked through the door. General Brodhead was occupied with rolling up some maps. He spoke without looking up.

"What is the purpose of your visit," he snarled.

"Sir, I would like to journey to Hannastown, to seek a lawyer for Mamalachgook," she began.

"Nate the publican was of no help to you then, I take it," General Brodhead responded.

"He was the one who suggested I go to Hannastown," Rebecca explained.

General Brodhead looked up from his desk. Now that his eyes were on Rebecca, his manner softened.

"Surely you don't plan to travel there alone?" He inquired.

"Yes sir, if you could provide me with a map. I have no knowledge of the country between here and there."

"I can't allow you to make such a journey alone. It's not safe. We continue to get reports of Indian deprivations against the farmsteads. Like as not they would capture you as they did before or even scalp you. Sending an unarmed woman beyond these walls is like feeding a chicken to the wolves." General Brodhead commented.

"Well this 'chick' can shoot. If you would but lend me a rifle, power, and shot."

"Ah, it is hard to fathom a delicate young lady like you even knowing which end of a musket to point at the enemy." General Brodhead chuckled.

"My father taught me," Rebecca started, then continued. "I can shoot the head off a snake at a hundred paces. I spect I can outshoot your best man here."

"Oh, this I have to see," the general began. Then he shouted: "Sentry"

The young sentry was in the door quick as a flash, saluting sharply across his chest, holding his rifle perpendicular to the floor.

"Yes, sir?"

"Go get Sgt. Rodgers and tell him to bring his rifle as well a spare musket, with powder and shot for both." General Brodhead ordered.

"Yes sir," the sentry answered, did an 'about face' and left.

"Well Miss Walker, we'll see how good a marksman you are." The General commented.

As they waited for the return of the sentry with Sgt. Rodgers, General Brodhead related the details of some of the reports of Indian attacks, which had recently been reported. Rebecca sensed the General was trying to scare her out of making the proposed journey. Rebecca was glad when a knock at the door finally interrupted the General's diatribe.

"Yes," the General bellowed.

"Sgt. Rodgers here," a muffled, gruff voice answered.

"Sgt. Rodgers here, what?" the general answered.

"Sgt. Rodgers here, sir," came the answered.

"Enter," General Brodhead commanded.

Rebecca's attention turned to the door. As the sergeant entered, she immediately recognized him. He was the gruff speaking man she'd asked about the cannon and whom she shied away from when he'd asked to call on her. In each hand he carried a rifle and, draped across his chest were straps connected to two power horns and two bullet bags. The rifles were unlike the ones she'd seen the other soldiers carrying. The major difference was both rifles had longer barrels.

"Are we going hunting, General?" Sgt. Rodgers asked.

"No, just a bit of target practice," the general answered.

Sgt. Rodgers extended an arm with one of the rifles, offering it to the General.

"I think you'll find this a fair piece, sir. I borrowed it from one of the local boys in my platoon. It's nearly as good as mine and I think you'll find it more accurate than any of the military muskets here– begging your pardon sir."

The general took the offered rifle. He tested the weight, then he put the butt to his shoulder. After sighting down the barrel at some imaginary target opposite Rebecca and the sergeant, he lowered the weapon to a position diagonally across his chest.

"And heavier, also," General Brodhead commented.

Then the general held the rifle out to Rebecca.

"Take it, and see what you think," he ordered.

Rebecca took the rifle from the general and repeated the same motions. After bringing the rifle to a resting position across her chest, the general pressed:

"Well?"

"Sire, it's a might more awkward than my father's; but it will do." Rebecca answered.

"What's she talking about?" Sgt. Rodgers asked, giving the general a perplexed look.

"This young lady has challenged you to a shoot'n match."

"Me? I hate to brag sir, but I'm about the best shot at this post." Sgt. Rodgers responded.

"And some say in the Pennsylvania Militia," the general added, then, he continued. "Rebecca here wants to travel to Hannastown, and she wants to prove she can shoot her way out of any trouble. So we're going to see how good she is."

The sergeant stood dumbfounded. General Brodhead strode over and pulled a three-cornered hat from a post on the wall. He then headed toward the door, announcing:

"Let's see what she can do."

Sgt. Rodgers hastily opened the door for the general. The general walked out. The sergeant then tipped his hat to Rebecca, with a sweeping motion of his arm that gestured her to the door. Rebecca followed the general. She had to lower the rifle to keep it from hitting the top of the doorframe. Once outside, however, she cradled it comfortably in her arms. She noted that, once outside, Sgt. Rodgers held his weapon in a similar fashion. They followed behind General Brodhead who strode briskly across the compound toward the main gate. Since it was daytime, the gates were opened, but two sentries walked back and forth across the gate opening in opposite directions. When the general neared, one of the sentries yelled:

"Present arms."

Rebecca watched as both sentries stopped, brought their rifles to a position straight up and down in front of their bodies. The general then saluted and ordered, "Carry, on." He then walked out the gate. Once the general, Rebecca and Sgt. Rodgers had passed, the sentries continued their march back and forth across the gate opening.

Rebecca and Sgt. Rodgers continued to follow the General until they reached a spot near the riverbank. There, Rebecca observed the stumps of several trees. Each of the stumps were remnants of trees which had been felled by cutting them at about 5 feet above the ground. All of the stumps were riddled by holes, obviously the size of rifle balls. The site was apparently a practice range for the soldiers in the fort. The general stopped, turned and looked at Sgt. Rodgers.

"Fix a target." He ordered.

Sgt. Rogers dug into one of the bullet bags and pulled out a patch of cloth. He went to the center stump and forced the small piece of cloth on to an existing nail. The general then ordered.

"Mark off 100 paces."

The sergeant then strode back in a direction perpendicular to the post, counting as he walked. When he reached 100, he stopped and scratched a line in the dirt with the heel of his boot.

"Done sir," he announced.

"Very well," the general said, then continued: "Miss Walker can you see the target?'

"Yes sir," she replied.

"You shoot first," General Brodhead ordered.

Rebecca looked at Sgt. Rodgers.

"May I have power and shot?" she asked.

The sergeant removed one of the power horns and bullet bags he carried and offered them to her.

"I presume you know how to load," he snarled.

"Yes," Rebecca answered. She took the horn and bag and proceeded to load the rifle. Ramming the ball and wadding home took some effort and she saw the sergeant smirk as she loaded the rifle. Then she stood on the line, raised the rifle to her shoulder. She found it hard to steady the piece, but after, a deep breath, followed by an exhale, she fired. Cradling the rifle in her arms she advanced toward the target with General Brodhead on her left and Sgt. Rodgers on her right. When they were close enough to observe the results, Rebecca could see her ball has just nicked the cloth on the bottom side of the wadding.

"Not bad," the general announced sounding both surprised and pleased.

"The rifle shoots a little low," Rebecca said in a matter-of-fact manner. "Do I get another shot?"

"Of course," General Brodhead started, then continued: "But the sergeant gets to shoot next."

The three returned to the firing line. Rebecca paid no attention to Sgt. Rodgers as he loaded and fired. She busied herself with loading for the second round. After the report of his rifle, the three again advanced to the target. When they reached it, Rebecca saw that his round had clearly penetrated the patch a little above dead center.

"Good shooting," General Brodhead commented. Then he ordered: "Place a new patch for a target."

The sergeant did as ordered. Rebecca noticed, however, that he picked up a stone, knocked out the nail and hammered it in about 3 inches higher than before. He then affixed a new patch to the nail. The three returned to the firing line. Rebecca observed that Sgt. Rodgers was clearly agitated. She decided he was worried that her shot had come so close to his.

"Why don't we let the sergeant go first this time?" Rebecca proposed.

"As you wish," General Brodhead responded. "Sergeant you fire next."

Sgt. Rodgers loaded and fired. When they three examined the wad of cloth, it was clear he had placed the ball dead center. The sergeant, noticeably relieved said:

"Your turn, miss."

They returned to the firing line. Rebecca took careful aim and squeezed off a round. When they went to examine the results, all that was visible was a single hole in the wadding where the sergeants round had struck previously.

"Seems you missed the target entirely, miss," Sgt. Rodgers proudly announced.

"I can't see how," Rebecca protested. Then she ran to look up close.

"Sergeant, do you have a jackknife?" She asked.

"Yes, why?" he asked.

"Please dig in this hole and tell me what you find." Rebecca requested.

Sgt. Rodgers looked at General Brodhead.

"Humor her," the General ordered.

Sgt. Rodgers shrugged his shoulders. He took a knife from his pocket and began to dig away at the hole. In a few moments he produced a somewhat flattened ball of lead. He held it up for Rebecca and the General to see.

"Is there anything else?" Rebecca asked.

Sgt. Rodgers shrugged again and went to work with his jackknife. A few moments later he produced a second chunk of lead, apparently flattened on both sides.

"I guess this is my ball. The first one I dug out must have been Miss Walker's," he conceded.

"Good shooting, both of you." General Brodhead complemented. "Well I've seen enough. Sgt. Rodgers you are dismissed. You may return to your usual duties. Rebecca give the sergeant the rifle and accouterments. You and I will discuss your request on the way back to my office."

Rebecca handed her rifle, powder horn and bullet bag to Sgt. Rodgers. He immediately departed for the gate to the fort. General Brodhead started striding quickly in the same direction. Rebecca hurried to catch up with him.

"Well, sir, have I convinced you?" she asked the general when she caught up with him.

"I am convinced you are an excellent marksman," the general began. Then he went on. "However, I would be reluctant to send a single soldier on a trip, such as the one you propose, with so many renegades creating havoc hereabouts."

"But general," Rebecca began.

General Brodhead interrupted before she could continue.

"I will be sending a party of soldiers to Hannastown day after next. You may accompany them. Can you be ready to leave at sunrise?"

"Oh thank you sir, yes." Rebecca responded.

"Come back to my office then. You can pick up your things. I will have the Quartermaster issue you a musket, power and shot for the journey. Mind you, the musket won't shoot as true as the fine piece you just used."

"It'll do," Rebecca responded.

"And I expect you to return it in good condition upon your return." General Brodhead admonished.

"Yes, sir," Rebecca answered.

Rebecca walked alongside the general the rest of the way to his office. When they arrived, he ordered the sentry to send for the quartermaster. The general told her to take a seat. The quartermaster turned out to be a grizzly old man— too old for military service Rebecca thought. He didn't wear an army uniform but buckskin breeches, a calico tunic shirt and coonskin cap. As soon as he entered General Brodhead's office, the general began giving him orders.

"Take this woman to your armory and outfit her with a musket, and power and ammunition. Provide enough for a week's march, same as you would for the average soldier. Oh, and provide her with a pistol also."

"A pistol?" Rebecca asked, perplexed.

"Yes," General Brodhead responded. "And I want you to keep it concealed at all times, unless, of course you must use it as a weapon of last resort. You'll be traveling with 12 men and I can't vouch that all will treat you with proper respect. Do you understand?"

"Yes, I think I do," Rebecca answered, remembering the trouble she had with Sam McCain's men.

The general then turned to the armorer. "And mind you not let anyone else know about the pistol."

"Yes, sir," the armorer responded.

"You may go now," the general started, then he followed: "but be in front of the flagpole in the compound by first light– ready to travel."

"Yes, sir," Rebecca responded with a courtesy, and then she scurried to catch up with the armorer who had already reached the door.

The armorer strode rapidly across the compound with Rebecca following at his heels. He didn't look back to see if Rebecca was with him or not and said nothing. Every few feet he spat a bit of chewing tobacco out, so she was reluctant to get too close. Presently they reached a small hut, built of rough-hewn logs, with a door formed of log slabs. The armorer produced a key and unlocked a padlock securing the door. Rebecca hesitated as he disappeared inside. Within a moment she heard him growl:

"Get in here missy."

Rebecca entered. In the dim light provided by a single window in the back of the hut, she saw a double rack of rifles stacked back to back. The armorer walked around it slowly, the pulled one of the flintlocks from the rack. He jostled it up and down as though testing its weight.

"This un oughta do ya," the armorer said as he handed it to Rebecca.

She took it. It was heavy; but not as heavy as the rifle she had used in the shooting match. The armorer then took a deerskin bag from a peg of several on the wall and offered it to Rebecca.

"The bags got shot, paddn' and spare flints– should do ya." He snarled, then continued: "Powder horn's on the wall, take one."

Rebecca took one of the power horns off the wall. From the weight she felt it was full; but she checked it just to make sure. The armorer grunted with displeasure as Rebecca inspected the power in the horn, then spoke:

"You should be equipped to go where you're goin," he commented.

"Yes, sir," Rebecca responded, then quickly left the armory. Once outside, she remembered the pistol. Reluctantly, she turned back to the door. The armorer had just opened the door to leave. When he saw Rebecca was returning, he grumbled:

"What is it now, Missy?"

"The pistol, sir, I forgot the pistol. Remember the General…"

"Oh, yeah," the armorer interrupted her. "Come on."

Rebecca followed him back inside. She watched as he pulled a drawer open from underneath his workbench. The armorer pulled out a flintlock pistol. He held it out at arm's length, as though testing its weight. Snorting, he put the pistol back in the drawer and pulled out another. Rebecca noticed this one had a shorter barrel. The armorer held the weapon out again like before. Apparently satisfied, he twirled the pistol around in his hand so the butt end faced Rebecca.

"Here you go," the armorer said, offering the pistol to Rebecca. "It takes the same size ball as your rifle and you should have flints enough for both."

"Thank you," Rebecca responded and took the pistol from the armorer. She quickly backed to the door, anxious to be free of this gruff old man.

"Take good care of them weapons, mind you. I expect them back in the condition they is now."

"Yes, sir," Rebecca answered and darted out the door. She walked briskly toward blacksmith shop, anxious to see Hanna again. The trip across the compound with her belongings, the rifle, pistol, and accessories left her feeling quite tired. She wondered how she would keep with the soldiers all the way to Hannastown toting all that gear. When she arrived at the blacksmith shop, she dumped all her gear on her bed and sat down to catch her breath. Hanna came in with Charity in her arms. Hanna spied Rebecca and asked:

"Is something amiss? I expected you would be on your way to Hannastown by now."

"The General wouldn't let me go alone. He did, however, say he would allow me to go with a contingent of soldiers he is sending there. They depart at dawn," Rebecca responded.

"You look dejected, is there something else?" Hanna asked.

"I'm worried about keeping up with the men with all this equipment," Rebecca answered her.

"I think Henry can help you with that," Hanna began. She continued: "He knows how to pack for a long march." "Henry," she called.

A few moments later, Henry Easton came out of the residence, cleaning his teeth with a little sliver of wood. "What is it dear?" he asked.

"Can you help Rebecca figure out how to carry all these things on a journey to Hannastown without collapsing from fatigue?"

Henry looked at the pile on the bed and answered: "I think so. She's a healthy girl. I can make her a pack frame from willow branches that will allow her to carry most of the weight on her back– the rifle too. I'll see if I can get one of the soldiers to fetch me what I'll need." Then he disappeared outside the blacksmith shop.

Hanna looked at Rebecca. "He will fix thee up, I'm sure. Come help me with supper."

After supper, there was a knock on the door. The soldier had returned with the items Henry requested. Rebecca assisted him as he formed a frame from willow branches and leather thongs and straps that fit her form perfectly. Henry even showed her how to attach the musket to the frame so she wouldn't have to carry it in her arms or on her shoulder.

"It won't be as available if you should need to use it, but it won't be as big a strain on your stamina. If the need to use arises, most likely the other soldiers can keep the enemy at bay long enough for you to get at it. Keep it loaded at all times. Now what shall we do about the pistol?" he asked.

"The colonel insisted I keep it concealed. I suppose I could just carry it in the pack." Rebecca answered.

"Aye, that's true; but thee will not be wanting to be a fumbling in the pack should you need to use it," Henry responded. "I have an idea," he continued.

"What's that?"

"I'll fashion a special holster that will allow you to carry it strapped on the outside of your thigh. It'll mean you'll have to pull up your skirts to get at it. Does that bother you?" Henry asked.

Rebecca blushed. The thought of pulling up her skirts in the presence of a group of men embarrassed her. Nevertheless, it seemed a most practical solution.

"I can deal with that, go ahead and make the holster."

About an hour later Henry had fashioned a holster. It was made to fit the flintlock pistol with two straps to tie it to her thigh. As he presented it to her, he commented:

"I think you should be able to walk with this. I'll step out while you try it out. Come out when you have it in place and try walking with it."

Rebecca waited until Mt. Easton had departed. Then she raised her skirts and strapped the holster with pistol to her bare left thigh. Then she stood up and shook her skirts back in place. She looked down at her left side. She thought she perceived a bulge in her skirt on the left side. She reached under her outer skirt to check and see if her shift had caught on the weapon; but it hadn't She decided she would just have to accept the unsymmetrical appearance and hope it wouldn't attract attention. Rebecca then decided to try walking with the pistol attached. She stepped out onto the fort grounds and walked to the main gate and returned. She felt herself leaning to the right all the way as though to compensate for the extra weight on her left side. During the walk, she watched the faces of the few people, mostly men, she encountered. She felt as though all were staring at her. Rebecca worried that on the trail to Hannastown, sooner or later someone would surmise she carried the secret weapon. When she returned to the blacksmith shop she found Mr. Easton back at work. He was busy pounding away at a wheel rim tire and didn't see her approach. She had to tap him on the shoulder.

"Mr. Easton," Rebecca began.

"Yes, Rebecca, how does the holster work?"

"Well I feel the bulge is visible and I feel like I lean to the right as I walk." She answered.

"I watched you for a short time after you left. I think the bulge is only noticeable because you and I know it is there. As for the walk, I did notice you favored one side; but I think we can fix that if you sling the rife on your right shoulder instead of strapping your rifle on the side of your pack so you are more balanced during the march. Just try not to do a lot of strolling about when you are not carrying the pack."

"Thank you, Mr. Easton. If you'll excuse me I think I'll take the pistol off now."

"I don't think that is a good idea, Rebecca."

"Why not?"

"I think the more you wear it, the quicker you'll get used to it." Mr. Easton explained.

"Do you think I need to keep it on in bed?"

"Well you could remove it tonight; but you'll definitely want to sleep with it while you are on the trail." Mr. Easton instructed.

"Yes, I guess you're right. Thank you." Rebecca replied.

Rebecca then went to assist Hanna.

Rebecca spent a restless night; partially because she decided to sleep with the pistol attached in order to get used to it, and partially because she was nervous about the upcoming trip. She arose and left the Easton's residence early the next morning. All the family members were still sleeping. Rebecca longed to say good-bye but didn't want to awake any of them.

Rebecca arrived at the rendezvous location first. Only a short time later, however, she spotted the figure of a man in Army uniform approaching. As he drew near, she recognized him as the young Ensign she met when they first arrived at Fort Pitt. He had a rifle in a sling on his shoulder and a saber dangling from his left hip. She could also see he had a pack strapped to his back. When he came near enough, he tipped his hat, and said:

"Good morning, Miss Walker, I am Ensign Butler. I will be leading this mission."

"You may call me Rebecca, Ensign. I'm not encouraging familiarity; but I think the traveling will be easier if we are not too formal." Rebecca replied.

"Then I would appreciate it if you called me Joshua, Rebecca." The Ensign countered, with a big smile.

"Where are the others, Joshua?" Rebecca asked.

"The sergeant is kicking them out of bed. The Colonel doesn't allow spirits while we're on a mission so they tried to drink enough whiskey last night to last the trip. I If they're not here soon, I'll be checking up on them."

Just then, Rebecca's attention was diverted by the sound of someone yelling. She looked across the field where she'd first spotted Ensign Butler. She saw a single line of men, rifles shouldered, and carrying packs. They were walking along more or less in step. Alongside the line was a single man, dressed in an Army uniform, but not carrying rifle or pack, shouting at the line of men:

"Left, right, left, right... Get in step you miserable mongrels."

The sergeant marched the group to where the Ensign stood with Rebecca. He then gave the command to halt followed by:

"Left face."

The line of men now stood shoulder to shoulder instead of one in front of each other. Then the sergeant saluted the Ensign and said:

"They're all yours now, God help you, Ensign."

Ensign Butler returned the salute and responded.

"Thank you, sergeant, you are dismissed."

The sergeant did an about face, and walked off. Then Ensign Butler turned to address the line of men.

"At ease," he commanded.

Rebecca watched as the men removed the rifles from their shoulders and lowered them to their sides, resting the rifle butts on the ground. The men also assumed a more relaxed stance. She noted none of them wore uniforms. Several wore buckskins and others wore shirt and trousers much like her father wore on the farm. One had a beaver hat and the others either a dusty looking three-corner felt or fashioned from animal skins. Ensign Butler began to address them:

"Men, our mission is to march to Hannastown and provide security for supply wagons being sent to Fort Pitt. There are bands of Indians raiding in these parts and they would love to get their hands on the powder and shot which will be part of the supplies we will be guarding. This young lady is Rebecca Walker. She has urgent business in Hannastown so she will be accompanying us. Colonel Brodhead has special interest in seeing she arrives there safely and unmolested so mind your manners with her."

Just then one of the men in the ranks mumbled something undistinguishable.

"Did you have something to say, Private Johnson?"

"Yes sir. If we take a woman along it's likely to add a day to the march. Also, if we run into Injuns on the way there; one of us is going to have to make sure they don't get aholt of her."

"Well, General's orders are to take her along," Ensign Butler started. Then he continued: "I don't know if she will slow us down; but Colonel Brodhead assures me she can handle a rifle in a fight. As you can see she carries her own. Now do any of you other men have a problem?"

The other men looked at each other. Then each said: "No, sir," in random order.

"Ok, that's settled. Now for the order of march. Corporal Winowski, you take point. I will follow. Rebecca, you fall in behind me. The rest of you men can choose your positions among yourselves; but whoever is the last man, I want you to keep a sharp eye on the trail behind us. I don't want the redskins sneaking up on us from behind. There will be no talking while we're on the march and when we stop for rest or meals keep your voices low. They'll be no cooking. You've all received rations of biscuits and jerky. Now line up."

The man whom Ensign Butler referred to as Corporal Winowski stepped out of the line several paces. Then he faced toward the gate of the fort. Ensign Butler told Rebecca to follow him and the ensign took his place behind the corporal. Rebecca followed the Ensign. A few minutes later the small column departed the gate and began the trek.

Weighed down by pack and rifle, Rebecca found it difficult to keep up behind the ensign. Before long, her undergarments were soaked with her sweat. It also felt like the holster containing the pistol was slipping down her thigh. Rebecca scurried up behind the ensign and spoke very softly.

"Joshua, could I have just a minute or two of privacy?"

Ensign Butler turned slightly. Rebecca could see he had an exasperated look on his face. Then, by use of hand signals, he ordered the squad of men to stop. He looked at Rebecca and said in a low voice.

"Do what you have to do and hurry back. And don't go too far from us."

Rebecca spotted a bush she thought would conceal her and disappeared behind it. She pulled up her skirts to expose her legs, undid the leather things securing the pistol holster. She re-tied them as tightly as she could stand. The white skin of her thigh bulged on each side of the thongs. Rebecca hoped she wouldn't lose circulation in her leg; but didn't want the pistol to fall off either. She stood up, shook her skirts back in place and returned to the squad of men who had taken advantage of the unexpected break by sitting down. When Rebecca returned, they all rose to their feet. Rebecca whispered a quick: "Sorry, thank you," to Ensign Butler. The line reformed and the march continued.

By midday they were deep into forest. Ensign Butler signaled the column to halt and quietly told them to take off their packs, eat and rest. When Rebecca removed her pack it felt as though the weight of the world had been lifted from her shoulders. She sat on the ground and leaned back against the pack. She too a few sips from her water bag and sighed a sigh of relief.

Ensign Butler, who had also been leaning against his pack alongside her, looked over to her and commented:

"You've done well, Rebecca. I was afraid you would not be able to keep up with us."

"To be honest, Joshua, I feel exhausted; but I'm determined not to be a burden."

The ensign smiled back and winked. "I'll stretch this break out as long as I can; but we must reach Hannastown and return on schedule or the General will have my ass."

Rebecca smirked at Ensign Butler's use of the word, ass. Then she saw his face turn red and he apologized:

"Please excuse my language, ma'am. I'm not used to having ladies along on the trail. It was just a slip of the tongue."

"You're forgiven, Joshua," Rebecca responded, giving him a big smile.

Very shortly after that, too short a time for Rebecca, Ensign Butler ordered the group to its feet again. The ensign helped Rebecca put on her pack before he put on his. Rebecca could feel his breath near her ear as he adjusted the pack into place. She discovered she was becoming aroused, so she nervously pulled away.

"Thank you, I'm fine now, Joshua," she whispered.

The ensign put on his pack, never taking his eyes from her. Rebecca was sure the closeness had aroused him also. Then the image of Mamalachgook entered her mind. *She must not forget why she was making this journey. It's just that up until her capture, she had been sheltered from contact with men other than her father. She hadn't experienced the feelings that the presence of a man might arouse in her. Ensign Butler was a handsome man too. He had a face with an attractive cleft in his chin. He had broad shoulders; but his upper torso didn't portray a man with prominent muscles. He was more the lean, wiry type. There was one exception. His tight breeches revealed powerful thighs and his calves bulged beneath his stockings, indicating he'd spent much of his life walking. Rebecca worried that it might be too easy to surrender herself to this man.* Her thoughts were quickly interrupted by the ensign's order to resume the march.

As dusk began to fall, Ensign Butler gave the order to stop and make camp for the night. Again, Rebecca welcomed the relief of being able to drop her pack. She then busied herself with spreading out her bedroll and looking over her rifle to make sure it would be ready to fire. Then she got out her biscuits and jerky. One of the men, she hadn't learned his name, came over to her and said:

"Me and the boys would be pleasured ifin you'd join us for supper."

Rebecca looked behind him. She could see the rest of the men were in the process of gathering around in a circle, including Ensign Butler.

"I would be glad to accept, sir," Rebecca responded.

The man extended a hand to help her up. Rebecca stuffed her food into her pockets and took the offered hand. He pulled her to her feet, and then he offered his arm to Rebecca. Rebecca wasn't sure what the gesture meant; but she had seen other women at the fort holding a man's elbow as they walked, so she took hold of his arm and he escorted her to the circle.

As the group ate, the men talked about things like the quickest way to skin a deer and which rifle shot the truest. After a while, the man who escorted Rebecca to the circle asked.

"Would ye tell us how ye come to be here?"

Rebecca thought for a moment. She wasn't sure how much to tell them or even if she should tell them anything. Rebecca decided she needed their trust, so she told them basically her life story, including her capture and why she was making the journey with them. When she finished, the man who had escorted her to the circle commented:

"I don't understand how a white woman could love an injun enough to risk getting her scalp lifted in these woods; just to find some lawyer that probably won't do her no good."

Rebecca felt a rush of different feelings: anger, despair and worry. The she answered:

"You don't know Mamalachgook. You are judging him by the action of others. Anyway, remember he saved my life and prevented me from becoming some sachem's slave."

The man she was addressing was about to make another comment when a shot rang out. It was followed by several blood curdling shrieks. The man she had been talking to slumped over. Red liquid oozed from his chest.

"Defensive positions," Ensign Butler barked his order.

Rebecca watched, stunned, as all the remaining men grabbed their rifles and scrambled to take positions behind tree trunks and stones in a rough circle around her. Rebecca was now sitting in the middle of this giant circle. A moment later, a painted Indian came crashing through the brush and attempted to snatch her. She rolled away adroitly; but the Indian turned to make a second attempt. The next thing she knew, he was lying on top of her gasping and choking. Rebecca rolled, taking the dying body with her. Once free again, she got to her feet, observing that Ensign Butler was returning his saber to its scabbard.

"Get your rifle, Becky," he shouted.

Rebecca bolted to her pack. She was glad she had taken the trouble to look over the rifle earlier. It was free. She donned the power horn and bullet bag. Then Rebecca began scanning her surroundings for a target. She didn't have to wait long.

<h1 style="text-align:center">CHAPTER 8</h1>

INDIAN ATTACK!

Rebecca could make out a feather moving through the trees toward one of the positions occupied by one of the men of her squad. She estimated where the head would be located from the movement of the feather. She aimed and squeezed the trigger. She heard the click of the flint striking, followed by the blast of the rifle and then a cry of pain. She'd hit her target.

With several of their brothers now dead, the war party decided to rush the camp rather than exchange fire from a distance. A few moments later every member of Ensign Butler's squad found himself engaged in close combat. They were using their rifles as clubs to fight off their attackers, who now attacked with tomahawks and knives.

Rebecca quickly reloaded, chose a target and fired again. Another Indian fell and his intended victim waved his appreciation at Rebecca. That man however received only a brief respite from the battle. He soon was attacked by two more braves. One of the braves managed to get behind this man and the brave struck a killing blow with his tomahawk.

Rebecca was busy reloading. She couldn't do anything to save the man. However, once she'd reloaded, she dispatched his other attacker to the happy hunting ground. Rebecca then started reloading again.

As Rebecca was reloading again, another of the squad was killed. The ensign himself was madly trying to fight off four Indians with his saber. At first he was only able to parry blows from their tomahawks. Soon, however, he was able to take the offensive. With the stroke of his saber, he cut off one of the tomahawk filled hands and, with a backhanded movement he sliced the jugular vein of a second attacker. The ensign was sprayed by a stream of blood. The third Indian tried to fend off the ensign by picking up a rifle from the ground and using it to parry the saber blows. The ensign became preoccupied with his assailant, the Indian with the rifle, for a brief moment, allowing the fourth Indian to strike with his tomahawk. Ensign Butler caught the movement out of the corner of his eye and leaned back in an attempt to avoid the deadly hatchet. This movement saved his life; but the tomahawk sank deep into his left thigh. Seized with pain, he swung his saber back toward the fourth Indian. The blade caught this attacker just below his rib cage, ripping a foot long gash. Blood flowed and part of the Indian's intestines emerged. Undaunted by the gaping wound in his side the Indian raised his tomahawk to strike again. Then he fell. Ensign Butler wasn't even cognizant of the sound of the shot that brought the Indian down. Rebecca had done it again.

The third Indian took advantage of the momentary diversion, dropped the rife he had been using to defend himself, and drew a large knife from a scabbard attached to his calf. He lunged toward Ensign Butler and took him to the ground. This forced the ensign to drop his saber in order to have both hands free to defend against the knife attack.

As Ensign Butler rolled and wrestled with the knife wielding Indian, Rebecca started to reload her rifle. Another Indian decided it was time to put this female sharpshooter out of business. With a scream he came running to her with raised tomahawk. Rebecca dropped her empty rifle. She yanked up her skirts, baring the thigh with the pistol attached. Just as the Indian reached her, she had the pistol free and in her hand. Rebecca fired point blank. The ball struck the Indian in the chest; but he fell, knocking her over, and landing on top of her. He withered and squirmed on top of Rebecca for what seemed to be an eternity, then stopped. Rebecca struggled to get out from under the lifeless body.

Finally, she managed to bend her left knee enough to allow her to push against the ground and roll over, leaving the corpse on the ground and her on top.

Rebecca pushed herself to her feet. Her breast heaved from the exertion of freeing herself from the Indian. Pistol still in hand, she looked around her. The fighting was over. Ensign Butler sat, legs spread on the ground, examining his wounded thigh. Another figure, whom Rebecca recognized as Corporal Winowski, staggered over to the ensign holding his right shoulder with his left hand.

"How bad is it, sir?" Corporal Winowski asks, weakly gesturing at the ensign's thigh with his right hand.

"It's a deep wound, but I should survive. How are the others?" Ensign Butler asked looking around.

"Dead sir. It's just you, me and the lady. On the positive side, all them redskins are dead." The corporal answered.

Just then Rebecca reached Ensign Butler. She dropped the pistol. Then she dropped to her knees to examine the ensign's wound.

"You're hurt, Joshua," she cried.

"Yes, Rebecca," the ensign started. Then he went on: "But I'd be dead for sure if you hadn't been such a crack shot with that rifle."

"Aye, she's a wonder with firearms," Corporal Winowski started. Then he continued: "She saved us both by evening up the odds."

"I must attend to that wound," Rebecca announced.

Rebecca then sat back, hiked up her outer skirt, and tore some strips of cloth from her undergarments. She was oblivious to the fact she exposed both of her bare legs immodestly in front of two men. Neither of them attempted to avert their eyes either. After retrieving the bandage material, she went to work on Ensign Butler's thigh. After she was satisfied she'd done her best, she stood up, bandage in hand and turned to Corporal Winowski.

"Now let me look at that shoulder." Rebecca said.

"Ah, ma'am, I don't knows as you can do much for me. The bleeding's stopped; but I' think a sinew's cut from the bone.

"Well sit down and let me attend to it," Rebecca commanded.

The corporal did as ordered. Rebecca examined the wound. Then she bandaged it. He had been right it appeared the shoulder muscle had at least been partially separated from the bone. Rebecca was now stuck in the wilderness with two nearly helpless men. She knew she needed to get both to a doctor. She only hoped they both weren't already permanently crippled.

"We need to push on to Hannastown. You both need professional medical care. Can you stand, Joshua?" She asked.

"Hand me one of those rifles," Ensign Butler commanded.

Rebecca looked around and picked up the nearest one. She offered it to Ensign Butler. Using both hands on the rifle, he struggled to his feet. He hobbled a few steps, then announced.

"I think I can walk; but it will be mighty slow going. Why don't you go on with Corporal Winowski. You can sent a party back for me. They can also bury the dead of our party."

"I don't think it is right to leave you here alone. What if other Indians come looking for the ones we killed? There must be something else we can do." Rebecca scolded him.

"I know, we can build a travois," Corporal Winowski proposed.

"What's a travois?" Rebecca asked.

"It's easier to build it than describe it. Come on I'll give you directions." The corporal answered her.

With that the corporal picked up a tomahawk and led Rebecca into the woods. Rebecca and the corporal took turns chopping, he with his good arm and Rebecca with both. The cut two long poles and a couple of short ones for cross members. They also found some vines to use for lashings. Rebecca and Corporal Winowski took the materials back to where Ensign Butler was waiting. Corporal Winowski directed Rebecca how to build it. Unfortunately they had to remove some of the clothing from the dead to stretch between the two long poles to provide surface for Ensign Butler to lay on. When it was complete, they helped the ensign on to it. Then Rebecca and the Corporal gathered up minimal supplies and three rifles and gave them to Ensign Butler to be carried on the travois. Corporal

Winowski had fashioned a crude harness out of some of the purloined clothing. He and Rebecca put it on. It was a single strap which ran from one pole, across both of their shoulders to the other pole. It would allow both of then to walk side by side to share the load. Just before they took off, Rebecca announced:

"Oh, I forgot something."

She then slid out of the harness and ran back to where she'd dropped the pistol. She picked it up and, turning her back to the two men, hiked up her skirt and returned the empty pistol to her holster. Then she scurried back to the travois and took her place in the harness.

"Ok, let's go," Rebecca said.

"What was that all about?" Ensign Butler asked.

"Oh, I carry a little personal protection under my skirt," Rebecca replied bashfully.

"I wondered where you got that pistol," Ensign Butler commented.

CHAPTER 9

HANNASTOWN

The journey was long and tedious. It took a day longer than it would have without the two wounded soldiers. Where the trail was wide enough Corporal Winowski and Rebecca shared the harness. When it narrowed, they took turns. Rebecca found the extra strain of bearing the full load particularly taxing; but she knew she needed to do her share as Corporal Winowski seemed to be weakening with each hour that passed. On one of their breaks, Rebecca took the time to examine both men's wounds. Both showed signs of infection; Ensign Butler seemed to be suffering the most from his. He had a fever and the thigh was badly swollen.

About the time Rebecca started considering whether to leave the two to rest while she pressed on to find help, the trail they'd been on merged with a wagon road. A few hours later, they could see smoke from multiple chimneys in the distance.

"That should be Hannastown up ahead," Corporal Winowski announced, now staggering under the load of the travois.

"Let me take it by myself," Rebecca pleaded. Then she continued: "You look about ready to drop and I don't want to be toting both of you.

"Thank you very much, Ma'am," Winowski answered, stepping out from under the makeshift harness.

"You may call me Rebecca too, we've been through too much together to be formal with each other."

"Thank you, ma'am, I mean Rebecca."

Traveling along the road was much easier. The skids of the travois glided across the ground. Before long they could make out the buildings of Hannastown. They passed a partially plowed field. Looking out over the field Rebecca could see a farmer behind a horse drawn plow heading away from them. Rebecca thought to call out to him; but he'd appeared too far away to hear her. Just then she heard a child's voice from behind her.

"Where are you folks going?"

Rebecca stopped and turned her head. A boy, perhaps about 8 years old, dressed in a cotton shirt and buckskin breeches, but barefoot, came running up, then stood in front of her.

"What's your name?" Rebecca asked.

"Caleb," the boy answered. Then he questioned. "Why are you pulling that man?"

"He was wounded in an Indian attack. So was Corporal Winowski here," Rebecca answered. Then she went on to explain: "They are soldiers from Fort Pitt. They need help. Do you know if there is a doctor in Hannastown?"

"I don't know; but maybe Pa does." Caleb answered.

Before Rebecca could say anything else, Caleb darted off, across the field heading toward the farmer. Rebecca set her load down and checked Ensign Butler. He was unconscious and burning with fever. Rebecca mopped his brow with the little water they had left. Then she stood up to watch Caleb. Corporal Winowski sat down to rest. Rebecca continued to watch as the boy crossed the field at a dead run. She saw him run up to the farmer. The farmer stopped plowing and, after a brief conversation with his son, unhitched the horse from the plow. He then hoisted his son up on the horse's back and hopped up behind him. In a few moments they were riding toward Rebecca. When the farmer reached them, he dismounted and helped his son down.

"My son, here says you need help." The farmer said.

"Oh, yes sir. These two men are what are left from a party of soldiers who were attacked by Indians. We were traveling from Fort Pitt to Hannastown."

"How can I help you?" the farmer asked.

"These men need medical attention. How far is it to Hannastown? Is there a doctor there."

"It's only about two miles further along this road. We don't have a doctor; but there is a woman in the town, the tavern owner's wife who knows of potions and things. She's helped many of the settlers around here who've been sick or injured. I'll take you there." The farmer responded.

"Oh, thank you, Mister...."

"I'm Justin Whitfield. Please just call me Justin." The farmer interrupted.

"I'm Rebecca Walker. You may call me Rebecca."

"Well Rebecca, let's just rearrange things here a little and we'll be on our way." Justin responded.

Justin immediately took charge. He arranged the harness so the horse could pull the travois. Then he helped Corporal Winowski onto the horse's back. He instructed Caleb to run home and tell "Ma I'll be late for supper." As Caleb took off over the plowed field again, Justin started leading the horse with Rebecca alongside started off down the road to Hannastown. As they walked, Rebecca told the story of the Indian attack to Justin. Naturally curious Justin asked:

"But why were you traveling with that squad of soldiers?"

Reluctantly, Rebecca told Justin about her capture and her relationship with Mamalachgook. She also explained that her purpose in traveling to Hannastown was to find a lawyer to help Mamalachgook. When she finished she asked:

"Do you know of a lawyer?"

"Well Rebecca, we have Squire Hanna who sometimes serves as a justice in court; but I doubt you could ever find an attorney in Western Pennsylvania that would defend an Indian. I don't understand why you would even want to continue to look for one after what happened to you on the journey here." Justin responded.

"I love Mamalachgook."

"Ah, love. It gets us all in trouble of one kind or another. It was my wife who convinced me to leave a successful harness business in Philadelphia to scratch around in the ground in the wilderness. She claimed it was a better environment for Caleb to grow up in."

"I think you understand," Rebecca replied and took hold of Justin's arm.

Justin led them to a tavern called the Wild Raccoon. Then he stopped outside and said:

"Let me go in and talk to the innkeeper. It's not proper for a single lady to be in such a place."

"You are with me," Rebecca protested. "It is not like I'm walking in there alone."

"Very well," Justin acquiesced. Then he turned to Corporal Winowski.

"Are you up to looking after the ensign?"

Corporal Winowski nodded his assent.

Inside, Rebecca and Justin looked around. Behind the bar was a middle-aged man, stout and with a receding hairline. He looked at Justin and Rebecca.

"Well Justin, haven't seen you in here for a long time. Who's your friend?"

"O'Neil, we need some doctoring. Is the misses about?"

"Is she the patient?" O'Neil responded, looking at Rebecca.

"No sir, there two men outside who were wounded in an Indian attack, one suffered from a leg wound which is badly infected," Rebecca pleaded.

O'Neil shouted: "Kathleen, we need you out here, toute de suite."

"What's it now, Patrick," a woman answered from some back room beyond the common room of the tavern.

"Just get your lovely face out here," Patrick O'Neil shouted back.

In a moment a woman stepped into the room. She had dark hair, graying at the temples and despite some lines of aging in her face, one could tell she must have been extremely attractive in her younger years. She wore a gray dress with white frills on the sleeves and a white apron. She looked at her husband and spoke:

"What is it now? Another drunk with a belly ache?"

"No, we have two men outside in need of the doctoring, would you look to them?" Her husband asked.

Mrs. O'Neil glanced at Rebecca. Then she looked at Justin.

"Who's the wench? I've not seen her hereabouts. You haven't been cheat'n on that lovely wife of yours have you?

"Please ma'am, your services are needed badly," Rebecca interrupted.

"Lead on my dear," Kathleen responded.

Outside, Kathleen rushed to the travois.

"Ah, Saints preserve us. You are in a bad way. We must get you to a bed at once." She exclaimed.

Kathleen O'Neil looked first at her husband and then at Justin. Then she shouted.

"Are you two just going to stand there? Fetch that man inside at once!"

Justin took Ensign Butler underneath the shoulders and O'Neil by the knees. Winowski and Rebecca followed.

Once inside, Mrs. O'Neil ordered:

"Get him up to bed. There's an empty room just upstairs to the right."

Kathleen then faced Winowski. "Up to the room with you also. I tend to you as soon as I can."

"I'd like to be of service," Rebecca pressed.

"Well then come with me," Kathleen O'Neil ordered.

Rebecca then took the corporal by his good arm and escorted him up the stairs. They followed Justin and Patrick carrying the limp body of Ensign Butler.

❧

Once Kathleen with Rebecca's assistance had done all they could to treat the patients, they joined Patrick O'Neil and Justin who were waiting at a table downstairs in the tavern.

Kathleen asked, "What happened to those men?"

"Seems they met up with tomahawks," Justin started. Rebecca decided she'd best tell the story.

"We were on our way to Hannastown from Fort Pitt, she began.

Then she related the story of the Indian attack. When she finished, O'Neil commented.

"That must have been an awful experience for such a young lady. And I think our mayor, Squire Hanna should know about it. We may need to take action. He'll know what to do."

Then O'Neil looked at Rebecca.

"You look like you are in need of a drink. I have some straight cider – unfermented." O'Neil proposed.

"That would be nice, thank you," Rebecca responded.

O'Neil went behind the bar and produced a jug and a pewter cup. He poured a cupful and brought it to Rebecca. Then he turned to Justin.

"How about you? I have stout, Jamaican rum, and some whiskey. The whiskey is a little raw. It hasn't been properly cured."

"Nothing for me, thanks," Justin started. Then he continued: "I need to be getting back to the wife. She's probably already put out at me for neglecting the plowing to come here. She's a slave driver, you know. She'll probably want me to continuing plowing after supper until the darkness descends." Justin responded.

O'Neil laughed at Justin's comment on his wife. Then he offered his own comment.

"Tis true the bonds of marriage are but bondage to the husbands."

Justin then looked at Rebecca and then at O'Neil.

"Would you look after the miss? I don't know if she has means to pay you for accommodation, but I can repay you when the crop comes in."

Rebecca butted in.

"Don't worry about me. I'll see the innkeeper is repaid for his kindness. You go home to your wife; and thank you for all you have done."

With that, Rebecca reached up and kissed Justin on the cheek.

"Miss, remember he's a married man," O'Neil joked.

"And so are you," Rebecca responded giving O'Neil a quick peck on the cheek also.

Kathleen broke in.

"Will you two men quit flirting with the girl and get about your business," she scolded.

"Right, Kathleen," Justin responded and left the tavern.

Mrs. O'Neil then looked to her husband.

"I'll be looking after the young lady here. Now here's a list of things I need for you to get for me so I can attend to those injured men."

Patrick O'Neil took the list from his wife and looked it over. Then he complained:

"Some of this stuff grows in the woods. It'll take me awhile to find it."

"So it'll be an hour or so before the regular customers start showing up and it wouldn't hurt to close the tavern until you return, even if it means it delays their intoxication for a couple of hours longer."

Patrick O'Neil said nothing more. He just slammed his three cornered hat on his head and left, list in hand.

"Can I help in some way?" Rebecca asked.

"Yes, we should bathe the men. Come to the kitchen and I'll show you where to get a pot for heating the water and a wash tub. When all is ready you can bring them to the room. I'll tend to the bathing. It wouldn't do for an unmarried woman to see a naked man."

Rebecca did as instructed. After delivering the wash tub, the hot water and several buckets of cold water to the room that held the two soldiers, she waited outside the door for further instructions. A short while later, Mrs. O'Neil appeared with a bundle of clothes and handed them to Rebecca.

"Will you launder these? You'll find lye soap in barrel by the back door to the tavern and a wash board and tub near the barrel also. There is a clothes line out back."

Rebecca was busy washing the clothes behind the tavern when Patrick O'Neil returned. Once she had all the garments washed and hung up to dry, she entered the tavern and found it bustling with patrons. Patrick O'Neil spotted her and took her aside.

"The locals and a few odd travelers have come in for food and drink. Could you help me serve them?" He requested.

"Yes, sir," Rebecca replied.

Patrick O'Neil gave her an apron and Rebecca began to wait on the customers. As she worked, she felt the stares from the all-male crowd. A few asked her questions like: "What is a so comely wench doing in a place like this?" Some also asked her if she would be available to meet them later. Rebecca did her best to brush them off without being too impolite. Then she heard Kathleen bellow:

"Patrick James O'Neil!"

Rebecca looked toward the sound of her voice.

Mrs. O'Neil was behind the bar arguing with her husband. In a moment, Mrs. O'Neil came straight for Rebecca, took her by the arm and escorted her to the kitchen.

"What's the matter?" Rebecca asked, perplexed.

"It's that husband of mine. He had no business sending out there, a lamb among wolves. Most likely all of those men have indecent proposals on their mind and some of them will try to pursue them." Kathleen O'Neil explained.

"But don't you ever serve the customers?" Rebecca asked innocently.

"That's different. The locals know better that to proposition a married woman, and the strangers that do get a piece of my mind. Anyway, you must be exhausted. Let's get you up to bed."

Mrs. O'Neil then led Rebecca up to an empty room with a bed and night stand.

"Wait here a moment," Kathleen said.

Kathleen was gone for a minute or so. Then she returned with a white garment draped over her arm.

"You may use this nightgown. It will be a little big for you since it is one of mine and I no longer have a slender figure like you. Now strip off all your clothes and put this on. I'll clean your things and hang them out to dry overnight."

Rebecca did as ordered. She was a little embarrassed when Mrs. O'Neil saw the holster with pistol strapped to her leg. But when she explained why she wore it and how it had saved he life, Mrs. O'Neil nodded her approval and commented:

"There's been a time or two I may have found use for the same. My mother, however insisted I carry a sheiliegh when I was out unescorted; and I found that weapon to be quite useful."

The nightgown fit very loosely; but the fabric felt so good against her skin. When Mrs. O'Neil left with the bundle of her clothes, Rebecca blew out the candle which illuminated the room. She crawled into bed. The mattress and pillow felt heavenly compared to sleeping on the hard ground. In a flash she was engrossed in deep slumber.

Rebecca slept until noon the next day. In fact she might have slept longer if she hadn't been awakened by Kathleen O'Neil knocking on her door. Rebecca sat up in her bed and entreated Kathleen to enter. Mrs. O'Neil had her shortgown, petticoats and shift draped over her arm. She walked over and began laying the garments on the foot of the bed. As she did so she described the garments:

"Your outer shortgown cleaned up nicely and only needed minor mending; but your under things were scarcely more than rags. I happened to have some of my old ones packed away in a trunk. I washed them out to rid them of the musty odor. I hope they will do."

"I'm sure they'll be fine. I'm afraid I had to use parts of my petticoats as bandages." Rebecca explained.

"I thought as much," Kathleen began. Then she continued, "When you are dressed, come to the kitchen. I've a pot of stew on the fire. You look as if you could use a good meal."

Rebecca dressed and went to the kitchen. After a meal of stew and tea, Mrs. O'Neil sat down at a table with her.

"Well what are we to do with you now?" Kathleen O'Neil asked.

"I need to hire a lawyer and get back to Fort Pitt. I have a friend imprisoned there." Rebecca began.

"Now why would a slip of a girl like yourself be involved with a criminal?" Mrs. O'Neil gasped.

"Oh, he's not guilty of anything except being an Indian," Rebecca protested. Then she went on to tell the whole story of her capture and the subsequent events, right up to her arrival at Hannastown.

"My dear, you have been through a lot." Mrs. O'Neil commented. Then she continued: "I suppose it is your duty to stand by this man, Mamalachgook; but we have no lawyers in this town except Squire Hanna. The only learned man outside of our mayor, Squire Hanna, is Simon Dubois. He's an ex-minister of some church and is inclined to the drink. In fact, he's nursing a mug of spirits in the Tavern right now."

"Do you think Squire Hanna would help me?" Rebecca asked.

"Not very likely, he's a justice and most probably will be called to preside as judge in the case."

"How about Mr. Dubois?" Rebecca pressed.

"I couldn't say. If you ask me though, dealing with him might be nearly as bad as dealing with the devil himself. Still, he's never done anyone any harm around here. On the days he's sober, he earns his keep helping with the planting and harvest among the farmers. He also makes a little cash preparing legal documents, mostly for land transactions."

"Would you introduce me?" Rebecca asked.

"It's better I bring him in here to talk business. Being seen with him in the tavern will give you a reputation, if you know what I mean. He'll come back if I offer him a free bowl of stew and the spirits to wash it down. You'll be on your own then. I've got the chores piling up on me, especially with the sick men upstairs."

"By the way, how are they doing?" Rebecca asked.

"The Corporal's showing good signs of recovery. His fever's broke and it looks like his shoulder is on the mend; but I doubt he'll ever regain the full use of it. The Ensign is conscious; but still has the fever. If the fever breaks, he should be up and around in a few days. He's asked about you and he keeps going on about returning to Fort Pitt. He's worried about not completing his mission." Mrs. O'Neil explained.

"Yes, they were to escort a load of supplies to the fort." Rebecca commented.

"My husband passed on the word to Squire Hanna about the Indian attack and the wounded soldiers. I believe the local men will be meeting here tonight with the Squire to discuss what action they should take. Now I'd better fetch Mr. Dubois." Mrs. O'Neil said and left the kitchen.

A short time later, Mrs. O'Neil returned to the kitchen. She was followed by a lanky man dressed in a tan brocade jacket, with brown knee breeches with tan brocade cuffs, dark red vest front, white jabot and the ruffled lace cuffs. His clothes, however, looked in need of a good washing. He had graying hair tied in a ponytail and at least two days' worth of whisker stubble on his face.

Mrs. O'Neil was about to say something; but the man spoke first.

"Allow me to present myself, Mademoiselle, I am Simon Dubois. And you are?"

"Rebecca Walker," she answered, arising from her chair.

Simon Dubois took Rebecca's hand and kissed it. She was a little perplexed at this gesture; but she felt he meant it only as a sign of politeness. Simon spoke next:

"I understand you wish to have a word with me. Shall we sit?"

Rebecca sat down again, followed by Mr. Dubois. He then asked:

"Now my dear Lady, what can I do for you?"

"I need a lawyer. I understand you have some knowledge of such things." Rebecca responded.

"Well, I have not been admitted to the Westmoreland County Bar; but I've had some study of the subject. I actually am more adept at linguistics. I studied Latin and Greek at Princeton College in preparation for the Presbyterian ministry. I can also read, write and speak French, Spanish and some German. Most of my law practice, if you can call it that, consists of helping people around here prepare documents such as land registrations. I've had no practice in litigation. What did you have in mind?"

"I have a friend who in imprisoned at Fort Pitt. I came to Hannastown to see if I could get a lawyer." Rebecca explained.

"Ah, how it that such a young wench as yourself came to associate with a criminal?" Dubois asked.

"He's not a criminal!" Rebecca spat, "He didn't do anything wrong. The General put him in jail to keep him from being lynched."

Rebecca then went on to tell the whole story of how she'd been captured by the Delawares, how Mamalachgook helped her escape and how he saved her life. She also told the story of her journey from Fort Pitt to Hannastown. When she finished, Dubois commented:

"You've been through a lot, miss; but I doubt I could do much to obtain the release of an Indian when so many settlers in these parts have suffered from their raids. I sympathize with you, though. As a Presbyterian minister, I lived with some of the Delaware tribe at a village called Coshoton in the Ohio territory. I found most of them to be quite decent people; but the relations between Indians and whites were strained there also, with neighboring tribes urging war against the whites to regain lands lost."

"So you were a minister?" Rebecca probed.

"Yes, was. I'm afraid I developed an affinity for spirits that got me ousted from the ministry. I headed back east in hopes of hiding my shame in a more populated area; but, alas, I haven't made it beyond this community. They seem to accept me, faults and all, so I've decided to stay here for a time. Men of education are rare in these parts so I received some monetary compensation for rendering those legal services I've described." Dubois explained.

"Would you go to Fort Pitt with me?" Rebecca asked.

"Ah, the request to accompany such a beautiful young lady on such a journey entices me; but, since I am nearly devoid of funds, what payment might I expect for my services?" Dubois asked.

Rebecca felt uneasy about the idea of traveling alone with this man. Nevertheless she had her concealed pistol and she was desperate to get help for Mamalachgook. She made her proposal.

"I have no cash; but I would be willing to indenture myself to you for a reasonable time."

"What skills do you have Miss Walker?" Dubois asked.

Rebecca thought a moment. Then she responded: "I can cook, launder and mend your clothes, and I know how to make whiskey."

Dubois' eyes brightened when she mentioned whiskey. Rebecca immediately regretted she'd mentioned it. Quickly she offered an alternate proposal.

"But, if Mamalachgook were free, he could pay you back in beaver hides and other furs you could trade for cash. He's an excellent hunter."

Dubois stared at the ceiling. Then he spoke: "Ah, whiskey and furs, they are the coin of the realm in these parts. I must consider your offer. But, as you know, the way to Fort Pitt is wrought with danger. How do you propose we get there and retain our scalps?"

Rebecca answered. She knew she was assuming a lot; but she tried to sound convincing.

"The two soldiers I came here with were sent her to escort supplies back to Fort Pitt. We could travel with them."

"My dear, I understand they are bed ridden from the wounds they suffered in the ambush coming her. What makes you think they will be physically able and willing to make the return?" Dubois asked.

"I know Ensign Butler. He has a devout dedication to duty. He will complete his mission or die trying. Corporal Winowski will follow his orders."

"But the ensign lost most of his squad on the trip here. Are you suggesting that two men, weakened by recent wounds, you and I, and perhaps a couple of wagon drivers would be able to defend against an Indian assault?'

"I'm willing to take the chance," Rebecca started. Then she continued: "But chances are just as good that we won't run into Indian raiders again. After all, we killed all of the party that attacked us."

"Ah, the optimism of youth, I will give your proposal some thought. In the meantime, I suggest you and I wait to see if, indeed there will be an effort to re-supply Fort Pitt. I understand there's a meeting to be held in the tavern tonight. I shall attend. I'll let you know what transpires." Dubois answered.

"I plan to attend that meeting also, even if I am the only woman in the tavern." Rebecca responded.

CHAPTER 10

PROCURING AN ATTORNEY

Rebecca spent the rest of the afternoon helping Mrs. O'Neil with her chores. As the time for the public meeting drew near, Rebecca working in the kitchen, could hear the volume of noise in the tavern increase. Mrs. O'Neil was in and out of the kitchen repeatedly taking food orders for the tavern clientele. She had promised Rebecca to let her know when the meeting would begin. Finally, Mrs. O'Neil entered and announced:

"Squire Hanna just finished his supper. He should be starting the meeting soon."

"Thank you," Rebecca responded, dried her hands on a dish towel and entered the public room of the tavern. She looked around. Most of the tables were filled with men who looked like they'd just come in from the field. Men also sat on a couple of benches along two opposing walls. Rebecca chose to remain standing in a near corner. Rebecca watched as a man, presumably, Squire Hanna since he was attired in expensive looking coat, waistcoat, and breeches, stood up from his place at a table and hammered on the table with a pewter mug.

"Hear ye, Hear ye, I call this meeting of the citizens of Hannastown and neighboring landowners to order." He said.

The tavern noise abated, as the men turned their attention to Squire Hanna. Rebecca noted that Mr. Dubois sat at a table by himself. She thought to sit with him; but decided the gesture might be misinterpreted by both Mr. Dubois and the others in the tavern. Before Squire Hanna could continue, everyone's attention became focused on the stairway. Corporal Winowski was assisting Ensign Butler descending the stairs. They were both dressed in the recently laundered uniforms. Corporal Winowski helped the ensign to the table where Mr. Dubois sat. Once they were seated, Squire Hanna continued.

"By now you've all heard of the recent deprivation inflicted on the party of soldiers led by the two men over there," he said, pointing to the table. "Would you gentlemen introduce yourselves?"

Corporal Winowski helped Ensign Butler to his feet and the ensign spoke.

"I am Ensign Butler and this is Corporal Winowski we were ordered by General Brodhead to Hannastown to escort supply wagons carrying supplies for Fort Pitt. Our squad was attacked and the corporal here, myself, and the young lady standing in the corner were the only survivors. It is important we get those supplies to Fort Pitt, so I ask for any assistance you can provide."

Ensign Butler and Corporal Winowski then sat back down. The Squire continued:

"It seems we have three issues here to deal with: First, we need to form a militia to deal potential Indian attacks, second, we should form a burial party to give the dead soldiers a Christian burial, and third, there is the matter of getting the supplies to Fort Pitt. As to the first issue, how many of you are willing to join a militia?"

Nearly every hand shot up. Mr. Dubois, and of course, the ensign and corporal, declined. Then Squire Hanna asked the second question: "How many of you will join in the burial detail?'

About a dozen hands were raised, including Ensign Butler and Corporal Winowski. The Squire, upon seeing the two military men raise their hands, questioned:

"I suggest we start at daybreak tomorrow, are you gentlemen well enough to make the trip?"

Corporal Winowski stood up alone and spoke: "The ensign here needs a couple of more days to recover; but I can lead a burial party to the ambush site."

"Good, all you men volunteering for the burial party, meet in front of this tavern at sunup. Now to the problem of getting the supplies to Fort Pitt, how many of you wish to volunteer?"

No one raised their hand. One of the men stood up and addressed the Squire:

"Squire, I like to help; but there's a big difference in maybe a two day journey round trip to bury the fallen soldiers, and taking almost a week to get to Fort Pitt and back. I've got a powerful lot of plowing still undone, I can't afford to be gone that long."

Squire Hanna looked around the room, then asked: "I suppose you all have business to attend to which precludes you from making the journey to Fort Pitt?"

Heads nodded around the room and there were grunts of concurrence. The Squire looked at Ensign Butler and spoke.

"I'm sorry sir, we can't accompany you."

Ensign Butler rose from the table.

"I understand. I will see the supplies get to Fort Pitt. I plan to leave as soon as Corporal Winowski returns from the burial detail. If any of you change your minds in that time, your company will be most welcome."

As the meeting turned to the organization of a militia, Corporal Winowski and Ensign Butler headed toward the stairs. Rebecca hurried to them.

"Would you come to the kitchen with me?" She asked.

"Sure, Rebecca," Ensign Butler responded.

She grabbed two extra chairs from the tavern public room so they could all sit at the kitchen table. Once they were seated, Rebecca began.

"I want to go back to Fort Pitt with you. I think I might have found someone to defend Mamalachgook in court."

"Who is that?" Ensign Butler asked.

"Simon Dubois. He was the man sitting at the table with you."

"Him? He was pretty well on his way to intoxication. I also notice he didn't volunteer for anything." Ensign Butler said incredulous.

"Well I have a few days before we leave. He hasn't said no to me yet. I think I might be able to convince him." Rebecca pleaded.

"Corporal, fetch that man in here," Ensign Butler ordered.

Corporal Winowski was gone only a moment. He returned with Simon Dubois staggering before him.

"Sit down Mr. Dubois," Ensign Butler entreated.

"What can Simon Dubois do for you gent..gentlemen," Dubois slurred.

"You can accompany us to Fort Pitt." Butler responded as though the matter were already settled.

"Wait a minute. I never told this young wench I would go. I was also at the meeting. Do you think I want to make that journey with no armed escort?"

"Corporal Winowski and I will both be armed and this 'wench' as you refer to her is probably the best marksman in Western Pennsylvania. I've seen her in action. She saved my life and the corporal's." Ensign Butler retorted.

Simon Dubois stood up and bowed toward Rebecca.

"Sorry miss, I meant no offense. I will accompany you with these gentlemen to Fort Pitt, if you can provide some compensation for my services."

Ensign Butler spoke up: "I can provide you a private's wages for the trip there, payable when we reach the fort."

"And I will find some way to pay you for your services when we get there, if you'll but trust me. What do you charge?" Rebecca asked.

"Well I usually deal with documents so I charge a flat fee which depends on the type and complexity of the document. For your case I must charge 5 shillings a day or fraction thereof for time spent on the case. That means one beaver pelt will get you two days of my time." Dubois answered.

"That sounds reasonable, I'm sure Mamalachgook can trap enough beaver to cover your fees if he is acquitted." Rebecca responded.

"And if he isn't?" Dubois pressed.

"Then I will find another way to pay you. I told you I know how to distill whiskey." Rebecca countered.

"Ah, a very useful skill indeed, Miss Walker your credit is good with me." Dubois responded. Then he added: "Now that our business is concluded, I would like to return to my tankard of rum. I don't think you will have any trouble locating me when it comes time to depart for Fort Pitt. I'll keep the tavern owner apprised of my whereabouts."

With that statement, DuBois left the kitchen. After he departed, Ensign Butler commented:

"Rebecca I think it's risky to put your trust in him."

"Joshua, I have no choice. He's the only man around here with knowledge of law who is willing to defend Mamalachgook."

❧

The next four days went much too slowly for Rebecca. She continued to help Mrs. O'Neil with the chores; but the second day after Squire Hanna's meeting, Ensign Butler had recovered enough to walk, albeit with a noticeable limp. Rebecca then accompanied him as he made preparations for the return journey to Fort Pitt. He acquired two wagons and horses from the owner of the livery stable. When this was done, he took Rebecca out on the road on one of the wagons and taught her the rudiments of driving a team of horses. He explained: "If we run into trouble on the way to Fort Pitt, you may need to drive the team by yourself."

With wagons acquired; they went to the trading post and got the supplies. The proprietor was surprised the ensign was able to pay in hard

171

currency instead of Continental Greenbacks, which were seriously devalued. After the supplies were loaded, Ensign Butler confided in Rebecca:

"General Brodhead came up with the cash for the wagons, horses and supplies. From where, I have no idea. There is little hard currency about these days. Whiskey and animal skins are the usual currency around here."

Searching for wagon drivers turned out to be an exercise in futility. Mr. O'Neil said they were expecting some traders to come with wagons from Philadelphia one of these days; but had no idea when they would arrive. He also informed Rebecca and Ensign Butler that:

"Most likely they will want to return to the east; rather than go to Fort Pitt."

Ensign Butler then made the rounds of the town and neighboring farms. He returned to announce to Rebecca.

"I can't find anyone willing to take the job. They are all aware that our party is small and not likely capable of fending off an Indian ambush."

"Does that mean you have to cancel the trip?" Rebecca asked anxiously.

"No, Corporal Winowski and I are duty bound to go. We'll have to drive the wagons; but I think you should consider staying here. It could be a perilous journey and we might not make it." Ensign Butler responded.

"No, Joshua, I have to get back to Mamalachgook. We've been through peril before. I'm only worried that Simon Dubois will refuse to go along. We really can't ask him to risk his life."

"In that case, I'll have a personal talk with him; give him the facts, and allow him to back out if he wishes." Ensign Butler explained.

"I really should be with you when you do, Joshua. I must let him know I won't think the lesser of him." Rebecca responded.

"Very well." Ensign Butler concurred.

As it turned out Simon Dubois was willing to go even though they would only be a party of four. He told Rebecca he looked forward to the challenge of defending Mamalachgook. He explained that, if he were successful, it might open up a new career for him. Perhaps word would get around and he could practice law on a full time basis.

The evening of the fourth day, the burial party returned. Corporal Winowski sought out Ensign Butler and the two took a table in the tavern to discuss the journey to Fort Pitt. Ensign Butler was also anxious to know details of trip the corporal had made with the burial detail. Rebecca, carrying some clean mugs in to give the innkeeper, spotted the two and went over to the table. She sat down and asked.

"How was your journey?"

Corporal Winowski started: "Well ma'am…"

Ensign Butler interrupted: "Rebecca, don't you think we should move to the kitchen?'

"Why, Joshua? I've been seen all over town with you. I don't think I need to worry about being seen here with you."

"Very well, continue corporal," Ensign Butler responded.

Corporal Winowski resumed talking about the trip. Rebecca became nauseous when he described the state of decay the bodies were in; but she continued to listen. They had buried each white man in their own grave, and the Indians in a mass one. Ensign Butler commented.

"The fact that Indian bodies were still there is important. It likely means no one will be looking for who killed them. It's a sign that our trip to Fort Pitt may not be as risky as I thought."

"When do we leave?" Corporal Winowski asked.

"Tomorrow at daybreak. I've made all the preparations." Ensign Butler answered. Then he continued: "There will only be four of us; you, me, Rebecca, and Simon Dubois. I couldn't find any one to drive the wagons, so the four of us will have to take our turns at it."

"Can you handle a team?" Corporal Winowski asked, looking at Rebecca.

"I think I'll be alright. Joshua, I mean Ensign Butler has been giving me lessons."

Corporal Winowski shook his head in disbelief; but said nothing more. Ensign Butler then addressed Rebecca.

"You'd best go to bed and rest up. It's back to sleeping on the ground the next few days. The corporal and I will finish our drinks, and be off to bed ourselves."

CHAPTER 11

BACK TO FORT PITT

The foursome, Ensign Butler, the corporal, Dubois and Rebecca made completed the journey to Fort Pitt safely. The only incident along the road occurred when Ensign Butler caught Dubois trying to tap into a barrel of whiskey that was part of the shipment. He threatened Dubois with 30 lashes when they got to Fort Pitt if there was a repeat occurrence.

They arrived the afternoon of the fourth day. The party drew stares from the soldiers and others within the fort; primarily because Rebecca was driving one of the wagons. Riding with her was Corporal Winowski. He was grateful that Rebecca could drive as his right shoulder still pained him some.

They drove the wagons to the Quartermaster Stores. There Ensign Butler ordered Corporal Winowski to oversee the unloading and obtain the Quartermaster's receipt for the goods. The ensign then announced to Rebecca and Dubois.

"I must report to General Brodhead. I think he will be anxious to talk to you, Rebecca, and I suppose you with him. You are both welcome to accompany me."

"Gladly," Rebecca responded.

The three walked to the headquarters building where the single guard snapped to attention and performed a "present arms" salute to the ensign. Ensign Butler gave him a hand salute and spoke.

"Inform the general that Ensign Butler requests permission to report."

When the guard entered the building to announce Ensign Butler's presence to the general, Butler turned to Rebecca.

"You should wait outside until summoned."

Rebecca nodded her concurrence. The guard came back out and announced:

"The general bids you enter."

Ensign Butler remained inside for a period of 5 to 10 minutes; then he appeared in the doorway and motioned for Rebecca and Dubois to enter. Inside the general's office, the general was the first to speak.

"Ah, Miss Walker, you seem to be getting to be something of a legend. Would you do us a favor and tell me what transpired on the journey from here to Hannastown?"

"Hasn't Ensign Butler already made his report?" Rebecca countered

"Yes, but I'd like to hear the story from your point of view. I will require the same of Corporal Winowski when he becomes available."

So Rebecca told the tale to the general. When she was done, General Brodhead remarked:

"You tell the story with such richness and passion. Could I prevail upon you to repeat it to a scribe so that we might use the story to pay homage to the men who were killed on the way to Hannastown? I am planning to arrange a memorial ceremony tomorrow or the next day for those soldiers.

"Yes, sir, I would be glad to," Rebecca responded.

"Now is there something I may do for you?" the general asked.

"Yes, sir, this man with me is Simon Dubois. He has come to defend Mamalachgook as his legal representative. Could we meet with Mamalachgook?"

"Harrumph," General Brodhead cleared his throat. Then he answered: "That Indian, yes it would be good to dispose of that matter as soon as possible. Mr. Dubois, are you willing to defend this Indian in an environment that is likely to be quite hostile?"

Dubois hesitated. Then he asked: "Would you elaborate on what you mean by a hostile environment?"

"I mean my men who guard Mamalachgook are the only thing which has prevented him from being lynched. You make run the risk of being tarred and feathered or worse once your purpose be known." General Brodhead explained.

Dubois gulped. Then he continued: "What are the charges against him?"

"I formally charged him with being an accomplice to murder on the basis that he came from a tribe that killed Miss Walker's family. The same tribe is suspected to have been in on other killings. Perhaps members of that tribe also attacked Ensign Butler's detail."

"Sir, the ones who attacked us had the markings of the Seneca," Ensign Butler chimed in.

"Well you may have to testify to that at trial, ensign, if there is a trial." General Brodhead responded.

"What is the evidence against this Mamalachgook?" Dubois asked.

"Well Miss Walker's description of the attack on her family is the most damming evidence. Yet there is no specific evidence to show Mamalachgook has attacked or killed any whites. I had him imprisoned here as much for his own protection as for being a suspected accomplish to murder."

Dubois replied: "I think I will risk taking on his case. May I, that is Rebecca and I converse with the prisoner?"

"Yes, but let's first discuss trial arrangements. What do you propose?" General Brodhead asked.

"I would like his case to be presented in a court of Oyer and Terminer." Dubois answered.

"That court is usually held at the county seat in Hannastown. If I transfer the prisoner there; which I am reluctant to do because of a scarcity of manpower, he will likely be in greater danger because I will no longer have control over his confinement. He will be held in whatever passes for a local jail and the risk of lynching will likely be greater."

"Could the court be convened here?" Dubois asked.

"I will send a messenger to Squire Hanna. He is one of the justices. I will inquire if he and/or another justice are willing to hold court here. It will likely take some time to get a reply. I will keep you informed." General Brodhead replied. Then the general addressed Ensign Butler:

"Ensign, take these two to the guardhouse and instruct the guard there to let them have as much time as they wish with the prisoner."

"Yes sir," Ensign Butler replied and the three left the general's office.

They crossed the compound to the guardhouse where Mamalachgook was confined. Ensign Butler instructed the guard who undid a latch and opened the door for Rebecca and Dubois to enter. Inside, Rebecca was immediately affected by the darkness that prevailed in sharp contrast to the sunlit grounds of the fort. She was also repulsed by an offensive smell within. As Rebecca's eyes readjusted to the change in illumination, she called out.

"Mamalachgook?"

"Watch where you step," Mamalachgook's voice came back.

Rebecca scanned the interior as her eyes adjusted to the new environment. There was a floor made of roughhewn logs, in the middle of which was a large hole dug in the earth with an open trap door. A ladder formed of lashed logs led into the pit. Rebecca, seeing the ladder, immediately descended into the hole. She found Mamalachgook, threw her arms around him and drew him to her breast. Then she kissed him hard on the lips and drew her head back to look into his eyes.

"Oh, Mamalachgook, I've missed you. How have they been treating you?"

"Oh, very generously, I get a ration of bread and water twice a day; and if there are leftovers from the soldiers mess which can't be preserved, a little meat and vegetables." Mamalachgook answered.

"You poor dear. I've got to get you out of here." Rebecca cried.

"You don't like these accommodations," Mamalachgook joked, sweeping his hand around to present his cell to Rebecca. Then he continued: "You see there is room for two or three more."

Just then they were interrupted by the voice of Dubois, who had chosen to remain above.

"Could we get on with our business, Miss Walker? It rather smells in here."

"Alright, we'll come up," she answered.

Rebecca led, climbing the ladder and taking a seat on the perimeter of the hole, her feet dangling into the pit. Then she gestured for Mamalachgook to sit beside her. Following their lead, Dubois took up a similar position on the wooden ledge across from them.

"Will you do the introductions, Miss Walker?" Dubois entreated.

"Mamalachgook, this is Simon Dubois. He has journeyed here from Hannastown to help you get released."

Mamalachgook surveyed Dubois from head to ragged shoes.

"How can this man help?" Mamalachgook asked.

"Let him tell you," Rebecca responded. It suddenly hit her she had no idea what the plan was.

"I've been giving the matter some thought. The fact is that there is no real evidence against Mamalachgook here; just presumed guilt by association. Still any jury assembled here will likely be composed of men prejudiced against Indians in general and Delawares in particular. I have lived among peaceful Delawares. We ought to see if we can find any potential jurors who are aware of the peaceful tribes. They may listen with a more open mind." Dubois began outlining his strategy.

"There's a blacksmith named Easton here at the fort. He's a Quaker. I think he would judge the case on merit rather than prejudice." Rebecca offered.

"That's a start. I hope we might find others. Next we should consider whether you should testify, Rebecca."

"Why shouldn't I testify?" Rebecca protested.

"Because your testimony is a two-edged sword. Your support of Mamalachgook will help, of course, but you will likely be cross-examined on the subject of the massacre of your family. That may turn sentiment against Mamalachgook"

"I must testify. There is no one else to speak for Mamalachgook," Rebecca pleaded.

"Very well," Dubois acquiesced. Then he continued: "I think it might be useful to summon Ensign Butler as a witness."

"But why? He has no relationship to Mamalachgook." Rebecca queried.

"Yes, but his testimony on your actions during the recent raid on the detail Butler commanded may convince the jury that you are committed to defending whites against Indian attacks." Dubois explained.

"How does that help?" Rebecca asked.

"It could convince the jury that you are only interested in freeing this particular man; that you have a firm belief in his innocence. You would not be looked upon as one who has some naïve commitment to avoiding conflict with Indians at all costs." Dubois explained.

Dubois then turned to Mamalachgook and asked: "Are you willing to stand before the bar and testify in your own defense?

"I will do so."

"Ah, good," Dubois started. Then he continued: "It is best if the accused confronts his accusers with his own rebuttal to their charges. It is even better that you are able to speak English. Of course, you will be subject to cross-examination. I must spend some time coaching you on what to avoid saying lest you inflame the jurors."

Mamalachgook looked puzzled. Dubois picked up on this and added: "Don't worry. In time you will understand."

Dubois then looked down as though he wished to avoid talking about the next subject.

"Now, about payment for my services. Rebecca, you indicated that Mamalachgook might be able to make payment in furs. Mamalachgook do you agree to this?"

Mamalachgook gave Dubois a puzzled look. Then he answered:

"I have no cache of furs. If free, I could trap sufficient beaver or raccoon, or I could kill to acquire skins to make payment. How many of which do you require?"

"Miss Walker and I agreed on payment equal to one beaver pelt for each day I spend on your case or its equivalent in other species' hides. As I have no other clients at Fort Pitt, I must charge for idle time also until your case is settled." Dubois explained.

"That is reasonable; but you must understand I must be free to hunt or trap to make payment. What happens if I am not freed?" Mamalachgook asked.

"Then Miss Walker has agreed to repay me by performing some service of equal value."

Rebecca saw a look of disgust was over Mamalachgook's face.

"Such as what?" Mamalachgook demanded.

"She will have to produce the equivalent value in whiskey. She has already committed to do as much." Dubois answered.

Mamalachgook looked at Rebecca.

"You make that promise?" he asked.

"Yes dear, I did," she answered.

"I think it not good you make the whiskey for the white man. If he becomes drunk…"

Rebecca took his hand in both her hands and interrupted him.

"Darling, trust me."

Dubois got up. Then he announced: "Well I'd best be seeking some pen and paper. I need to outline the defense. I'd also like to learn some something of the locals. Is there a tavern at Fort Pitt?"

"Yes it's called the Thirsty Beaver. I'm sure you'll have no trouble finding it." Rebecca sneered.

Dubois called the guard to let him out. When he was gone, Mamalachgook asked Rebecca.

"What was that last comment you made about?"

"I'm afraid Mr. Dubois likes to imbibe in the spirits a little too much." Rebecca answered.

"So I have a drunk who is supposed to get me released?"

"Sorry, Mamalachgook; but he is all I could find."

CHAPTER 12

MAMALACHGOOK'S TRIAL

Nearly two weeks passed before the trial commenced. General Brodhead commandeered the *Thirsty Beaver* for a site to hold court. He also served as the prosecutor since he was the one who had charged Mamalachgook with participating in the murder of white settlers. The closing of the Thirsty Beaver for the purpose of conducting the trial caused resentment among the innkeeper as well as the customers accustomed to dropping in for a meal or drink during the day. Two justices had arrived for the trial from Hannastown the previous evening and took up lodging at the tavern.

When Rebecca entered the tavern it appeared all the residents of Fort Pitt were there. Mr. Dubois noted her arrival and went to greet her. Then he escorted her to a bench before the bar where Ensign Butler was already seated. She smiled at Ensign Butler and sat down. She was about ask the ensign why she didn't see Mamalachgook when the tavern door opened and two soldiers with rifles appeared with Mamalachgook walking before them. It appeared he had been allowed to bathe before the trial. He stood straight and tall in his breechcloth and leggings; but was thinner and paler then when Rebecca had first seen him what now seemed like a lifetime ago. His hands were bound in front of him. The soldiers escorted Mamalachgook to a small table where Dubois was now seated. He sat down and the two soldiers moved to the closest wall to the table and remained standing.

Then General Brodhead entered with a man Rebecca recognized at the scribe to whom she had previously related her story. The General and the scribe sat down at table in front of the bar near the opposite side of the room from Dubois and Mamalachgook. The scribe started removing writing material from a pouch he'd carried in. The General turned and looked toward the tavern entrance. In a moment he stood up and announced: "This court of Oyer and Terminer is now in session. All rise. Justices John Moore and Hugh Brakenridge will preside over the hearings."

Two men, elegantly dressed compared to the others in the tavern, walked in and took up seats behind the bar.

"You may be seated," one of the justices said. "I am Justice Brakenridge and this is Justice Moore you will address us accordingly separately or collectively as 'The Court'."

Then the Justice Moore asked: "Will the prosecutor stand and state the charges?"

General Brodhead stood up. He motioned with his hand toward Mamalachgook.

"This Indian from the Delaware Tribe, Mamalachgook, is charged with abetting in the murder of settlers in this region." The general stated.

Justice Moore then continued: "The accused will stand and enter his plea."

Dubois nudged Mamalachgook. Then they both stood up. Mamalachgook looked straight at the two justices and said: "Not guilty."

Justice Moore continued: "You may be seated. We will now proceed with the selection of a jury. Prosecutor call the first man to the bar."

"Mr. Henry Easton", General Brodhead announced.

Henry Easton hobbled forward on his crutches to the bar and stood before the justices.

'State your full name and occupation," Justice Brakenridge ordered.

"Henry Ernest Easton, blacksmith."

"How is it that you are crippled?" Justice Brakenridge asked.

"I lost my leg during the battle of Harlem Heights in New York. A British cannon I believe."

"Have you any relationship with the accused?"

"No sir, this is the first time I've ever seen him, although I've known of his presence at Fort Pitt for some time." Henry Easton answered.

Justice Brakenridge looked toward Dubois. Then he ordered: "Counsel for the defense will approach the bar.

Dubois got up and moved to a position alongside Easton. Then Justice Brakenridge ordered: "State your name sir and your position in this court."

"I'm Simon Dubois, counsel for the accused, Mamalachgook."

"Have you any questions to ask this potential juror?" Justice Brakenridge asked.

"No sir."

"Do you have any objections to his serving as a juror?" Justice Brakenridge asked.

"No sir."

Justice Brakenridge then addressed Easton: "You will serve as a juror. You may take a seat on that empty bench along the wall."

The selection process continued until six men had been selected. Rebecca watched with intense interest, trying to guess whether each man would decide with an open mind. She noted that all the men General Brodhead called except Mr. Easton seemed to be newly arrived settlers. Was the general trying to stack the jury in Mamalachgook's favor? Dubois offered no objections and all of the first six called were seated as jurors.

Justice Moore then ordered General Brodhead to present: "That evidence or testimony against the accused."

General Brodhead proceeded to call forth 'witnesses'. They all turned out to be settlers who had been victims or whose relatives had been victims of Indian raids. Each witness told their story on an atrocity trying to convince the justices that all Indians in the vicinity were guilty of the murder of someone and the one being tried in this court was no different.

Dubois quickly dispatched each witness on cross-examination by demanding they "Swear to God" that they had seen Mamalachgook himself perform the atrocity. This, of course, they could not do. Those who had actually survived an Indian assault insisted it was impossible to tell one warrior from another.

Dubois then called Rebecca to stand before the bar and tell her story. As she told the full story of the massacre of her parents and the killing of her brother, she glanced from time to time at the jurors to see their reaction; but they all seemed to have neutral facial expressions. She continued until she had told all up to her arrival with Mamalachgook at Fort Pitt.

General Brodhead then cross-examined Rebecca. He tried to get the point across that in her captivity she had accepted Indian ways and was now reluctant to speak out against them. All knew of women who had been captured and released after a treaty signed only to return to the tribe who'd captured them. Rebecca protested to the point of tears that this was not true in her case.

Dubois stepped in and asked the Rebecca be excused. He called Ensign Butler to the stand to tell the story of the incident on the way to Hannastown. When the ensign was finished, Dubois addressed the jurors: "Now does that sound like a woman who has been intimidated by Indians?"

Then Dubois asked Butler: "Do you think Ms. Walker fears the accused and fears some sort of retribution by his tribal brothers if she speaks against him?"

"Sir Rebecca is the bravest woman I've ever known and, as handy as she is with a rifle, the Delawares would be wise to fear her instead."

Ensign Butler's comment brought a roar of laughter from what up until now had been a somber courtroom.

When Justice Moore had gaveled the court back to order, Dubois stated: "I rest my case."

Justice Moore then instructed the jury and ordered them to decide the case.

The juror's talked among themselves for about half an hour, the Henry Easton stood up.

"Justice Moore and Justice Brakenridge, we the jury have decided that no conclusive evidence was presented that the subject Indian was guilty of any crime."

Justice Brakenridge spoke: "Thank you. The accused will approach the bar."

Mamalachgook did as ordered. Justice Brakenridge then looked toward the two guards and ordered: "You will unbind his hands."

They complied. Then Justice Brakenridge addressed Mamalachgook:

"You are free to go. I would advise, however, that you depart Fort Pitt at your earliest convenience. There are likely some here that don't think justice has been done today and may wish to administer their idea of frontier justice."

Rebecca rushed to Mamalachgook and hugged him. She then led him over to Dubois and hugged Dubois. The three left the tavern together. Once outside the tavern, Dubois asked Mamalachgook.

"Where do you plan to go now that you are free?"

Mamalachgook looked around, surveying the interior of the fort and breathing deeply, sampling the air of freedom. Then he responded.

"I must go. You both know I am not wanted here. I will go into the woods and make camp for myself. Then I will hunt to get the animal skins you seek for payment. Where shall I find you, Dubois to make payment?"

"I will return to Hannastown. I can usually find work there as I know most of the locals. I reside in a small shack behind the trading post. When you come, I would advise you to avoid being seen. The people in that area are edgy since the party Rebecca was traveling with was attacked. If caught and not lynched on site; you may have to go through this legal process again. I can't assure you the outcome would be the same. And now, Miss Walker, what will you do?"

Rebecca didn't hesitate.

"My place is with Mamalachgook."

Dubois responded: " I beg you consider what people will think if they learn of you traveling with an Indian man. You know gossip travels fast."

Rebecca thought a moment. Then she addressed Mamalachgook.

"How do your people legitimize a relationship between a man and a woman?"

"We have no formal ceremony. Presents are exchanged between the family of the man who desires the woman and her family. Then the man and woman cohabit. If she be a good woman who desires the man and he be a good man who provides for the woman, they spend a lifetime together. If not, they will separate." Mamalachgook explained.

"Since I no longer have a family, I would expect you to give me a present if you wish to marry me." Rebecca proposed with an impish grin.

"Who said I want to marry you?" Mamalachgook teased back.

Rebecca slowly twirled around.

"Do I not appear to be good wife material?"

"You attract me as the flower does the bee; but an attractive woman is not necessarily a good wife."

"What else is required?" Rebecca continued with the contest of wits.

"She must have strong limbs and womb to carry child. She must have strong back to plant and sow crops. Most of all, she must desire to serve her husband."

"You mean I must be a slave to you?" Rebecca asked, her temperament now growing somber. She then took Mamalachgook's hands in hers. He responded.

"I do not mean you need satisfy my every whim; but you prepare food when I am hungry, nurse me when I'm sick, comfort me when I am troubled, and humor me when I desire the pleasure of your body."

The Rebecca spoke: "I will promise to do these things if you will promise to provide meat for me to cook, care for me when I am sick, comfort me when I am troubled, and pleasure me when I desire your body."

"I now pronounce you man and wife." Dubois piped in.

Mamalachgook smiled and Rebecca chuckled. Then she turned to Dubois with a look of sudden enlightenment.

"You could marry us, couldn't you, Mr. Dubois? You are an ordained minister."

"Was an ordained minister, my dear Miss Walker, the Presbyterians would not recognize the marriage to be legitimate."

"I don't give a fig about the Presbyterians," Rebecca started. Then she continued: "I just want people in general to recognize we are man and wife."

"A civil ceremony would do as much. I expect either one of the Justices who presided at the trial could perform an acceptable marriage ceremony." Dubois responded.

Rebecca grabbed Mamalachgook by the hand and yanked him back into the tavern. Inside she spotted the justices standing at the bar enjoying a tankard of spirits. She pulled Mamalachgook and rushed up to them. A little winded, Rebecca asked.

"Justice Moore and Justice Brakenridge are you authorized to marry people?"

Justice Moore spoke first: "Yes, we both do that rather routinely."

"Would one of you perform a marriage ceremony for us?" Rebecca asked.

Justice Brakenridge asked: "You mean you wish to be married to this Indian?"

"Yes."

"My dear, you must consider what you propose," Justice Brakenridge began. Then he continued: "You will likely be ostracized by your race and he by his race if you become man and wife."

"I don't care. My family and I had little contact with society before I came to Fort Pitt." Rebecca responded.

Justice Brakenridge then addressed Mamalachgook.

"What about your people?"

"My brothers no longer will accept me as one of them as I disobeyed our sachem in bringing Rebecca here."

"I see," Justice Brakenridge started. Then he continued: "Where do you plan to live?"

Rebecca looked at Mamalachgook.

"We could live on the homestead my father started. What do you think Mamalachgook?"

"That is possible, if you will accept the fact that I am a hunter and will not likely be satisfied as a grower of crops."

"Isn't that pretty much the way of the Delaware? The men hunt and the women tend to the field. I can accept that."

Justice Brakenridge then asked.

"Do you love each other?"

"Yes." Rebecca responded.

"Yes." Mamalachgook concurred.

"There is the problem of witnesses," Judge Moore chimed in.

"What do you mean?" Rebecca asked.

"In a normal marriage another man witnesses the marriage for the groom, who in this case is Mamalachgook and another woman witnesses for bride, that being you, Ms. Walker."

"I'll be the best man, that is witness for Mamalachgook, providing of course he wishes me to do so." A voiced boomed from within the tavern.

It was Dubois he had followed Rebecca and Mamalachgook inside.

"Will you expect more beaver to be witness?" Mamalachgook asked.

Rebecca punched Mamalachgook's shoulder then said.

"Do you think white men put a price on everything?"

Then Rebecca looked at Dubois and asked: "Would you?"

"No, that service would be free." Dubois responded.

"I accept you as my 'best man', then," Mamalachgook answered.

"I think Mrs. Easton would serve as my witness," Rebecca proposed.

Justice Moore then spoke.

"Justice Brakenridge and myself planned to return to our residences this afternoon. We both have business there we are neglecting while we are here."

"I will stay one more day and perform the ceremony if everything can be arranged before noon tomorrow." Justice Brakenridge offered. Then he continued: "Of course there will be a fee for my service."

Rebecca's emotions spiraled downward. Then another voice from within the tavern asked.

"How much is your fee?" A voice within the tavern asked.

"I normally charge 5 shillings; but since I will be detained here an additional day I must make it 10 shillings." Justice Brakenridge responded.

Rebecca thought the voice of the person requesting the amount of the fee was familiar. It was Ensign Butler. He walked up to the justice. Took a small purse out from underneath his shirt, retrieved some coins from the purse and handed them to Justice Brakenridge.

"It's two and a half days pay for me; but I owe this young lady my life. I wish to see her on the road to a happy future." Ensign Butler explained.

Rebecca rushed to the ensign and kissed him on the cheek.

"Oh thank you, Joshua," she gushed.

"I just hope you find happiness." Ensign Butler responded.

"I expect you have preparations to make, Miss Walker," Justice Brakenridge broke in. "I will conduct the nuptials here at 9:00 a.m., if that is satisfactory." He continued.

"Yes, sir," Rebecca replied.

She then turned to Ensign Butler: "You'll come won't you?"

"If my captain will release me from my duties, yes." Ensign Butler replied.

Rebecca then took Mamalachgook by the hand and said:

"Come, I want you to meet the Eastons."

CHAPTER 13

THE WEDDING

Hanna Easton was thrilled when Rebecca broke the news to her.

"Oh there is so much to do and very little time. I must get some friends to assist. Will you look after the children for me?"

"Yes, of course; but do you think other women at Fort Pitt will be help prepare for a wedding between a white woman and an Indian?" Rebecca asked.

"The women of my sewing circle will not want to be cheated out of a wedding. It's a social event we rarely have at Fort Pitt. Any wedding, even a mixed marriage, gives them a good excuse to throw a party. I would hate to face any of my friends if I refused to include them in the preparations." Hanna answered.

Mamalachgook who was standing alongside Rebecca gave her a dumbfounded look.

"Come, let me introduce you to Mr. Easton, Faith, and Hope," Rebecca entreated.

Rebecca led Mamalachgook to the shop where Henry Easton was now back at work. Faith and Hope were just outside the exposed entrance to the shop drawing pictures in the dirt. When the children saw Rebecca and Mamalachgook approaching their father, they stopped what they were doing and followed them. Apparently they were curious to know who the strange man was. Rebecca began the introductions:

"Mamalachgook, this is Henry Easton. I think you remember him from the trial."

Henry Easton extended his hand and Mamalachgook shook it.

"I am pleased to know thee," he said.

"And I am pleased to know the man who helped me achieve justice." Mamalachgook answered.

"I can't see Rebecca here associating with anyone but a just person. I'm glad we settled that business. What are your plans now?" Henry Easton asked.

"Rebecca and I are to be married tomorrow."

"So that's why Hanna went flying out of here. You know women and weddings." Mr. Easton chuckled.

"I'm afraid I am not aware of that white custom." Mamalachgook answered.

"Well, after tomorrow, you'll not likely forget," Mr. Easton laughed again.

"Let me introduce you to the children," Rebecca said.

Then she picked up each of the two girls in turn. She told Mamalachgook their names and told them his. The girls each were shy and had difficulty repeating his name. After the introductions, Rebecca suggested.

"Why don't you and I take the girls for a little stroll, Mamalachgook? Would that be alright with you Mr. Easton?"

"I'm sure they would enjoy it," Mr. Easton responded. Then he continued: "But Charity is within, and I'm in the middle of a job and do not wish to stop to attend to her. Could you entertain Faith and Hope in the house?"

"Oh, certainly. Where was my mind? Hanna would never forgive me if I left Charity unattended." Rebecca responded.

So Rebecca led Mamalachgook and the two girls into the house. She led Mamalachgook to the crib where Charity was busy playing with her toes.

"This is Charity," Rebecca announced.

Rebecca and Mamalachgook had no problem entertaining Faith and Hope. Curiosity overcame the girl's shyness and they began to fire questions at the strange man before them. Mamalachgook found himself talking about everything imaginable from why he wore his hair so funny and didn't wear a shirt to the legend of the origin of the Delaware. The two girls as well as Rebecca were engrossed in his stories. Rebecca was impressed with his ability as a storyteller. He was telling a story about a snake and a turtle when Hanna returned with two other ladies.

"Mamalachgook, will you excuse us please, we have woman matters to take care of?" Hanna asked.

Mamalachgook got up from his position on the floor where he had been sitting with Rebecca and the girls and walked out into the shop. Both he and Hanna were surprised to see Faith and Hope followed on his heels. Out in the shop, Faith begged.

"Please finish the story."

Mamalachgook took the girls by the hand and sat them down on the ground where they had been drawing pictures earlier and continued. He finished the story; but they begged for more, so he continued his storytelling. He found it useful to draw images in the dirt as he went along.

Meanwhile, back in the house, the women had stripped Rebecca of the clothes she'd been wearing, dressed her in an old wedding dress one of the women had brought and were busy figuring out how to alter it to fit Rebecca's figure. As the two ladies who had come with Hanna worked on the dress, Hanna prepared a cauldron of hot water and brought in a bath tub. After the locations for alterations had been noted, they took the dress off and a moment later Rebecca was naked in the tub. While one of the women worked on altering the dress, the other scrubbed Rebecca's back, then handed her the wash cloth so Rebecca could wash the rest. After the bath, Rebecca dressed in clean undergarments Hanna had provided. Hanna offered her a chair and began to work on Rebecca's hair as the work continued on the wedding dress. Hanna finished Rebecca's hair first. Rebecca felt a little embarrassed sitting in her shift waiting for the final fitting. She worried that either Mr. Easton or Mamalachgook might come in at any minute. When the dress was finished the women helped Rebecca back into it. Then the women stood back and admired their work.

"You look lovely," Hanna replied.

The other two women nodded approval. Rebecca could see they were pleased with their work.

"Thank you very much," Rebecca responded. Then she said: "I should show it to Mamalachgook."

"Oh, no. It's bad luck for him to see you in it before the wedding. Now take it off and put your other clothes on." One of the women answered.

Rebecca did as ordered. Then the two women bid Hanna farewell, saying they must go and help the other ladies prepare for the meal for after the wedding. As the ladies departed, Hanna asked.

"Rebecca, would you help clean up in here and help with the supper?"

"Sure, Hanna," Rebecca answered.

Rebecca started by getting a bucket and disposing of the dirty bath water. When she had emptied the tub, Hanna asked.

"Do thee think Mamalachgook would like a bath?"

"I suppose he might. I think he would like to cleanse himself of the smell accumulated during his imprisonment."

"Well, after the supper, you ask him. How about clothes for tomorrow? Should I see if I can procure some?" Hanna asked.

"I think Mamalachgook would prefer to be married in his native dress." Rebecca responded.

"Hmmm," Hanna responded. Then she continued: "I'm sure his leggings and breechcloth could do with a good cleaning, and I think it would be more proper if he wore a shirt. If I can come up with a shirt, do thee think thee can convince him to wear it for the ceremony?"

"I'm sure I can get him to concede to that much." Rebecca giggled.

After a supper of salt pork, potatoes, turnips and cornbread where Mamalachgook gorged himself, Rebecca led him outside where they could talk in private.

"Mamalachgook, the mistress of the house, Mrs. Easton asked if you would like to have a bath."

"Yes, that would be nice, but if I go to the river, the guards at the gate may not let me return." Mamalachgook answered her.

"Hanna, that is Mrs. Easton and I can prepare a bathtub with water here. She also asked if you would like your leggings and breechcloth cleaned." Rebecca continued.

"Does the white woman know how to clean those things?" Mamalachgook asked.

"I don't know."

"Then I will do it myself if she can provide soap for the breechcloth and brush for the leggings." Mamalachgook answered.

"I'll see what we can do. Oh, she also asked me if I could persuade you to wear a shirt tomorrow at the ceremony." Rebecca pressed.

"Do you desire that I do so?"

"Yes, Hanna thinks she can find one to loan you."

"Very good." Mamalachgook answered.

Rebecca took him back into the house and Mamalachgook carried the tub to a corner of the shop. Then Hanna and Rebecca arranged some blankets on a rope around the tub for privacy and went to prepare the water for the bath. Once Mamalachgook entered the bath, Rebecca returned to the house and helped Hanna clean up after supper. After a time, Hanna asked Henry Easton to check on Mamalachgook. When Mr. Easton returned, he announced:

"He's finished bathing and is cleaning his clothes. Thee can go to him. He's wrapped in one of the blankets."

Rebecca went to him. She found Mamalachgook, blanket wrapped around his waist, brushing his leggings. His breechcloth hung, drying, from the rope. When she approached him he said.

"Ah that bath felt good. You must thank the Mistress for me."

"I will."

Rebecca then set about emptying the tub. As she worked, Mamalachgook asked:

"Do you think I could stay here this night? The breechcloth is wet and it would be better if I allow it to dry before I wear it again so the air may freshen it."

"I'm sure you can sleep here in the shop. I'll ask. I'll probably sleeping out here also. This is where I slept before." Rebecca said then entered the house. When she returned, she announced.

"Hanna says you are welcome to the bed in the shop; but I must sleep inside. She said it is highly improper for a bride and groom to sleep in the same place until <u>after</u> they are married. I know we have slept together in the woods before; but I must humor her. She will provide me with a blanket and pillow to sleep on the floor."

"If that is the white custom, so be it," Mamalachgook sneered.

Rebecca sat on the bench beside Mamalachgook put her arms around him gave him a lingering kiss on the lips. He responded by holding her tight in his arms. In a moment Rebecca's body began to become flush from the sexual arousal caused by the kiss and embrace. Rebecca pushed herself free. She stood up and said.

"Hanna is right. This is no place for me tonight; but tomorrow night you and I will be free to sleep together. Good night."

"Yes, Rebecca, I look forward to tomorrow night; but there may be little sleep then." Mamalachgook answered with a big grin.

Rebecca then rushed into the house. She immediately prepared her bed for the night; but it was an hour or more before the arousal caused by the embrace died down enough for her to drift off to sleep. She was unaware that Mamalachgook had the same problem.

Rebecca was awakened by Hanna the next morning. Hanna had been the first one up in the house and awoke Rebecca so she could dress before

Mr. Easton arose. She helped Rebecca into the wedding dress. Rebecca offered to help Hanna with breakfast; but Hanna refused her help saying.

"Thee is not going to mess up that dress we worked so hard on by doing housework this day."

Rebecca then headed out to the shop to see if Mamalachgook had awakened yet. He wasn't there! A blanket lay in a heap on the bed and the breechcloth and leggings were gone. Rebecca rushed back into the house. Hanna saw the alarmed look on Rebecca's face and asked.

"What is it, dear?"

"Mamalachgook's gone." Rebecca answered as tears began to well up in her eyes.

Hanna moved to Rebecca and put her arm around her.

"Now I'm sure he had something he wanted to do. I'm sure he'll return soon. The way he eats, I think he'll be back by the time breakfast is on the table."

"I hope so," Rebecca sobbed.

"If he really loves thee, he'll be her for the wedding." Hanna consoled. Then she continued: "Now don't go messing up that pretty face and gown with tears."

Rebecca waited anxiously through breakfast and afterwards. She found herself unable to eat. Hanna had been wrong about Mamalachgook not missing breakfast. The hour set for the wedding was now fast approaching. Hanna was busy dressing up the girls for the ceremony and preparing a basket of food– her contribution for the feast afterwards. Then she came in with a buckskin shirt.

"This used to belong to Henry. He outgrew it some time back; but I think it will fit Mamalachgook." Hanna announced. Then she continued: "It is now time for us to depart. We don't want to be late."

Rebecca was feeling the lowest she had ever felt in her life. What had happened to Mamalachgook? Did he decide that marriage was a burden to avoid? Did he not love her as Rebecca thought? Nevertheless, Rebecca walked with the Eastons across the compound toward the *Thirsty Beaver*.

Hanna carried Charity in her arms, Henry, the basket of food, and Rebecca held the hands of Faith and Hope. For all appearances it looked like a family outing except for the wedding dress Rebecca wore. They arrived at the tavern entrance just as Justice Brakenridge approached. He tipped his three-cornered hat to the ladies and entered the tavern. The Eastons and Rebecca followed. Inside, Rebecca immediately noticed there were about a dozen women; but only a couple of men who appeared to be early patrons, Justice Brakenridge and Simon Dubois. Rebecca was wrought with anxiety. She sat Faith and Hope at a table and hurried toward the exit.

"I'll wait outside," Rebecca shouted back to Hanna.

Mr. Easton turned to his wife.

"Perhaps thee should go to her," he said.

"No, it is in God's hands, husband. His will be done, despite the consequences." Hanna replied.

Rebecca's eyes scanned the grounds of the fort, looking for anything familiar. In the distance, approaching from the gate of Fort Pitt she saw four figures. It was only moments later she identified two of the figures, Ensign Butler and Mamalachgook. The other two appeared to be soldiers of the militia carrying muskets. They walked alongside Mamalachgook as though guarding a prisoner. A though raced through Rebecca's mind: "What kind of trouble is Mamalachgook in now?"

When the party finally reached Rebecca, she noticed Mamalachgook carried a large bundle of flowers. Ensign Butler spoke first.

"Good morning, Rebecca, we've returned Mamalachgook for his lifetime of imprisonment.' Ensign Butler joked.

"His what?" Rebecca screamed.

"Yes, I understand he is to be your prisoner for life." Ensign Butler laughed.

"Mamalachgook, where have you been?" Rebecca scolded. Her anger was now at a peak.

Mamalachgook, with a big grin on his face, calmly explained.

"While talking with Faith yesterday evening, she asked if there were to be flowers at the wedding. I managed to catch Mrs. Easton's ear a little later and asked what the meaning of the flowers was. She explained that normally there were flowers at a wedding; in particular, the bride carried a bouquet. Well remember you said you expected a present if I was to marry you, did you not?" bouquet probed.

"Yes, but are you telling me that you disappeared this morning to pick flowers?" Rebecca asked.

"Exactly. I went to General Brodhead's office this morning to ask if I would be able to leave the fort and return without being refused reentry at the gate. He assigned Ensign Butler and these two men to escort me so there would be no trouble." Mamalachgook explained.

"And we were ordered to attend the marriage ceremony and feast afterwards, to ensure order prevails," Ensign Butler added.

"Mamalachgook, I don't know whether to hit you for disappearing this morning without telling me or to kiss you for this beautiful bouquet of flowers."

"I'd prefer the latter," Mamalachgook replied smugly.

"Later," Rebecca started. Then she continued: "Now get your heathen body in there, put on the shirt Hanna has provided and let's get on with this wedding." Rebecca ordered.

Mamalachgook handed her the bouquet of flowers and entered the tavern. A few moments later, Mamalachgook and Rebecca stood before Justice Brakenridge with Dubois alongside Mamalachgook and Hanna alongside Rebecca.

The ceremony was short and immediately afterward Justice Brakenridge took his leave to return home. Ensign Butler, the two soldiers, Simon Dubois and Mr. Easton took advantage of their privilege to kiss the bride. Mamalachgook was somewhat chagrined at this and asked.

"Why do you kiss them Rebecca?"

"It is a wedding custom among whites; but your kisses are the only ones that count, Mamalachgook," Rebecca consoled.

The party went on for a couple of hours until Nate the publican informed them they needed to leave so he could serve his noontime customers. Rebecca, Mamalachgook, and the Eastons returned to the Eastons' residence. When they got there, Mamalachgook was the first to speak.

"Rebecca, you must prepare to leave Fort Pitt."

"Couldn't you stay through the night?" Hanna asked.

"No, Mamalachgook's right. We are married now and it is time for us to seek our own place to live together." Rebecca answered.

Mamalachgook started to remove the shirt.

"Please keep it," Mr. Easton said. "It no longer fits me, so consider it a wedding present."

"Thank you," Mamalachgook responded.

"Where will you go now?" Hanna asked.

"I will go where Mamalachgook wishes," Rebecca started. Then she continued. "However, we have a debt to pay to Mr. Dubois, so we will probably make camp somewhere in the forest between here and Hannastown to reside until Mamalachgook obtains enough fur pelts to repay the debt. I am uncertain as to what happens after that; but I trust that Mamalachgook will provide for us."

Rebecca then asked Mamalachgook to wait for her and she entered the house with Hanna. She removed the wedding dress and put on her old clothes. Then she and Hanna prepared a pack with provisions for the trail. She also gave Rebecca two rolled up blankets.

"I can't deprive you of your blankets," Rebecca protested.

"Nonsense," Hanna started. Then she continued: "You and Mamalachgook can't spend your wedding night on bare ground. One is for under you and the other for over. I'll tell the ladies of my sewing circle I need two more quilts. They'll only be too happy to oblige. Quilting bees are one of the few social activities we have here."

Rebecca then made her farewells to the Hanna and the girls. She left the house to join Mamalachgook who was busy talking to Henry Easton. Mamalachgook had a rifle in his hands and Mr. Easton was busy explaining its origin.

"This is the musket I carried when I fought the British with Washington. Since I lost my leg, I have little use for it. I can't go hunting like I used to. Please take it as a wedding present. You will need something to hunt game to feed your new wife."

"That is very generous of you Mr. Easton." Mamalachgook responded.

Then Henry Easton took down a power horn and bullet bag from a peg in the shop. He handed them to Mamalachgook, saying: "The rifle isn't much good without these. I had fresh power put in the horn."

"Thank you, again," Mamalachgook replied.

Mamalachgook then noticed Rebecca.

"Are you ready?" he asked.

"Yes. You carry these." Rebecca responded, handing the blankets to Mamalachgook.

"What are these?" He asked.

"They're blankets. It's our bed for time being, until you can build a proper one," Rebecca answered.

As Rebecca left the shop with Mamalachgook she was surprised to see Ensign Butler.

"What are you doing here?" Rebecca asked.

"The general ordered me to escort you and Mamalachgook to the gate, to make sure neither of you are molested." Ensign Butler replied.

"Thank the general for me," Rebecca started. "Let's go Mamalachgook."

CHAPTER 14

CAPTURED AGAIN!

After Rebecca and Mamalachgook bade farewell to Ensign Butler at the gate, they followed the Monongahela until they came to Turtle creek. They began to follow the creek upstream. The sun was getting low in the sky by now and Mamalachgook suggested they look for a place to camp for the night. They found a spot a hundred yards or so from the creek where the ground was flat enough to lie comfortably on.

"Let's stop here," Mamalachgook proposed. "We're not far from the creek and I might be able to catch fish in the morning."

Rebecca took off her pack and Mamalachgook spread one of the blankets on the ground. Rebecca dug in the pack and found some biscuits and deer jerky. As they ate she brought up the thought she had been thinking since they had left Fort Pitt; but was reluctant to suggest to her new husband.

"Mamalachgook, what would you think of settling down at my families' old homestead?"

"Why would you want to live there? Does it not bring up unpleasant memories?" He asked.

"Yes, I would have those memories; but it was a lovely location and, as far as I know, the cabin is still there. I would prefer to have a roof over my head." Rebecca answered.

"In time I could acquire tools and build us our own lodge," Mamalachgook countered.

"But living at the cabin would save you all that work," Rebecca responded with a sweet coaxing voice.

"I will keep that thought in my sleep tonight; but consider it may have since been destroyed. Also, it is not close to Hannastown. Perhaps we should a place to camp closer to Hannastown until I repay the debt to Dubois.'

"Speaking of sleep, perhaps it is time we bedded down," Rebecca suggested.

Rebecca then began to unroll the second blanket. As she did so, she felt Mamalachgook come up behind her and start caressing her shoulders. She then he reached around and started to pull the pins from her short gown. Rebecca slapped his hands and said.

"Stop, let me do it. You're likely to tear something."

Mamalachgook sat back on his heels to watch. Rebecca removed her short gown, scarf, outer petticoat and then the under one and pockets. When she was down to her shift, she leaned forward to kiss Mamalachgook. He began to rub his hands up her bare thighs under the shift, then he stopped abruptly.

"What is it?" Rebecca asked.

"We are not alone," He answered and rolled over to reach for the musket.

Rebecca grabbed the top blanket and wrapped it around her. As Mamalachgook stood up to survey the woods behind them, four Indians came forward. They were dressed and painted like members of Mamalachgook's tribe and had rifles pointed at the two newlyweds. Mamalachgook appeared to recognize them and lowered his weapon. They did likewise.

"Mamalachgook," one of them said in a tone of recognition.

"Xèli Chikënëm , what brings you here?" Mamalachgook asked.

"My brothers and I hunt and scout."

Mamalachgook turned toward Rebecca.

"This is Xèli Chikënëm, or, roughly translated in English: Many Turkeys," Mamalachgook announced.

Rebecca, clutching the blanket around her, just nodded. Then Mamalachgook asked.

"What are you scouting?"

"The sachem wishes to know about movement of white soldiers to and from Fort Pitt. He wishes to know what he may be up against if we attack white settlers nearby." Many Turkeys answered.

"He's not going to attack Fort Pitt, is he?" Rebecca cried out.

"Who is this woman? She looks familiar." Many Turkeys asked.

"She is my woman. I have taken her as wife." Mamalachgook answered.

"Big mistake, brother, white woman not have the stamina of Lenape women. Still she very pretty, understand your mistake." Many Turkeys commented. Then his facial expression turned to one of recognition.

"Isn't she the one we captured many days ago?" He asked.

"She is the one," Mamalachgook admitted.

"This is not good. The sachem is very angry she not delivered to Maghingua Tscholens. He told us if we should find this woman on our travels to capture her and bring her back." Many Turkeys continued.

"Mamalachgook, you're not going to let them take me are you?" Rebecca protested.

Mamalachgook raised his rifle, pointing it toward Many Turkeys. This caused a similar reaction from the other three Indians. Mamalachgook held his position for a moment.

"I could kill you," he announced.

"And my brothers here would kill you. What would be gained? We would still take the woman." Many Turkeys responded.

"Couldn't you forget you found us?" Mamalachgook asked.

"That is not possible. We have our duty to the sachem. However, you could plead for this woman to the sachem. Now that you have taken her for wife; perhaps he will accept that." Many Turkeys proposed.

"That is a good plan," Mamalachgook started. He lay his rifle down and continued: "Rebecca and I will never really be free as long as we are being hunted by my brothers. I would like the sachem's blessing on our marriage, if not his blessing, at least his tolerance of it."

"Oh, Mamalachgook do you think you can convince the sachem to acknowledge our marriage and leave us alone?" Rebecca asked.

"I must try. Right now, it seems the only thing to do."

Mamalachgook then spoke to Many Turkeys: "If I give my word we will accompany you to our village without resistance, may we travel as brothers?"

Many Turkeys lowered his rifle and the other Indians followed. Then he smiled and continued: "True to my name, I bagged a big gobbler today. Let us enjoy it as brothers. Can your woman cook for us?"

"I will cook it if all four of you fetch fire wood and start a fire." Rebecca responded.

"All four of us?" Many Turkeys asked, perplexed.

"If you want me to cook, all four of you need to disappear for a few minutes," Rebecca repeated.

"Trust us Xèli Chikënëm," Mamalachgook reassured them.

When the Indians had their backs to Mamalachgook and Rebecca, heading for the woods to get firewood, Rebecca ordered Mamalachgook:

"Hold my blanket up while I get dressed."

Mamalachgook did as ordered. Rebecca hurriedly pulled her clothes back on. It was good she did it quickly because the four Indians did not spend long gathering the firewood. Many Turkeys handed her the dead bird, and she began plucking it as they built a fire. As the turkey roasted on a spit of green wood, with Rebecca turning it from time to time, Mamalachgook and his brothers engaged in conversation. They spoke in the Lenape language so Rebecca couldn't understand them. Mamalachgook, noticing that Rebecca looked distressed, spoke out.

"Rebecca, I haven't introduced you to my brothers. You already know Many Turkeys, of course but there is Tëmakwe Kèhkëlahikès, that is Beaver Trapper, and beside him is Sikhay Elahtunikèt which means Salt Seeker, and finally we have Ashëwìl Alàhshi Namès or Swims Like Fish. Brothers, this is my wife, Rebecca."

As Mamalachgook introduced each one, they each nodded and smiled at her. She smiled back to be polite, while thinking that each one who smiled today could just as easily kill a white man or woman tomorrow. The thought made her shiver. Then there was Mamalachgook. He looked completely at ease among them like a relative at a family reunion. Could it be she had made a mistake in marrying him?

When they had eaten, it was now completely dark. Rebecca announced she was going to sleep. Surprisingly, Mamalachgook just nodded at her and stayed with the others around the fire. She lay down between the two blankets and started to drift into slumber. As she began to nod off, she felt the strong hand of Mamalachgook on her waist and heard him say.

"Will you not give your husband a good night kiss?"

Rebecca responded: "You'll not be enjoying the pleasure of the matrimonial bed with your 'brothers' only a stone's throw away."

Mamalachgook sighed and lay back. In a gesture of consolation, Rebecca snuggled up alongside him and put her head on his shoulder. Then she fell asleep.

Rebecca woke up in Mamalachgook's arms. She discovered he was already awake and had only been waiting for her to wake up.

"My wife had a good sleep?" He asked.

"Yes, did you hold me all night?" She asked.

"Yes, but holding you I did not sleep well. There is a tingling in the arm you lay on. Come let's get up." Mamalachgook answered.

They both arose to find the other Indians were roasting freshly caught fish on a fire. Mamalachgook and Rebecca approached them and Many

Turkeys offered each of them a cooked fish. When all had eaten, Many Turkeys announced it was time to go and Rebecca and Mamalachgook packed up their belongings for the trip. Rebecca noted that none of the four Indians objected to Mamalachgook carrying his rifle.

The journey to the Indian village where Rebecca has first spent her captivity took six days. It might have been made in four; but time was spent in hunting to provide food for the party of six. Mamalachgook had taken his turn at hunting without any of the other Indians showing concern that he might escape or turn on them.

When they reached the village, Taskemus was first to see the group. She had just offered her father a bowl of food. The sachem was sitting with his back to the approaching group that included Mamalachgook and Rebecca. Taskemus immediately spotted Rebecca and ran to her. The sachem rose to his feet and turned to see what had drawn his daughter away. Taskemus gave Rebecca a hug and said: "It is good to see you again."

Rebecca hugged Taskemus back and responded: "I enjoy seeing you also; but I am not happy to be here. I was forced to come."

Taskemus broke the embrace and stood back with a look of dismay. She started to ask why; but the sachem spoke.

"So, Mamalachgook, you return after many days with the woman you were to deliver to Maghingya Tscholens, you will explain."

He then took Mamalachgook by the arm and led him to the place where he'd been sitting. Rebecca tried to follow but many Turkeys restrained her.

"The sachem wishes to speak with Mamalachgook privately," he said.

Taskemus took Rebecca's hand and led her away from the group of four saying: "I wish to speak to you privately."

Taskemus led Rebecca into the great lodge where Rebecca had resided in captivity. As soon as they were inside, Taskemus said: "You must tell me everything that has happened since I saw you last."

"I will if you promise not to repeat anything to your father that I ask you not to," Rebecca responded.

"You can trust me. Now talk." Taskemus demanded.

"To begin with, Mamalachgook and I are married." Rebecca started.

Taskemus' faced beamed upon hearing the news.

"Please, tell me all about it." Taskemus pleaded.

So Rebecca told her all that had happened since she left the Delaware village. She asked Taskemus not to repeat anything about the Indian attack on the party led by Ensign Butler. When she finished Taskemus commented.

"Oh, you have been through a rough time."

"Well I fear the worst may be yet to come. What do you think your father will do to Mamalachgook and me?" Rebecca asked.

"I cannot say. If Mamalachgook had taken an Indian woman for wife, he would let Mamalachgook and his woman live together in peace. Having a white woman for a squaw is no disgrace. It has been done before. But defying my father's wishes and taking you for his woman will not sit well with father. It is an affront to his authority as sachem. I could talk with him; but it may do little good."

"Would you?" Rebecca asked.

"Of course, you and I are friends, are we not?" Taskemus answered.

"Yes, and I wish I could always be near you to enjoy that friendship." Rebecca responded.

Just then, Taskemus' father entered the lodge, a stern look on his face.

"You will leave us alone, daughter," he ordered Taskemus.

Taskemus demurely arose and left the lodge. The chief then spoke to Rebecca.

"I have sent Mamalachgook away from the village for three sunrises to pray and fast. He has a big decision to make."

"What decision is that?" Rebecca asked.

"If he is to rejoin our community, he must pledge his allegiance to me and his brothers. He must obey my decisions in all things as his other brothers do. The white men have become fewer as the war among the whites in the east has drawn many away. We have an opportunity to regain control over our lands. Mamalachgook must commit to join his brothers in the war against the whites. If he will do so, he may live among us and the union between you and him will be respected."

"What if Mamalachgook chooses not to war against the whites?" Rebecca asked.

"Then he will be banished from the village." The chief answered.

Rebecca figured she knew the answer to the next question; but had to ask: "If he is banished, will I be allowed to join him?"

"You will remain my captive if he is banished. You will be sent to Maghingya Tscholens as before." The chief answered and left the lodge.

Rebecca slumped back against a lodge pole, pondering the future that lay before her. She would be willing to live with Mamalachgook in the village; but not as a wife of a warrior dedicated to killing settlers whose only crime was to eke out a living on the land. And if Mamalachgook were banished, would he try to come for her and somehow wrest her away from these savages or would she be handed over for a life of slavery? Immersed in these thoughts she didn't notice that Taskemus had returned.

"I see that the talk with my father has you greatly troubled." Taskemus remarked.

"Yes, Taskemus, there appears to be no way Mamalachgook and I can live in freedom. He will either be bound to kill whites in allegiance to your father or I will be bound to serve Maghingya Tscholens the rest of my life." Rebecca answered.

Taskemus sat down by Rebecca and took hold of Rebecca's hand.

"I tried to talk to father, explaining that he should not cause such pain to people who are in love with each other; but he said the matter was none of my concern. He told me of the ultimatum he gave to Mamalachgook. If Mamalachgook is banished, I will help you to escape. I think you two will find each other."

"Oh, Taskemus, I mustn't make trouble for you." Rebecca responded.

"Don't worry. Father will not forget I am his daughter. In time he will forgive me. Now come help me with the work. It will help the time pass while you are waiting for Mamalachgook to return."

Taskemus was wrong. As much as Rebecca tried to keep busy, the hours drug on. In addition she slept little.

When Mamalachgook finally returned, Rebecca was tending the fire under the cooking pot. A small group of warriors followed him as he approached the log the sachem was sitting on. The sachem stood up and asked.

"What have you decided?"

"I have decided to choose banishment. I ask that I may take my wife with me. Is there not some way I might purchase her freedom?"

The chief ordered two of the warriors standing behind Mamalachgook to bring Rebecca to him. They went and seized Rebecca roughly and took her to the chief. In a moment she was standing facing Mamalachgook with the chief standing alongside. She looked at Mamalachgook. The strain of the three day fast showed on his face; but she could see his desire for her in his eyes. The chief circled the two lovers, rubbing the back of his head. He circled several times then stopped.

"Face your sachem," The chief ordered.

Both Mamalachgook and Rebecca turned to face the chief. Then the chief spoke.

"Woman ever since you were brought to this camp, you've caused trouble. It is best I be rid of you."

Then the chief faced Mamalachgook as said: "You will take this woman from the village and I don't want to see either of you again."

Rebecca was so elated she kissed the sachem on impulse.

"Oh, thank you so much," Rebecca said.

The chief, shocked, backed back a step after the kiss. Then he shouted: "Go!"

Mamalachgook took Rebecca by the hand and led her toward the edge of the village. Just before they were clear, Many Turkeys appeared and handed Mamalachgook the rifle, power horn and bullet bag which Mamalachgook had carried into the village. He said nothing, just turned back toward the center of the village.

CHAPTER 15

HOME AT LAST

Rebecca and Mamalachgook said nothing to each other until they were nearly a mile from the village, then Rebecca grabbed Mamalachgook by the arm, spun him around to face her and kissed him hard on the lips. He responded by drawing her tight to him with the arm that wasn't carrying the rifle. The embrace was prolonged but they had to breath so eventually it was broken. When Mamalachgook released her, Rebecca asked:

"Will we have any more trouble from your 'brothers'?"

"No, banishment works both ways. The people of the village are not allowed to have any kind of contact with us either." Mamalachgook answered.

"Then we are free?" Rebecca gasped at gave Mamalachgook another kiss.

She took his arm and started walking again. A moment later she asked: "Do you remember the way to my parent's homestead?"

"Yes, we will go there."

⁊⋲

It took five days for them to reach the homestead. Time was required for them to find food and cook meals along the way. The first night Mamalachgook pressed Rebecca to make conjugal love; but she put him off saying: "We have only the hard ground to lie on. Please wait until we reach the cabin." Mamalachgook respected her wish. She did enjoy the comfort of his shoulder each night though.

It was the early morning of the sixth day when they arrived. The first thing Rebecca noticed was the weeds which had sprung up in the portion of the field which her dad had managed to plow before he was killed. Her mother's vegetable garden had been invaded by weeds also. However, vegetable sprouts were visible among the weeds. When they entered the cabin, they had to evict a family of raccoons that had taken up residence. Rebecca surveyed the mess. Her mother had always kept the place so tidy. Tears began to well in her eyes; but she fought them back. Instead, she turned to Mamalachgook.

"I'll be most of the day cleaning this up. Come." Rebecca ordered.

She led him to a lean-to shed behind the house. She found her father's saw and an ax.

"Here, take these and start cutting firewood, you see the remnants of the old wood pile over there." Rebecca ordered.

Mamalachgook took the tools and looked at the old wood pile with an expression of disdain.

"I'd rather hunt and see if I can find meat for supper," he said.

"You can do both. Just make sure you get us enough wood to last through the night and tomorrow; that is if you want regular meals." Rebecca conceded.

Mamalachgook said nothing and headed for the woods, cutting tools in hand. Rebecca returned to the house and began the task of cleaning. She found that some of the plates, cooking and eating utensils still remained. She restored the bed her parents used to sleep in. The sheets and blankets were dirty but cleaning them would have to wait until tomorrow. About noon, no longer hearing any sawing of chopping sounds, Rebecca looked out to discover, Mamalachgook heading into the woods with rifle in hand. It pleased her to see he had cut and piled a fairly decent pile of firewood.

Mamalachgook returned a couple of hours later with a deer. He began to dress it; but before completing the work he brought her some choice cuts to prepare for supper. He asked Rebecca if she had salt. She pointed to a barrel which she had discovered was still half full. Mamalachgook maneuvered it outside. When Rebecca looked out later she was pleased to see he was preparing jerky from the rest of the deer meat.

As the sun was setting, Rebecca called Mamalachgook in for supper. They had a fine supper of roast venison and some potatoes and onions which had survived in her mother's root cellar. Rebecca had also discovered a couple of jugs of cider left there.

After supper Mamalachgook returned to drying the venison until darkness began to fall. Then he returned to the house. Rebecca met him at the door.

"How is it going?" she asked.

"It is done well enough. Will you help me to collect it so the creatures of the night don't steal it?

When they had collected and stored the meat within the cabin. Rebecca announced:

"Well there is only one more thing to do."

"What is that?" Mamalachgook asked.

Rebecca took him by the hand and led him just outside the cabin door.

"You have to carry me inside. It is an old custom for the husband to carry his bride over the threshold." Rebecca replied coyly.

Mamalachgook picked Rebecca up and carried her across the threshold. Inside she told him to set her down. Then she latched the door. She began undoing the ties on her short gown.

"Now," she said, "We'll do what you've wanted to do the past nights on the trail."

❧ ❧ ❧

www.ingramcontent.com/pod-product-compliance
Lightning Source LLC
Chambersburg PA
CBHW061529310726
48972CB00008B/2379